I0594560

War Heart

The Five Furies of Heaven

Book 1

Ashley Capes

War Heart
The Five Furies of Heaven: 1
Copyright © 2020 Ashley Capes

Cover Painting: Marcel Mosqi
Cover Design: Christina P
Layout & Typeset: Close-Up Books

All rights reserved. No part of this book may be reproduced in any form by any electronic or mechanical means including photocopying, recording, or information storage and retrieval without permission in writing from the author.

ISBN-978-0-6487704-1-1

www.ashleycapes.com

Published by Close-Up Books
Melbourne, Australia

For Brooke

Chapter 1.

Kilek slid to a halt, his arm outstretched. "See? It's a sword. I told you."

Steel glinted beneath the noon sun. A blade protruded from the rockslide that lay beside the old highway where the road cut through rust-coloured hills. The village had already cleared most of the stone and mud but last night, a faint rumbling reached Kilek where he lay abed, listening to Camilea's wheezing snore from across the room. Even then, he'd nearly sat up and snuck out to investigate, certain it was a second slide.

But the risk was too great; Camilea would flog him if he was caught.

Yet his guess was perfect.

Tyar grinned. "Well, well. That's twice you've been right today," he said, pushing his blond hair back from his forehead and wiping at the sweat. He leant on his bow. "Sure you want to go down there? Doesn't look too stable."

Kilek unslung his pack, mostly water, food and bundles of *ballas* wood for the cleaning of the old temple. "I'll be careful."

"You'd better be. I don't want to explain to your sister that I let you get yourself killed clumping through that muck."

Kilek frowned at his friend. "Let? Exactly how much older than me do you think you are? And Camilea's only my half-sister – why do I have to remind you every time?"

Tyar sighed. "I'm hoping you'll give up soon."

Kilek started down the slide, testing each piece of mud-caked stone with his boot before putting his full weight upon it. "Well here's another reminder – she'll be too drunk to know any different, let alone care."

"Do you really think that?" Tyar's voice bore a trace of sadness.

Kilek didn't turn his head. "Yes."

He hopped over a twisted oak branch and landed on a slab of stone, dropping to a crouch to keep his balance. The muddy gravel, which had yet to set completely, gave way but not enough to send him tumbling down. He sucked in a breath. If it did, he'd break a limb at best and be buried alive at worst.

But the sword was close; the lion's head pommel clear.

Mud cloaked most of the blade but enough caught the light to see that it had barely been tarnished. He stretched forward. The slab of stone slid a little further. "Come on."

He gripped the handle and pulled.

The blade slid free with a rasp.

Kilek grinned as he lifted it to brush at the dirt. Numbers, etched into the blade. *Eighteen, nineteen. Twenty-three and thirty-six.* Were they supposed to be dates? Ages?

"Well?" Tyar called down.

"Got it." Kilek hooked the blade through his belt and

started back up the slide, presenting it to Tyar when he reached level ground.

"Looks old," his friend said. He peered at the engraving, flicking more dirt to the ground. "The numbers don't make much sense."

"Maybe they meant something to the owner? Like famous battles?"

Tyar nodded. "Mathi might know; she's obsessed with all that." He handed it back. "Let's hurry it up, I want to get this over and done with – I've got too much to do back at the inn."

"Sneaking wine isn't work, Tyar."

"Well, it isn't exactly easy, either."

Kilek chuckled as he collected his pack and started along the highway once more, Tyar at his side. Birdsong overhead competed with the crunch of their boots, and then, after a time, muttering as they climbed one of the steeper hills.

A dark wood waited beyond the crest but above the green treetops, peeked the tip of a stone tower – the old Temple of Avendria. Disused since before his grandfather's time to hear old Dorael tell it, and he was probably right given the condition of the place. While folk in the north hadn't precisely turned their back on the Goddess, she was certainly rarely worshipped further south either. Kilek hadn't been within since last spring, during the chore of their previous cleaning trek.

"Think it'll be overrun with paddots again?" Tyar asked.

Kilek nodded. "I packed extra ballas wood – if we have to, we'll smoke them out."

"Good, because my bow isn't the best for this sort of work."

The late spring air was cooler beneath the elms, shade

soon helping to chill the sweat on the back of his neck. The path quickly became overgrown by mud-weed and bracken where the half-buried stone branched toward the temple. A wooden sign burdened with lichen proclaimed the Temple of Avendria just ahead, but a crumpled shape lay beyond – too small for a person. Perhaps an animal?

Kilek slowed as he drew near, glancing to Tyar, whose own brow was furrowed.

Part of the shape was covered in orange fur – a motionless fox. Yet it was the... thing caught in the animal's jaws that gave Kilek pause. A huge insect, and it seemed just as dead as the fox. Pale purple ichor had burst from its narrow body, spilling across the fox's head and searing the flesh down to the bone. One of the creature's translucent black wings had been crushed and a faint acrid scent lingered in the air.

"By all the Gods... What is that?" Tyar said as he knelt, reaching out.

Kilek caught his friend's arm. "Don't touch it."

Tyar nodded. He drew his belt knife and lifted the insect's body. The underside gleamed; six jagged legs curled up, tiny white hairs visible. It was unpleasant, but far worse was the new, pungent scent the movement seemed to unleash, so strong that it began to burn Kilek's airways.

He turned his head as he coughed. "That isn't natural," he said when he looked back. "Have you ever even *heard* of something like this?"

Tyar had moved his blade to the head – yet he flinched away when his probing revealed red mandibles and an ichor-filled mouth beneath bulging eyes. They, too, had been dull purple orbs.

"No. And we should leave it alone," Tyar said, wiping his

blade on the ground before he stood.

"I think we should bury it."

"Why?"

"In case another animal comes across it and is killed. Or a person," he added, glancing away from the thing.

"Shouldn't we get to the temple? I want to be home before dark."

Kilek frowned. Burying the insect creature wouldn't take so long... but he had to admit, touching it wasn't so appealing, even with a boot. Not even ants or maggots wanted to come close – they'd confined themselves to the opposite end of the fox. "I suppose." He took the old sword and used it to slide the animal and insect from the trail. "That will have to do for now."

"We'll figure it out later," Tyar said, dragging Kilek by the shoulder.

Kilek stumbled after, unable to stop himself casting a glance back at the mute pile, patches of red and purple harsh beneath the bracken.

Chapter 2.

The stone temple reared out of the hillside, fallen leaves littering the earth before it. The face of the building bore nothing graceful; hard, square lines, dark stone and the whole thing empty of statuary. Only the large iron doors, blackened with age, spoke of the once-special nature of the place.

A figure had been carved there – Avendria herself, hair flowing rivers of leaves, joined by hawks, sparrows, winged serpents and even the great dragon Ceranec with his silvery scales – that carving was also clouded by long neglect. He paused to stare up at the dragon. In all the legends, Ceranec was a saviour, defender of the people, driving back hordes of darkness with his molten breath.

Kilek sighed. If only he could see the magnificent creature just once...

"Daydreaming again?" Tyar's voice broke Kilek's reverie.

"Sorry, I guess I was." Kilek used Servant Bastiem's key and a heavy click followed. Together, he and Tyar dragged the doors open, revealing pools of light within a large hall.

"You know, I think this is the last time I'll do this," Tyar said. "I'm getting too old. You too for that matter."

"That's a new excuse from you, Tyar."

"I'm serious. This will be my eighteenth Winter Carnival and your seventeenth – they should pass this cleansing ritual down to someone younger and besides, Gan needs me more and more at the inn."

Kilek grinned. "Then I guess we'd better enjoy being chosen, one last time."

"Enjoy chasing paddots out of every damn room? Sweeping droppings and breaking up their nests? And the stink of the ballas smoke sticks to my tunic for days afterwards. *Days.*"

"I see. You'd rather be chasing girls around the fields, right?"

Tyar sighed. "Not that Ganoit gives me much time to myself, but yes. I would much prefer that."

"Then let's finish up quickly."

Inside the temple, light streamed through circular windows to splash across thin, rat-eaten rugs. The rugs themselves were set in half circles, slipping between the stone seating that still faced a large dais where an empty, winged altar waited.

Between the spears of light the shadows seemed darkest, and already small, cat-like shapes were slinking away – the paddots. Hardly vicious creatures, they would flee when challenged but if one did bite, its jaws were like a vice.

"Heathens!" A voice shouted from outside. "Throw down your puny weapons and leave this holy place."

Tyar groaned. Instead of doing as the voice demanded, he dumped his pack to rummage through it.

It could only have been Mathila's voice. Kilek strode to the door and paused to draw the sword he'd found and shouted back. "Never! You Luargot-scum will have to come in and make us."

"Since I'm not Luargot, you can leave me out of this," a deeper voice replied.

Kilek grinned; Paxoph was with Mathi then, good. Kilek took a breath and leapt from the temple, rolling to his feet, blade ready. Dust swirled around his legs.

Mathi stood before him, arms folded, flanked by Paxoph and Alira. Like everyone else, Mathi was dressed in dark tunic and pants but her belt was weighed down by knives and her own sword. She also wore a blue headband that kept her blonde curls free from her face – something her mother made for her, so familiar that Kilek could hardly imagine Mathi without it.

Paxoph and Alira carried packs too. Pax appeared tired, wiping sweat from his dark skin while Alira – as ever – seemed so light on her feet, so at ease that it was as though the sun didn't bother her at all. She was fiddling with one of the small pouches of herb and powder she always carried.

"Where's Tyar?" Alira asked when she was done, her voice soft, almost sweet.

"Making a start," Kilek said.

"Start? You two must have crawled all the way here," Mathi said, a glint in her eye. "We thought you'd be half done by now."

He lifted the blade. "I found this in the slide."

His friends crowded in as Mathi took the sword, lifting it gently and turning it over. She traced the numbers on the blade, lips pursed – it was a cute expression but pointing it out wasn't worth the thumping it'd earn him. Up close, the handful of freckles across her nose and cheeks were visible – another thing he wasn't going to mention, since she often complained about them.

"It looks quite old," Paxoph said.

Mathi was nodding. "I think these dates relate to battles. Eighteen is the border skirmish with Sassehim and so is nineteen. Thirty-six is probably the Black Lake War."

"And this from the girl Father called his laziest student," Alira said with a small smile.

Mathi chuckled. "I like what I like." She handed the weapon back. "Great find, Kilek. Maybe I'll visit the slide myself on the way back, see if there's anything else there."

"Wait," he said. "Ah, you can keep it if you like."

"What?"

"You know swords better than me." He offered the blade to her.

Mathi took it with a smile. "Thanks, Kil. This is fantastic!"

"Hey." Tyar stuck his head out from around the door. "If you three followed us to help then quit mooning over that relic and get in here, will you?"

Kilek led everyone inside where they spread out and moved between patches of light. Squeaking followed as the creatures ran for exits – both the front doors and passages toward the rear chambers – preparation rooms for servants now long-since disused. Kilek stepped into the first hall, twin pieces of ballas wood raised. Striking the beasts was just as effective as smoking them out, and tended to kill far less often.

Hissing echoed from dark shadows as he approached a long bench. He'd cleared the very same room several times over the years; its stone bench, curved hooks and thin, well-like nests near as familiar as his own home. The paddot's feet scraped on stone as it burst forth, a ball of fur and claws scuttling from the chamber. Kilek let it pass, moving deeper to check each well for hatchlings. Empty, all of them.

He switched to his broom, collecting the fur, dried grass and twigs into a pile and sweeping it into the main hall.

Mathila's voice echoed as she shooed another creature out of a nearby chamber. "This hardly seems worth the trouble," she called. "Nothing ever changes. Every time we close up one hole, the paddots make another three before the next winter."

"It's important to Servant Bastiem, so that's good enough for me," Paxoph replied as he appeared from the opposite room with Alira, his voice calm.

"And it's not like he can do this work himself – he appreciates it, Mathi," Alira added.

"You're right, I suppose," Mathi said with a sigh. "Let's hurry then. I want to get back to training."

Kilek added his pile to the central heap, which Tyar had started and which the others were adding to with their own broken nests. By the sounds of muttering and squeaking, Tyar was upstairs already. "Sounds like I'd better help him," Mathi said with a grin, heading for the stairway.

"Nice try, Mathi," Kilek said. "We all know you just want to avoid the cellar."

"Exactly." She waved from halfway up the stair.

"Let's save her at least a nest or two, then," Alira said.

Paxoph nodded. "Sounds just to me." He led them behind the crumbling stone altar to a long corridor, which was in turn lined by closed doors. Each room contained a tiny window, space for a bed and a basin. Usually, paddots didn't find a way within but on the way back they'd check.

The bigger task was the cellar – or the roof. At least with three, it would be easier. One year, it had only been he and Tyar and the task had taken *much* longer.

Yet when they descended the stairs, it wasn't the dozen or so paddot nests or the huddled animals and their glowing eyes themselves that gave Kilek pause – it was the rubble. Broken stone lay scattered across the floor, piled beneath an opening. Light streamed in after it; most of the mess confined to a single corner. Even the ground sloped down there, the broad paving stones split and upheaved.

"That quake was more serious that I thought," Kilek said.

Kilek waved his ballas wood as he approached, almost an afterthought, and most of the paddots shot off for the stairs but one stood firm before her nest, hackles raised; a mother, no doubt.

He gave her some space; the wreckage was more interesting for now.

The damage was serious. A deep crack ran up the wall and across the ceiling, streaking from the point of the cave-in and revealing the edge of grass and blue sky beyond. Air flowed in – yet a chill rose from the floor where the stones were broken. A dark maw gaped up at him when he leant over.

"Something's shining down there," Alira said, moving closer to bend over the hole.

Paxoph stayed back. "Careful, you two."

A pale yellow glow waited below, faint yes, but no illusion. Was it some sort of holy ornament catching light from outside? "I thought this was the lowest point of the temple."

Alira still peered within, green eyes intent. "It feels like... like it's calling us."

Kilek glanced at her. "What do you mean?"

"I can't explain it."

"One of your feelings?"

She nodded, glancing away as if ashamed. "I know it sounds silly."

Paxoph crept a little closer. "Perhaps we should–"

Stone ground against stone. The floor slid forward. Kilek flung his arms out and caught something solid – Paxoph. The young man pulled Kilek back from the unstable ground with one hand, the other was wrapped around Alira's wrist.

When Kilek stood on firm ground, he looked back.

Pieces of stone had crashed down below and now dust rose up after, almost sparkling in the light.

"Thank you," Kilek said, his words echoed by Alira.

Paxoph nodded.

Footsteps clapped down from above and Tyar and Mathi soon joined them, eyes wide. "What happened?" Tyar asked.

"One of the quakes broke through. There's another room below," Kilek said. "Alira thinks there's something down there."

"Like what?" Tyar asked, though he hadn't approached yet, eyeing the broken floor warily. Then his expression changed. "Like, holy treasure in need of liberating?"

"It's a light," Alira said.

"Let's find out what it is then," Mathi said, straightening. "It's got to be better than cleaning this place."

Kilek took half a step closer, dropping into a crouch once more. "It looks like the rubble's made a bit of a ramp. It shouldn't be too hard to get in and out."

"Perfect," Mathi said. She glanced across at Paxoph. "Any objections, Mother Paxoph?"

"I object to that name," he said with a slight smile.

"Then it's decided," Mathi said. "I'll get a lantern."

Once she'd returned with lights, handing one to Kilek, she started her climb. One by one, they descended – even Pax – waiting for Kilek to join them. He followed, choosing his steps carefully, then raised his lantern at the bottom. The walls were cut from similar stone to the rest of the temple but the floor had been paved in a simple pattern – a line of marble headed into a corridor. When he knelt to examine it, the source of the pale glow became clear – gold vein had been set within the marble.

"I never knew something like this was here," Tyar said. "Think of what it must be worth."

"This is supposed to be a holy place for you," Paxoph said with a frown.

"I supposed if I believed in the Goddess, that would be true," Tyar said. "But I'm not going to rob the temple floor either, if that's what you're worried about."

"Good."

"No, I'm hoping there's something down here that's much easier to carry, actually."

Pax sighed.

"Hurry it up, you lot," Mathila said, striding along the line.

Kilek caught up quickly. The corridor was not long, and it soon turned into a spiralling staircase that led downwards, keeping the marble thread. After what seemed like a dozen flights, he was only guessing, Kilek slowed. "Just how deep will this go?"

Mathila shrugged. "Who knows? But we should explore a little further, we've got enough light left in the lanterns. And the day."

"Only if we find something soon," Paxoph said.

"Let's give it a little longer," Tyar urged.

Kilek nodded. "I'm curious too."

Mathi grinned. "Any more objections?"

Pax shook his head and Alira answered. "None from me."

"That's my girl," Mathi said, still grinning.

Chapter 3.

A vast, open well lay at the bottom of the stair, its sides full of climbing marble lines that glimmered in the light. The low wall reached Kilek's knees; each stone interlocked in a seemingly random pattern... almost giving the impression of strewn leaves. There was no bucket, only a black drop into silence – the shard of stone he'd tossed in did not offer an answering splash or clink.

Ten arched openings led from the chamber, flowing runes carved above each.

"Can you read them, Pax?" Kilek asked as he raised the lantern. "They look pretty old."

He shook his head. "They're ancient, that's all I can say, which is not much at all. It looks like a version of your Luargot script at least. Servant Bastiem would probably know."

"This is where we're meant to be," Alira said. "I'm sure of it."

"We are?" Mathi asked.

"Yes," Alira replied, hesitating. "I know this will sound

ridiculous... but I feel that we're supposed to be here. As though the quake happened in time for us to come here to clean the temple... it's as though we're *meant* to do this."

"Ah, is this another of your strange little feelings, then?"

Alira flushed.

Paxoph frowned at Mathi. "She's telling you what you want to hear, isn't she? You wanted to explore."

Mathi folded her arms. "So?"

"So let's do that," Kilek replied. "I believe her."

"The cornfield again?" Mathi asked.

"You'd believe too if you'd been there."

Tyar waved his hands. "Hey, enough, you lot. Now that we've found this place, let's figure out where we are."

"You're right," Mathi said with a shrug.

"I agree," Kilek said. They'd come this far; it'd be a shame not to learn anything more. And maybe there'd be something within that could help the village... he had no idea what, but if they *did* find something it would be pretty wonderful. The walls revealed little save for old lamps hung around the room. He moved to one and lifted it down, both oil and wick seemed good. "All right, how about this? We each take a light and choose a passage. If we find something we come back here to the well and wait for the others. If it looks like your path is just going to go on and on, come back here. Maybe give it a hundred paces?"

"You want to split up?" Tyar asked.

"Yes," Alira said. She strode across the room and took a lamp, lighting it from Kilek's and started down one of the passages, glancing at Mathila as she did.

"Wait, I'm sorry," Mathi called. "Ali?"

But Alira didn't turn.

"Let's just check the passages and see what we find," Tyar said.

Mathi snatched up a lantern, lit it without meeting anyone's gaze, and headed for a passage of her own.

Pax followed their example, sighing as he started across the room.

Kilek helped Tyar with his own light before giving his friend a nod. "Be careful, there could be more cave-ins." Somehow, that was easier to say than to discuss what had happened between Mathi and Alira.

"Right," Tyar said, and he almost bounced down his passage, no doubt at the slim chance of finding forgotten temple treasure.

Kilek moved to the opposite path, glancing up at the runes to choose one with a half-circle. The passage was narrow and straight, somehow free of dust or cobwebs. A small room soon appeared ahead and when he glanced over his shoulder, he'd walked far enough that he couldn't see the light from Tyar's passage.

The room was bare, save for a tiny dais and a patch of marble set in the floor before it. Once again, the pattern spoke of flowing leaves as if carried by a swift river – a common symbol of Avendria. Was this a ceremonial place for the old Servants? Kilek raised the lantern, checking the ceiling but there were no markings, no further clues as to the purpose of the room.

A heavy silence had fallen across the underground and his skin tingled as if the faint passage of air ran across his face and arms, almost expectant. He swallowed, then frowned. Even the faint sound of his swallowing had been muffled. What had they stumbled into?

The wall before him seemed to waver and he stepped forward to peer closer, footfalls soundless on the marble as he rubbed at his eyes.

Welcome, Kilek.

A woman's voice spoke within his mind. A crystalline sound that soothed him. His breathing eased and he set the lantern down, almost as if it had been a suggestion.

It is wonderful to hear the voices of my people in these halls.

A shimmering light of gold appeared on the dais, resolving into a slender figure. Her proportions appeared almost elongated, but it was still the form of a woman. A robe of feathers clothed her, a mixture of gold and orange save for a collar of black, mighty feathers that rose behind her head. Her pale hair shimmered bright against those dark feathers. She looked down at him, smiling.

He could not look away from her eyes – beautiful but terrifying... they had no pupils; instead shining with a warm glow. Despite the warmth, he shivered. Her eyes bored through him, as if tunnelling into his heart and mind, seeking his secrets, his hopes and wishes, searching every part of him from his failures to his worst moments and even, his future triumphs – yet these were vague and shadowy.

Kilek opened his mouth to speak but could not – the pure force of her presence was too much; he fell to his knees and gaped.

Kilek, do not fear.

Yet he could not help it, facing her had rendered him mute – here was a being unfathomable, someone who could wipe him from the earth with barely a glance, and she was telling him not to be afraid? His body began to tremble.

Ah. She waved a hand and a fresh wave of calm fell across

him.

His shaking eased. He swallowed, hard. "Are... are you the Goddess Avendria?" The question was stupid but he couldn't make his mind offer anything else.

Yes, that is the name given to me by your people but before the Luargot, all children simply knew me as the First Mother, the Gardener, the Great Bird.

"Forgive us for intruding," he said, lowering his gaze.

Do not fear, Kilek son of Kilek. I am glad. You and your companions are welcome and more – I have need of you.

"Of me?" He glanced up. Her expression was kind but still her gaze pressed down upon him, tightening his chest. "I have little to offer... b-but I offer it freely, My Lady."

You have more than you suspect, Kilek, but I will not force anything upon you – this must be your choice.

"What am I choosing?"

Do you recall what you and Tyar found on the path to my temple?

He blinked, a frown creasing his brow. "The strange insect!" Somehow, he'd forgotten about it. Had the others missed it?

Vast change approaches, and though such foul creatures are not the only harbinger, they are threat enough. All lands will be unsettled and great suffering will be visited upon all. I have called you here to fight such a grim future, Kilek.

"But... I don't understand. How will *I* help?" he asked, throat suddenly dry. "And what do you mean by great suffering – what's going to happen? Is it those things we found?"

Be calm, Kilek. Another wave of her soothing power washed over him. *I am permitted to change you so that you might aid in the struggle to come. If you accept this charge, it will be a cruel burden, you must understand.* She leant closer, and her voice grew soft. *But I have drawn you and your friends here because I see vast potential. It is up to you to fulfil the hope we have placed within you.*

Kilek clenched his hands together. "Please, I don't understand. Change me?"

Yes.

"I… I don't know if I want that."

Yet you must choose; I will not force it upon you.

"And you think I can help?"

We do not know for certain but I believe so.

"We? Do you mean… you and other Gods?"

Yes. And just as you are bound by a mortal lifespan, we Gods have our own bindings when it comes to our rivalries.

"But you are Gods, what could you fight over?"

Dominion. The world itself, belief, our own existence.

He frowned. "Are you saying that you are dying?"

That is a vague but suitable enough description of what might happen if I or my fellows are to lose this particular battle.

Kilek shook his head; none of it made sense truly, but he still had questions and the longer he spent with the Goddess, the easier it became to think. "And this time of change that you have said will bring suffering, is it because of whoever you want us to oppose?"

Yes. Sadly, in our bickering, mortals are often punished. But you can be the difference between suffering for many and suffering for all, Kilek. I know it is a grim choice and there can be little comfort in such choices but I will show you something that may help.

Darkness snapped over his vision.

It resolved into a green field bordered by tall forests... but a blight was crossing the grasses, a writhing mass of purple and black – the insects were devouring all in their path and he gasped even as a walled city with green flags replaced the image. Here, men in bloodied armour were waving the insects forward, unleashing them from cages so the insects flew overhead and swarmed across the walls. This image was soon replaced – now a river choked with bodies; man, woman, child, animal – even insects too, with larger, slower moving creatures that bore a similar look, picking through remains on the banks.

The chamber returned.

"That is our future?" his voice cracked.

If we fail.

"But, My Lady. You are a Goddess. Can't you stop them?"

She shook her head. *It is not permitted. Were I to lift my hand directly, certainly I could wipe the lands clean of the Cabeku and their masters but were that to happen, Kilek, the future I showed you moments ago would be a paradise in comparison. Each and every single living thing would be destroyed if we Gods clashed face to face, from man to insect, plants and even the mountains, the oceans and the sky itself.* A sadness emanated from her when she paused. *Then I would be responsible for the very thing I wish to prevent.*

Kilek exhaled heavily, a churning in his stomach growing. How could he possibly help? How? She was asking *him* to save the lands? And if Avendria was forced to use mortals to fight, then didn't that mean the other Gods would do so too?

That is correct, Kilek.

"So this other God will be sending their own charges into

the world? Who are they?"

That I cannot share – you must learn and strive and make your own decisions from here on, for every advantage I offer Javoteth is permitted to offer an equivalent. She reached out to touch Kilek's cheek, which sent a tingling through his entire body. *And know that HE has already chosen his five* Anesca *– or 'surrogates'. If you accept my call, you will encounter them, I hope not before you are ready.*

Kilek stared into her shimmering eyes, mind aswirl. Five surrogates? Wasn't Javoteth the Westerners' God of Harvest? Why would he send the *Cabeku* into the world? And by all the Gods, what manner of man would work with them?

Yet above all, there was a burning fear – did the Goddess truly think he was able to stand before all that she'd shown him? "But, My Lady, I am no-one."

She said nothing.

Her expression remained unfathomable. He squeezed his eyes shut. There was no way, no way surely... the images she'd shown him flashed in his memory. The insects, their mandibles tearing into plant and flesh alike... Refusal was impossible. No-one, *nothing* deserved such a future. His friends, his village, all the lands were in danger.

Kilek opened his eyes, resolute. "I accept."

Avendria leant closer still; feathers rustling, then placed a kiss upon his forehead. Her lips were cool like a mountain spring and now a sharper tingling ran across his limbs. She straightened and smiled down on him once more, it seemed touched with sorrow now. A new chill ran through him, even as he tried to still himself, tried to sense what it was that had been changed.

But once the sensation faded, he felt exactly the same

as before. He examined his hands with a frown. "Lady, I don't..."

The Goddess was gone.

"Avendria?"

What had she done? Maybe he *looked* different. Kilek lifted the lantern and started back along the passage, glancing over his shoulder a few times. But the Goddess did not reappear.

The others would be able to tell him; maybe they'd already figured it out? Was it great strength or speed? Skill with a blade? Visions of becoming a powerful warrior flashed within his mind, leading soldiers into battle against the insects, protecting his village and the royal city too – fear and exhilaration coursed through his body in equal measure.

Maybe then Mathi would take him more seriously.

Kilek slowed at the sound of unfamiliar voices from the well chamber. Excitement and confusion were clear but the words jumbled together. When he reached the chamber Kilek came to a halt.

Four strangers stood in the room, two men and two women.

Each had familiar features and hair colour, yes and one even had dark skin like Paxoph but they were...

Kilek's lantern crashed to the stone.

The four turned to him, stopping their conversation.

"Kilek?" The blond-haired man took a step closer. "You look the same." He carried a bow and though his clothes barely fit him now, they were of a familiar cut, just as his voice and expression were familiar. "Kilek, it's me – Tyar."

Chapter 4.

"We look so different but the same too," Alira was saying. "I can't believe it."

She was right. It took a moment, but if Kilek tried, he could detect traces of her younger self – the same delicate features, same green eyes but her cheek bones did seem more defined, even the shape of her body had changed, and he had to look away. It seemed the Goddess hadn't changed anyone's clothing, and so Alira and Mathi filled out their garments in a way they hadn't before.

And Mathi – his eyes were drawn to her constantly, even the way she moved had changed. Her curls were longer and fuller now, her blue headband still holding them in place. A certain cuteness had left her countenance, face no longer quite as round, her jaw line sharper and her freckles faded – even her bare arms were more muscled now; she was a woman.

Tyar and Paxoph had also changed, their shoulders had broadened and their faces were more composed of the harder lines of adults – they were themselves but so different.

Beneath the awe, Paxoph seemed even more serious and stern now; he even wore a dark beard! And when Tyar grinned, he almost looked like his old self but he was obviously drawing his own stares from Mathi and Alira.

And Kilek didn't have to ask them to know that he had not changed.

"Let's find a mirror," Mathi said. "I want to see myself."

"There's a pool behind the temple," Tyar said.

"Let's go," Alira pushed Tyar into movement and they started for the stairs, laughing with their new voices as they ran. Even Paxoph moved quickly this time, scratching at his beard as he did.

Kilek swallowed a lump in his throat before starting after them.

The climb was long and dull, the echoes of their joy floating down to taunt him. He fought a frown of resentment. The Goddess *had* changed him – she'd warned him it would happen so why hadn't she made him older and stronger like the others? Why would she lie? *Had* she lied? It didn't make sense and it wasn't fair.

When he reached the main hall of the temple it was empty – they were already outside. He hesitated. Did he really need to go out and watch them fawning over their reflections? They'd hardly notice if he wasn't with them. Kilek started gathering his pack and muttered another curse – he'd left the lantern below.

Should he go and get it?

Again, he hesitated. Did it even matter? The village wasn't going to run out of lamp oil any time soon... Kilek looked to the huge iron doors. Something seemed odd. There was no more laughter. Weren't they happy with the gift from the

Goddess?

"Kilek!"

It was Tyar – and there was true fear in his new but familiar voice.

Kilek crossed the floor at a dash, charging into the light. "What's wrong?" The four of them stood facing the road. He pushed between Mathi and Paxoph and froze.

A distant pillar of smoke rose from beyond the wood, an ugly black worm against the orange sky. It climbed from the direction of home. Was it an attack? Had the Goddesses' warning already come to pass? Gods, was everyone dead?

"That's coming from home, isn't it?" Tyar demanded.

"Come on," Mathi shouted as she took off at a sprint. Paxoph wasn't too far behind, nor was Alira, her expression tight with suppressed fear.

Tyar's eyes were blazing when he looked to Kilek. "If they've laid a hand on Ganoit..."

Together they ran into the wood, shadows growing around them, the others still ahead.

"What about what the Goddess said?" Kilek asked.

"I know."

They ran on and soon, the air began to rasp in Kilek's lungs – but he pushed himself harder. Green hills soon appeared through the trees ahead, and when they hit the winding road, Kilek had to slow to a jog and then to a stumble. Tyar glanced back. "I'm fine," Kilek called. "You go ahead; they need you."

Tyar nodded, expression grim, and kept running.

Kilek came to a halt, hands on his knees as he breathed hard. He'd pushed too far, trying to keep up with the others and now his limbs were like lead, even as early evening air urged him on with its chill.

He gripped the hilt of his belt knife, thumping his thigh with his other fist. If insects had attacked Hasere, he was better off staying behind anyway – he was no warrior. If only he was useful! But instead, he remained a child. Too slow to do anything for his village. Even Camilea, she might be a sour drunk who'd never once said a kind word but she didn't deserve to have her flesh seared from her bones.

Once he caught his breath, Kilek started again, a ragged jog he kept up until reaching the cornfields on Hasere's outskirts. There, he collapsed to his knees, tears in his eyes – two bodies lay in the middle of the road, arrows in their backs. Blood was already darkening their clothes. Blacksmith Oran and his apprentice Percyn; the smith's hammer nearby, haft broken.

Only a matter of hours ago, Oran had offered to sharpen Kilek's chisels.

He gagged as he stood, stumbling on and into the village; his heart thundering within his chest.

Smoke was fading, but it continued to rise from some of the wooden rooves – most of it from the Singing Maiden, the inn's upper storey a hunk of embers and twirls of smoke. The worst of the fire had obviously passed but the building was still ruined. Where was Tyar?

Nearby; Kilek's own door hung from the hinge.

He dashed inside. Aside from an overturned chair; everything appeared as it ought to, from the table cluttered with half-finished carvings and borrowed books where it sat beside their stove and the pan atop it, to the old chest where Camilea kept their meagre savings – whatever she hadn't drunk away – or 'hidden' from him beneath her bed.

A faint snoring came from the twisted sheets.

"Camilea!" he called as he leapt across the room, wrinkling his nose at the stench of unwashed clothing and wine.

A groan.

He shook her shoulder until her eyes opened, mere glints beneath the net of hair. She seemed to be having trouble focusing. "...away with you," she mumbled.

Of course she was dead drunk. "What happened?"

"They took everyone... away."

"Who?"

She growled, burying her face in the pillow, a snore rising once more.

He gave her another shake and shouted. "Gods damn you. Who did?"

"Westerners... they were..." Her eyes closed once more and she resumed her laboured snoring, no matter how he shook her then. Westerners? Did she mean people from the village of Limrade or further west – the nation of Minjao? Neither made any sense. Why would anyone from either place come to Hasere to kill or take people away?

What exactly had the Goddess said?

Her words did not return.

He ran outside, heading for the inn. Each home he passed seemed empty, doors open or kicked in, and no-one coming to meet him, to explain what had happened, to tell him where everyone had gone.

The scent of smoke grew heavier on the air as he neared the building. "Tyar?"

No-one answered but a regular sound became clear – a muted crunch and then a small thump. Digging. Someone was digging! He circled the home nearest the inn.

Mathila.

She was flinging loads of dirt onto a large pile. Two figures lay on the ground nearby – her parents. Her father's chest was soaked in blood, his longsword missing. His eyes were closed. Beside him, Mathi's mother, her face covered by a piece of cloth. Yet other than that, she seemed fine, her pale blue dress and white apron perfectly clean.

So clean that it couldn't possibly be true – how could she be dead?

"Mathi…"

She turned to face him. Tears ran down her face but her jaw was clenched. "Go find the others, Kilek," she snapped, turning back to the grave.

"I can help if–"

"Just go!"

He fell back. "I didn't mean to…"

Mathila stopped and her voice had softened – slightly. "I have to finish this myself, do you understand?"

"Yes."

But he didn't – he didn't understand any of it.

Kilek turned back to the inn. The front doors hung open, one broken, flattened in the street. Just two days ago, Ganoit had oiled the hinge, which had now been torn from the frame.

The others stood within, faces pale with shock as they spoke softly. Tyar had an arm around Alira and Paxoph was staring to the inn's upper storey, where the rooms for travellers were now skeletal frames of charred wood.

"What happened?" Kilek asked.

Tyar opened his mouth but no words came forth.

"Everyone who could walk and swing a blade was taken

by the Minjao," Paxoph said.

"By the..." He shook his head – that made no sense! "Taken where? And why?"

"They've been conscripted, Kilek," Alira said. Her voice was hoarse. "Father and Pax's uncle too. Ganoit and the rest of the town. They left the very old and very young behind... and killed anyone who tried to resist. It's all for some godsforsaken war in the west."

"But we're not part of the Minjao Empire."

"Tell us something we don't know, Kil," Tyar said, his voice flat.

Kilek blinked, the lingering smoke strong enough to sting his eyes. "Is this what the Goddess was talking about?"

"That hardly matters now, does it?" Tyar said, raising his voice.

Pax frowned at Tyar. "Servant Bastiem said that not everyone went quietly, Oran and Mathi's folks tried to stand up to them. The western officer told the village it was on the orders of some Minjao prince. Yan, perhaps."

"And now he's going to die by my blade." Mathila entered the common room, shovel still in hand. "As soon as we can, we're going after them."

Silence.

Mathi's eyes narrowed. "We can still save everyone else. Servant Bastiem said they turned south – they're obviously going to swing around to raid Birnvile before turning back toward the west because I doubt they will dare enter Sassehim, right Pax?"

"I can't imagine it, though they've come a long way for recruitment."

"Then we can cut them off if we take the Crioise River."

"I will go," Tyar said.

"And I," Alira added with a small sniff, her eyes were swollen with tears.

Mathi raised an eyebrow at Paxoph, who said only: "It will be dangerous – the most dangerous thing we've ever done."

"I know."

"There's a real chance we'll all die. Even after what the Goddess has done for us."

Kilek looked away but added his own voice. "I want to see Servant Bastiem before we leave."

"Fine," Mathila said. "Everyone else, find supplies – anything that might be useful."

"Servant Bastiem has the children in Jof's storeroom," Paxoph said.

Kilek nodded as he hurried through the darkening light to the tailor's home where it stood beyond the market square. The sign of the needle and thread was untouched, the steel catching the dying light. Had Jof, too, been taken? Unlike the other buildings, the door was not broken here and when he opened it and called softly, the elderly Servant soon limped through the storeroom door to the counter; his bruised face a mask of sadness – though it brightened when he saw Kilek.

"Kilek, my boy."

"You're hurt."

He rubbed a hand over his bald head. "They'll heal enough for me to get by."

Kilek produced the temple key. "I don't know if we locked the doors, I'm sorry…" A useless thing to say.

Bastiem accepted the key with his papery hand. "Do not

let it trouble you, lad."

"How are the children?"

"Most are sleeping, blessedly. Though a difficult tomorrow waits for them, and many more after that."

"Why did they come, Father?" Kilek asked.

He heaved a sigh. "They claimed it was to protect their people from war – I understand the urge if not the method."

"But from who?

"Perhaps the northern empire has returned from across the sea? There have also been rumours of border disputes between Minjao and Jasoria for some months."

"I see." He looked to his feet. "Did the others mention the... warning we received from the Goddess? You saw how they had changed?"

He nodded, expression becoming grim. "A cruel burden, despite what seems like a gift."

Kilek licked his lips before speaking. "Do you know why? I mean, do you think this invasion could be the suffering she mentioned?"

"It's possible." He paused. "But I fear we must brace ourselves for darker days still."

Kilek couldn't ask the next question – it was a selfish one, how could he ask when people had died, when people had been taken away? His friends – the pain on their faces. Blacksmith Oran...

"My boy?"

"I... I didn't know who else... or even if I should."

"Speak, you know you need not fear."

He nodded. "I wanted to ask... do you know why she gave me no gift?"

"Hmmm. Are you sure of that?"

Kilek gave a bitter laugh now. "Each time I see my friends I'm sure of it."

"What did she tell you? Her words, if you can recall them."

He took a moment. "That she would change me and something about being chosen because of 'vast potential'. There was more but I don't know, it's hard to remember."

"I know this will hardly seem satisfactory, my boy but I believe that, in time, her words will become clearer and for now, you must continue to be who you have always been."

Kilek met the Servant's kind gaze. "And who is that?"

Now he smiled. "Better if you come to your own realisation, I think."

Chapter 5.

Kilek trudged along the back lane that ran behind fields of waving grass. A warm wind whipped across the farmlands, many of them plots atop the hills themselves. Those same hills he and Tyar had run and laughed and hid amongst as children. But there was no-one left to chase them out of the stalks now, not even the ominous bark of Old Man Dorael's dogs.

His friends were just as silent. All the joy at their transformation torn away by the scenes in the village.

Grey filled half the sky as a cloudbank crept closer but there was no scent of rain on the air yet. He carried his bow with an arrow set to the string, which made it hard to untangle his cloak whenever it caught on the hilt of his old, borrowed sword.

Mathila led them south toward the river, following the invaders' trail – mostly a trampling of grass beside the road and the occasional discarded item; a broken blade forged in a mysterious pale blue and a set of snapped shoelaces. So far, they'd not seen any sign of the Minjao army but that didn't mean scouts weren't still in the area. Everyone kept watch on their surroundings, straining their ears for the sound of hooves, hands never far from weapons. Only Mathi seemed comfortable with a sword – the blade Kilek found in the slide. Tarvis had taught her every spare minute and before meeting the Goddess, it seemed Mathi would one day make the long journey to the royal city to train as a soldier.

How much closer to that dream was she suddenly – and yet, how much further?

Kilek glanced over his shoulder often. Several times he stumbled on the uneven ground, which was ridiculous. He'd made the trek dozens of times, knew every stone, root and ridge in the paths. Servant Bastiem's words echoed in his mind. *Better if you come to your own realisation, I think.* What had he meant by that? Had the Goddess… spoken to Bastiem too? Kilek would have asked the man but a cry from the children shortened their conversation – he'd hurriedly explained their plan and asked the Servant to look in on Camilea before leaving with a promise not to act rashly, despite the man's protests.

"How's everything back here, rear guard?" Tyar asked as he slowed his pace so Kilek could catch up.

"Fine."

"Good. Ah, Kil, are you all right? You know… with everything."

"I'm fine."

"I'm sure Avendria gave you something."

"Thanks, I'm sure she did too," Kilek said flatly.

"Hey, don't blame me. None of this was my idea," he replied with a frown.

Kilek stopped but before he could answer – he had no

idea what he was going to say – Paxoph called from ahead.

"Riders."

Together, Kilek and Tyar ran forward to crouch with the others at the edge of a farm, the wooden fence bearing fresh saw marks. Beyond, the hills fell away to the southern plains, which in turn sloped down toward the Crioise River, where it swept along in a dark line, scattered willows lining its banks.

Between the still-distant river and the edge of the farm a pair of horsemen approached. Their mounts tore clods of earth as the riders kicked, glancing over their shoulders. Shouts were lost in the wind but the pair was being pursued by a larger force of five. All wore similar clothing, a green uniform with white cinches.

The two in the lead turned sharply, heading for the river.

"Minjao," Alira said.

"And two of them deserters, it seems." Paxoph pointed with his bow. "They're going to be cut off."

Three of the pursuers were already angling toward the Crioise while the remaining two held their course. The deserters, if that was what they were, either did not see or were gambling that they'd reach the water first.

Even so, that was its own risk – the Crioise was old and deep, swift moving.

One of the pursuers readied a bow, steering with his knees only as he drew his string. He took aim, waiting for the right moment. Kilek held his breath.

The soldier fired.

One of the deserters stiffened and toppled from his horse.

Alira gasped and Paxoph muttered a prayer.

"Should we help them?" Kilek asked.

"We'll share their fate if we do," Mathila replied, her own expression grim.

Below, the remaining deserter had reached the water. More arrows were loosed, but they flew wide. The man flung himself from his saddle. He hit the surface with a splash and the current drew him away.

The horsemen fired yet more shafts into the river but it was impossible to tell whether the man survived, a thicker stand of trees soon swallowing the riders. Kilek stared after them, fists clenched.

"We should wait until they've gone," Paxoph said.

The Minjao did not search long before heading back to the southwest, toward Birnvile. As soon as the soldiers were out of sight, Mathi started forward, moving swiftly. Kilek ran in a half crouch, watching for any sign of the enemy but saw no-one – even a distant farmhouse seemed empty, no smoke rising from its roof, no animals moving about the yard.

When they reached the body of the deserter, they gathered around. The man was lying face down, blood from the arrow staining his uniform. The clothing did not fit too well and his belt was empty of sword or scabbard and he wore no armour, yet a winged helmet had rolled across the field.

Kilek couldn't look away; though he wanted to. Yet something caught his eye – the man clutched a rectangular pendant on a leather cord, the face showing a crude image of rain falling from a cloud. A charm sometimes used by farmers to the west of Hasere.

"He was a farmer," Kilek said as he pointed. "Look."

"They probably conscripted him too," Alira said.

"Shouldn't we check to see... you know?" Tyar asked.

Paxoph knelt and rolled the man onto his back. The conscripted soldier wore an expression of terror, eyes bulging, frozen in death. Blood seeped from his mouth.

Now Kilek looked away.

"No-one from home," Alira said, her voice barely above a whisper.

"We have to keep moving," Mathila said. "We need to save our families – we will avenge this man too."

"I hope we can," Kilek said.

Mathi frowned. "What do you mean? We don't have any choice."

He stared down at the deserter. "I hope we can protect each other too."

"We will." Her fierce expression had not changed when he met her gaze again.

"Do we bury him?" Tyar asked.

Mathi hesitated. "We should... and Goddess forgive me but I don't think we should risk the Minjao coming back."

When no-one objected, she started toward the river. Slowly, they followed. Kilek found himself the last to move. What were they going to do? How, by the Goddess, could they take on an entire army?

"I hope you're watching over us," he murmured.

They trekked in silence until they reached the intersection where the east road met the southern highway. There, the pale stone of the Crioise Bridge stretched across the river and a small post watched over a raft. The door to the wooden building was closed and no movement appeared behind the window. The faded planks of the pier stood empty too.

"Think they've taken Wilieu as well?" Tyar asked as they

approached, bows held ready.

"Would they bother?" Kilek asked.

"If the Westerners are such a large force, they wouldn't need the raft – and if they're sticking to the road this is out of their path, remember?" Mathi said.

She took them down the short flight of steps, calling for Wilieu. When no-one answered she peered within, then looked back. "Empty. And nothing looks disturbed."

"Should we leave now or look around a little more?" Kilek asked.

"I say we go now. It's still the best way to catch them, isn't it?" Tyar asked. "Assuming they're still heading for Birnvile."

"It seems likely, if they're trying to conscript as many as possible, Birnvile is closest," Paxoph said.

"Right," Mathi nodded.

Paxoph knelt to start on the mooring ropes. Kilek leapt aboard the raft, setting down his pack with its bread, fruit, water flask and blankets, and lifted the poles. He kept one for himself and passed the others to Tyar and Mathila when they joined him.

"Everyone aboard?" Mathi asked as she drove her pole into the green of the river.

Kilek joined her, leaning into it and slowly, the three of them pushed their way out of the shallows, reeds almost slithering against the wood. The current soon assisted but he kept up for a little while, long enough to break into a sweat. Paxoph offered to take over and Kilek thanked him, sitting to watch the banks slide by, a mixture of bright green grass and the somewhat more subdued willows.

Alira soon took over from Mathila, who joined him where they sat with their packs.

Kilek found himself staring; struck once more by how much she had changed and how much she'd stayed the same. Where once her smile had caused an invisible shiver within him, the very few times she'd smiled since leaving home had been... confusing. She was beautiful now and stronger too, if that was possible. She'd always been determined, diligent in her training but a simmering anger resided within now – both hands were clenched into fists where they sat in her lap and so he did not speak... yet it seemed she wanted to.

Quite some time passed before she finally did. "What do you think the Goddess meant by a 'great threat', Kilek?"

"Truly?"

"Yes, what did she tell you – the same as the rest of us?"

He shrugged. "I suppose," he said, and shared what he could remember. Each and every detail was difficult to bring back to mind – her golden eyes seemed most vivid in his mind, but he was certain he covered most of what had been said. "Did you see the insects?"

She nodded. "If that is the threat, then what of the Minjao?"

"Do you think they're connected?"

"Why not?"

He shivered.

"I have wondered the same," Paxoph said from where he worked.

"The creature Kilek and I found seemed deadly enough," Tyar added. "But it was a lot smaller than the ones the Goddess showed us."

"And if the Westerners *are* being controlled somehow?" Kilek asked.

"Then I hope the Lady Avendria gave us something more

than this," Alira said, her expression sombre as she gestured vaguely to her body.

Chapter 6.

The scent of wild mint filled their hiding place at the edge of the woods. Kilek moved the branch of a shrub aside, very, very slowly, gripping the smooth bark as the enormity of their task hit him anew.

He'd been far from confident before but now...

Men in the green and white uniform marched beneath the darkening sky, filling the road and spilling onto the grass, the rumble of their boots trampling everything. *Hundreds* of soldiers were headed west across the plain, their bearing watchful, hands on weapons. Most carried swords but just as many carried spears. All wore chain mail beneath their tabards and thin, leather cylinders hung from their white belts. He could not clearly see the faces of those on horseback, obscured by both the distance and their winged helms.

"There," Tyar whispered.

Figures marched in a line within the centre of the troops, their gait not as purposeful. Men and women, young and old, weighed down by packs, were almost being herded along. They, too, wore green, though no armour or weapons. Their expressions seemed slack and empty, though just as many were glaring at their captors.

Kilek's knuckles grew white on the branch as he squinted but none of the conscripted people seemed familiar. Mathila growled from where she'd leant forward. "It's not them – they must be people from outlying farms of Rams... or even Birnvile, they've probably already hit the town."

"There must be over four hundred without the conscripts," Paxoph said.

Silence fell across them.

"So, what now?" Tyar eventually said. Beyond the screen of trees, the soldiers flowed on. None seemed interested in the woods, but if someone did spot them, the plan was to flee back to the Crioise, which flowed on a little ways behind them.

"We could follow. Plan an ambush at night, if we could locate the officers' tents," Mathila said. "Maybe Prince Yan is with them."

No-one answered.

Her jaw was clenched.

Tyar shifted his position. "Someone in that force still might know where our families are," he said, offering a smile but Mathila was still staring at the army.

"Or maybe in Birnvile," Kilek said. "They would have left people behind again if they were too sick or old."

"It's not that far," Alira added. "We'd reach it before nightfall."

"And I bet we could catch up to this lot again easily enough," Tyar said. "With that many people they haven't been moving too fast."

Mathila was nodding now. "That's true – we need more information."

"We should stop a moment to eat," Paxoph said. "Let them get out of sight."

Their meal was a cold one, mostly bread and cheese taken from home. Every bite was dull and Kilek found himself drinking more from his water flask as he watched the flow of men on the road begin to recede. Why had they come? Had people from the distant northern empire truly attacked? Minjao was a giant nation... why did they have to steal people from Luargot?

Tyar stood the moment the soldiers were gone.

"Not yet," Mathila said, waving him down.

"Why not?"

"They might have rear scouts, fool."

He raised his hands. "Right."

Kilek wasn't sure how much time passed before Mathila finally pushed to her feet, but he blinked back sleep as he waited – and she'd been right about the rear scouts. Once the small unit of men had passed, she led everyone from the trees and started across the grass once more, running parallel with the road, heading away from the invaders.

Again, few words passed between them as they travelled.

When the stone rooves of Birnvile appeared below, spread around a small vale, Mathila had them crawling up the crest beside the road, peering around moss-covered boulders. The sun had not fully disappeared but the air was already cooling.

Warm light should have spilled from the windows.

Yet the town stood silent and cold.

"Is it safe?" Tyar asked, keeping his voice low.

"Let's find out," Mathila said. "Everyone keep an arrow

ready."

They started down the slope, spreading out. Kilek kept his bow half-raised, gripping it hard, glancing between the homes and the surrounding wood beyond the town, yet no-one appeared.

Relief was mingled in with the fear, the tension in every muscle – he'd never shot a man before, what would it be like? Hunting at least provided food for Hasere; what would killing someone provide?

But he knew, if attacked, he would fire.

Because the Minjao were wrong.

He circled the first home they came across, pausing to listen beside a window. Only silence from beyond the glass. Alira crept up beside him, one eyebrow raised. He shrugged as he whispered. "I think the house is empty."

Together, they moved through a sleeping vegetable patch and came to the next house and this time Alira peeked within, moving back to shake her head. Across the dirt street, Mathila and Paxoph were leaving a larger building, shaking their heads when Tyar met them. He, too, seemed to have found no-one.

Kilek waved to get their attention and then signalled deeper into Birnvile, toward the hulking shape of the Butterbread Inn. He'd visited it only twice before, once with Tyar while helping Ganoit haul grain after locusts struck the town's crops, and once with Camilea – she'd ordered ale and wine until she fell down, only to be hauled outside where she vomited and promptly began snoring. If only Camilea was his biggest problem once more.

But if any people had been left behind, the inn would be a good place to search.

And maybe rest too.

The others darted up the main street now. He glanced around as he ran, Alira following suit. They crossed an earth torn by the heavy tread of boots and hooves, closing on the quiet inn, reaching the carved doors just after Tyar.

"Think there's anyone here?" Kilek asked.

"I hope so," he said.

Mathila pushed the door open with her foot, her blade held ready.

Inside, chairs and tables had been reduced to kindling – all swept into one corner, seeming to draw attention to bloodstains on the common room floor, visible even in the dim light. They spread out once more. The central fireplace lay cold, the big mirror above it cracked. Pieces glittered on the floorboards below, catching the remaining light.

"Tyar, take Kilek and check upstairs," Mathila said. "We'll take the kitchen and the stables but we still need to be careful. Just because we haven't–"

Wood crashed against wood.

Men in green and white poured into the room – the first one knocked Paxoph to the floor so fast that Kilek didn't have time to raise his bow before a thin man, their leader it seemed, barked an order. "Throw your weapons down or die where you stand." His Minjao accent was light, a mere clipping of the words.

A trap! Kilek hesitated, Tyar too, he was scowling at the invaders but it was Mathi who lifted her sword and stepped closer. "We're not going to surrender to a pack of pigs like you."

He narrowed his eyes at her. Black hair peeked beneath his helm, which had a more ornate set of wings. "Ten of us and only five of you, lady. And one a kid at that. Sure you want to play that game?"

"Listen, if you come peacefully then you'll survive," another soldier added, his voice a little harder to understand. "Isn't that better than dying here?"

"Even if we die, half of you will come with us," Mathila said, her voice tight. Her jaw was clenched and her hand trembled ever-so-slightly, but was it fear or rage? Was she thinking of her parents? Everything her father taught her?

The leader grunted, muttering something in his own language before pointing a finger at her. "My orders are to recruit, not kill but I'll not hesitate if you force my hand."

"Mathi?" Alira's voice bore a note of worry.

A moment of silence passed before a new voice spoke. "Such tension!"

Kilek looked up to the staircase, where a tall figure peeked down with a grin. He was a spindly fellow wearing a long, dark cloak and gloves of white leather. His hair was a blond tangle, swept away from piercing green eyes.

Some soldiers shifted focus but did not attack; even the leader seemed dumbfounded.

The stranger started down the stairs, skipping the final few to land with a grin. "Quickly now, someone ask for my name – I love introductions."

Kilek gaped.

The leader of the Westerners spat. "It must be Fool, but if you know what's good for you, you'll be surrendering like these villagers here."

The odd man raised an eyebrow. "Or?"

"What?"

"Or. It's a *conjunction*, my dear Sergeant. We tend to use it to suggest options a person might be presented. Say, between honey *or* milk. I hope that helps dispel any confusion."

The sergeant's eyes were bulging. "Kill this imbecile!"

Two soldiers started forward, the faint-blue steel of their swords clear even in the poor light.

The stranger snapped his gloved fingers and the soldiers ceased moving – all of them – utterly frozen in place. Next, the man side-stepped to face the majority of the Minjao soldiers, then he glanced back at Kilek. His eyes were alight with suppressed excitement, as if he were about to reveal a great secret.

"This won't hurt you folks but why don't you cover your ears just to be safe – mistakes are so messy, after all."

"What do you mean..." Kilek trailed off when the fellow spread his arms wide and took a deep breath. Kilek slammed his hands over his ears just as the stranger's arms swung together.

Leather smacked against leather, the clap rocking the whole inn.

Soldiers flew back, smashing through the windows and walls. Their bodies bounced across the earth, still locked in whatever pose they'd held before being frozen. A mess of shattered glass and splintered wood lay behind.

Kilek found himself gaping like a half-wit once more. What magic had he witnessed? Who was the man if he could do such things? It was nothing like the tracking powers of the Hounds or the herb lore of Gile the Kettle Witch – not even the mysterious Cloud Painters of Jasoria could do such things.

"There we go," the tall man said with a grin.

"Are they... are they all dead?" Paxoph asked from where

he was climbing to his feet. Blood ran down his face from a cut on his temple.

"I'm not really sure," the fellow replied, still grinning. "But I don't think we should stay to find out, do you?"

Chapter 7.

"By the Gods, who are you?" Mathila demanded.

"Finally!" the man said. He dropped to one knee, spreading his arms as if to welcome her. "I am the great mage Florique, famous in all the lands for my feats, which are both many *and* varied."

Silence.

"Thank you," Paxoph finally said. "We appreciate you saving us."

Florique's expression fell a little. "Not one of you? Not even a single rumour?"

Tyar shrugged. "Sorry."

"This is hardly tolerable. How long have I been away?"

Alira's eyes were alight with curiosity. "Did you once live in this area?"

"Long ago, my dear." He rose, wiping dust from the knee of his pants. "I wonder, would you permit a travelling companion? In such dangerous times, it would be prudent to stay together – you no doubt agree."

Kilek glanced at his friends. Alira was smiling and

despite Mathila's silence, it seemed she could see the benefits of having such a powerful mage along. Pax and Tyar were nodding too. Especially considering how easily they'd fallen into the Minjao trap – how long would the sergeant have stayed, waiting for people to return to the town?

Alira placed her hands together. "I know we would feel safer having you along. I... I wonder what threat such men would pose you, if you will forgive me for asking, sir?"

He grinned. "I am but one man and they are many."

"Several hundred by our count, without the conscripts," Mathila said.

"Yes," Florique said, "and another two hundred at least have already headed further south, no doubt to gather the unwilling citizens of Gerdric village into their insidious cause."

"Gerdric? There's barely two dozen people there," Paxoph said.

Florique shrugged. "Perhaps less, but I wonder if their true destination might be the royal city. I overheard them nattering away in their sharp tongue and it seemed Alaycron was mentioned."

"Did they say anything about Hasere?" Paxoph asked.

"Hmmm... Perhaps something about recruits from there."

"Then it's possible they've been taken either north or west, as part of that sweep," Mathila said.

"Certainly," Florique replied.

"We saw no-one from home with the force heading west," Tyar said. "I don't think we should ignore the possibility."

"Then it's settled," Florique said, clapping his hands together with apparent glee.

Kilek flinched but no wave of magic cast him aside – and,

he was relieved to note, he hadn't been the only one to react with fear.

The mage offered a sheepish grin. "Apologies all."

"We should leave," Paxoph said. "There could be other soldiers out there."

Tyar led them from the building, bow half-drawn. Kilek readied his own, but beyond the mute shapes of the soldiers – still frozen – he could see little in the dark village. Glass crunched beneath their feet but their small group was soon on the outskirts of town, travelling down the paved southern highway with its shadowy trees.

Beside Kilek, Tyar glanced over his shoulder. "Do you think we should trust him?"

Kilek followed Tyar's gaze. A little ways behind, Alira was listening to Florique, most of the mage's words too soft to make out, though it seemed they were speaking about light. Her face was too hard to see properly, but the tilt of her head suggested the man was saying something interesting. Paxoph and Mathila were walking to the rear, weapons still held ready. "He saved us," Kilek said, "that has to count for something, doesn't it? If he meant harm, he could have let the soldiers take us or just used magic against us. He's obviously powerful enough."

"You're right, but... something seems odd."

"He's definitely odd."

"I know that but it's more. As Alira said, why would someone as powerful as him need to travel with us?"

"It's like he said, even a powerful mage would have trouble fending off a hundred spears or arrows."

"I suppose that's true but we wouldn't be that much help against a hundred men."

"Maybe he just wants someone to share a watch at night? Or maybe he's lonely."

Tyar chuckled. "Or maybe *you're* the odd one."

Kilek aimed a kick at his friend, but Tyar skipped away, still grinning.

By the time the moon had risen, Kilek found himself blinking back sleep once more, stumbling often. The shadowy fields and rows of elms had given way to stony hills and finally, ruins whose masonry gleamed in the moonlight. Merely a dozen buildings, all crumbling now. Rumour called it an outpost of the Moon-Wardens – magical people who had ruled the lands aeons past. According to Servant Bastiem's books, they spent only a short time in the lands before disappearing, supposedly dissatisfied with what they saw.

Most of the stones had an unfamiliar design, the few windows and doorways that remained were triangular, but with a tiny circle above the top point. Perhaps they had once held glass but when he'd visited the ruins years ago, Tyar at his side, they'd found nought but weeds and clumps of rotten wood.

"We could camp here," Mathila said.

"As no doubt the Minjao thought," Florique observed.

"Do you suspect another trap?" Alira asked.

"Not precisely, but it might be possible to learn something here if any had." He pointed to the centremost building, which boasted half a roof. "That one looks cosy enough, let's find some firewood."

"Is that safe?" Pax asked.

"You have my guarantee," the man said.

Tyar frowned. "How?"

Florique winked. "Magic, of course."

Mathila grabbed Tyar's arm. "Come on, I'm too tired for this. Let's just find what we can and set up camp."

Paxoph and Alira headed off in a different direction, leaving Florique standing before Kilek. The mage gave a nod. "Help me, won't you, Kilek?"

"Of course," Kilek said, following the mage around the side of a low, uneven wall. Tyar's suspicions echoed in Kilek's mind but he dismissed them. Florique was eccentric and quite powerful, but the mage had no reason to harm them. A fallen trunk, long-since turned hollow, lay against the stones. So pale as to be white in the moonlight, it would be perfect for firewood – as other travellers had assumed, if the half-broken shape was any indicator.

Florique kicked at an irregular piece, the crack loud in the night.

Kilek knelt to tear at more pieces, starting a small pile beside him.

"You seem troubled, young Kilek."

He kept his eyes on his work. "Do I?"

"Yes." Florique's voice was quiet and for the first time, utterly without any trace of sardonic humour. Kilek looked up. The mage's eyes appeared especially dark in the night. "It must be difficult being the youngest."

Kilek almost smiled. "They're not that much older than I."

"Of course." His tone remained understanding. "Well, I sense something about you that they do not. Something that has not yet flowered. Patience will help, though it will not seem enough, at times."

What did he mean–

A shout rang out.

Kilek spun to his feet. Mathi stood before the ruin, swinging her blade at a dark shape moving through the air. It buzzed in and out of her range, body and wings gleaming, too fast for her sword. An insect? Kilek fumbled with the hilt of his own weapon as he ran forward, but Florique caught his shoulder.

"Let me."

The mage raised a hand and silver light bloomed. A web shot forth. It tracked the creature through the air then struck, wrapping itself around the insect. It thudded to the ground, still aglow, though the light dimmed by the time Kilek neared.

"What is it?" Paxoph asked as he ran up, Alira and Tyar in tow.

Dark wings, six legs and bulging eyes faintly purple in the web's fading glow... an acrid scent. Kilek shuddered. "*Cabeku.*"

"Let's get it away from the camp," Tyar said.

Florique nodded as he skipped to the insect and flung his leg back – kicking it into the shadows. "There. So then, what are we having for the evening meal?"

Kilek glanced at his friends, whose expressions seemed to be mirrors of the shock that kept his limbs tense and his heart rate jumping.

"We're safe to stay here?" Mathi asked.

"I sense nothing else like the Cabeku nearby," Florique said, then snapped his fingers. Orange flames leapt up from the fire pit. The new light added a somewhat sinister look to his sharp features. "It is likely the only one. A scout, perhaps."

"For the Minjao?" Tyar asked.

"Possibly," he said. "After all, Javoteth is one of the western gods and he *is* known to command the insects, spiders and reptiles."

Kilek blinked. He'd forgotten the name but now, it was impossible not to recall the Goddess speaking it during her warning. Alira looked out into the night and no-one was willing to share what they'd heard, which was probably for the best.

Florique chuckled. "Worry not, I will cloak this place as we sleep."

"That would be most welcome," Paxoph said. Like the others, his expression may have contained a trace of doubt but weariness was far more visible.

"You can actually do that?" Alira asked, leaning closer.

"Certainly. Though not indefinitely, and we may wish to post a watch as well – for while no insect will find us, soldiers may still stumble upon this place."

"I will take first watch," Alira offered, then hesitated. "I would be honoured to hear more of such magic, if you would not mind?"

"It's no trouble," he replied.

"I'll take second," Mathi said.

"Give me the last then," Paxoph replied.

Kilek did not volunteer; he did not even wait for their meal, instead he kept his head down and busied himself with rummaging through his pack for blanket and bedroll. There was simply no way he could stay awake that long, even if his friends had been blessed by the Goddess and were obviously strong enough... yet his shame did not overwhelm him – Tyar had not volunteered either.

And so Kilek lay back and closed his eyes, letting the soft sounds of Florique and Alira's voices lull him to sleep.

Chapter 8.

No-one reprimanded Kilek for his weakness the next morning... yet he needed no help for that. He walked at the rear, slashing at weeds and saplings with a stick, scowling up at the sun where it fell across both road and field. Light sparkled on dew where it clung to the grass and leaves; everywhere he turned it was more pleasant views of the countryside in its greens and yellows, bright beneath the giant blue sky.

Even the trampled grass beside the road could have been – if he pretended – just signs of a farmer leading cattle from one field to another... but it wasn't that at all. They'd seen no-one all morning.

Everything had changed.

In just a single day.

Yesterday he'd woken to spring, to what would surely be just another regular day, the chore of the temple cleaning to be dealt with and then a fine meal at the inn to look forward to, and once his sister passed out, some reading or carving that evening...

Life was suddenly uncertain.

His own future? Just as unfathomable now. Or worse. If he believed the Goddess, it would be swallowed up by a time of darkness. Far darker than having to find his place in the village while dealing with Camilea. And no choice about his future had seemed quite right before... he'd even considered following in Servant Bastiem's footsteps. More often and more foolishly, daydreams about leaving Hasere with Mathi to become a King's Sentinel, the finest of knights, and there, he'd grow strong enough for her to notice him...

Such tiny, tiny problems compared to the Cabeku, compared to what was seemingly a dark war to come.

Now he sneered.

The dreams of a child.

But hadn't the Goddess seen something in him? He hacked his way through another pair of thistles. Why include him otherwise? If he couldn't stay up all night, well, he'd find something else he could do. He would *never* be a burden on his friends; he'd find a way to help.

Mathi led from the front. "We need to get ahead of the army somehow, we can't do anything unless we know which unit has our families," she said. "This isn't enough."

"But even if we do, how do we save everyone?" Tyar replied. "It's the same old problem, isn't it?"

Florique strode alongside them, seemingly content to listen.

But no-one else had any ideas and so they marched until noon, stopping to eat in a thin stand of juniper. It was not much in the way of cover, not if an enemy drew close, but from a distance it might help. As he ate his bread and cheese, staring across the green fields, Kilek kept half-an eye on the sky. Would the Cabeku return? And did the Minjao army truly use them as scouts? It couldn't be. The Westerners might have been warlike but they wouldn't stoop to using such creatures.

Supposedly, both Father and Mother had fought them when young, in the battle that took place in the ruined Wickerlands... but none of their letters ever spoke a bad word about their enemy. There was admiration for their skill, for the way they fought, with 'honour and grace' to use his father's words. It didn't sound like the kind of people who'd use foul monsters... so what by all the Gods was this Prince Yan up to?

"Kilek?"

He turned from the farmland. Alira stood nearby, dark hair falling around her hand where it shielded her eyes from the glare.

"Is something wrong?" he asked.

"No, I just wanted to check on you."

"Check on me?"

She joined him, and he had to look up to her now; they'd always been the same height. But she offered a gentle smile. "It must be difficult."

He swallowed the lump in his throat, a wave of emotion stealing his voice a moment. Her words were hardly cruel but they'd struck him a little hard with their kindness. He managed a smile of his own. "I suppose. What about you?"

She sighed. "Florique is... well, if I talk to him about magic, I don't have to think about Father as much. What he might be going through."

He nodded, and nearly said something reassuring but it

would have seemed... he didn't know. Empty? How could he possibly offer comfort? After all, his own family had not been taken. The task facing them was just so enormous. Instead, he asked her about Florique. "What does he say about the feelings you have?"

"He thinks I might be able to learn true magic," she said, and now her smile was one of joy, a flash of her former, younger self. "And that the way I can sense things sometimes is a sign of the ability. He said he can teach me."

"Well, we could use the help," Kilek said before lowering his voice. "But, do you trust him that much?"

"I think so."

Paxoph approached. "Ready to resume our trek?"

Mathi, Tyar and Florique were already moving along the road, seeming to stride tall beneath the weight of their packs.

"Yeah," Kilek said, as he lifted his own pack with a slight frown and started after his friend. Alira followed and though they did not speak any more of Florique, the mage was difficult to simply brush from his thoughts. The man *could* be trusted... because it all came down to a question of why? Why go to the trouble of saving everyone if he was just going to do something underhanded later?

That didn't make sense.

A soft wind swung across the fields as they travelled, not enough to stir much dust but it lessened the warmth from the sun and the breeze slowly grew stronger as the afternoon wore on. When they moved into a more wooded area, not quite a forest but still providing some shade, white and blue butterflies flocked to a patch of flowers. Kilek had started up a sloping hill, water flask raised, half-an eye on the butterflies, when he thumped into Tyar, who'd already reached the top. "What's wrong?"

The question hung in the silence.

He could not speak.

A large force of Westerners lay below, their tents spread across the road and even amongst the edges of the trees. The camp was easily large enough to contain the soldiers they'd been following – only this encampment seemed to include far fewer conscripts. A second force?

"Get down you fools," a voice hissed.

Too late.

The cry of a horn rang out from below – men in green and white uniforms pointing to the hill as they ran to the picket lines and their waiting mounts.

"What do we do?" Alira cried.

Mathi spun to Florique. "Can you stop them?"

He shrugged. "Not unless you want me to kill everyone down there – including the conscripts."

"Then hide us?" Tyar asked, his eyes wide.

The mage stretched his arms above his head. "Sorry, that's not one of my skills either – invisibility requires far too much concentration even to hide a single person, it's quite boring."

Kilek gaped at the man, then back to the approaching soldiers. "We have to do something now!"

Mathi had a hand on her sword but there was as much fear as anger in her gaze.

"I suggest splitting up," Florique said. "That way, whoever *isn't* captured can still do some rescuing. Well, good luck everyone." And then he was running, sprinting into the trees like a dark streak.

New shouts rose from below, the thud of hooves with

them. Kilek swallowed; his heart was beating way too fast and his legs were frozen. Move, fool!

"Go!" Mathi shouted.

He spun and hurtled down the hill. Footsteps followed but he didn't turn to see who owned them. Panic drove him on. At the bottom, he skidded across the loam beneath the trees, gripping the bark of an elm to execute an abrupt turn, flinging himself deeper. He swatted at branches as he crashed through the undergrowth, chest heaving.

Worse than a wild animal.

But his limbs refused to pay attention to his mind – he was making enough noise to bring the entire Minjao army down upon him!

The footfalls no longer kept pace with his. But the sound of the horses had neared and now the Westerners' voices seemed to share more words; coordinating a proper search rather than simple pursuit.

It drove Kilek on until the tree trunks began to thin. He needed more cover. He whirled once more and there, ahead, a hollowed log, near-buried in deep green moss.

He charged forward then slung himself inside. He slid on damp leaves, weapons scraping wood. But it was enough; the dark interior covered him, cloaking him enough that the adrenaline began to ease despite his still-straining lungs. Even the rich scent of earth was somehow soothing. It was a good hiding place, but would it be good enough? If the soldiers glimpsed the direction he'd taken, it would be useless. He had to be still. Quiet. Had to control his breathing. Had to stare at the circle of light that revealed the rest of the woods, and strain his hearing for any sound that seemed out of place.

He gripped the hilt of his belt knife.
And waited.

Chapter 9.

Voices drifted closer.

The western language. Triumph mixed in with the harshness of barked orders – but Luargot words too, a deep voice echoing between the unfamiliar phrases.

"Leave her. We've already surrendered, haven't we?"

Pax.

Kilek closed his eyes even as he gripped his knife harder. "We'll free you. Both of you." Though exactly who he meant by 'we' remained unclear. One thing he was sure of, without Florique there was no chance of actually succeeding. The Minjao numbers were simply too great. What was King Hadeon doing? Did he even know what was afoot in his kingdom's north?

New voices were joined by new footsteps and both neared swiftly. Kilek shrunk further into the log. How close were they?

Now the clink of steel against steel. Muttering and the creak and swish of branches being moved.

Still the opening to the log remained clear.

Two voices, very distinct now.

"Leave, leave, leave," Kilek breathed.

A shadow covered the opening, the man's face indistinct but he raised an arm to gesture for Kilek to come out. He spoke a few words, his tone sharp. Impatient.

Found.

A sinking feeling in his gut washed over Kilek and he ground his teeth.

The soldier thumped the log. Dirt filtered down, slipping between the neck of Kilek's tunic.

He still had his knife... but he was trapped. And he'd be useless against the soldiers even if he could use it. No choice but to give up – for now. "I'm coming."

Kilek dragged himself toward the light. When he neared the entry, strong arms gripped his own, hauling him free and tossing him to the ground. He hit the loam with a thud and a grunt. His knife bounced free. Before he could even move, something dug into his back. Someone gripped his hands and wrenched them behind, rope swiftly wrapping his wrists.

He ground his teeth, fighting back a rush of panic. What would they do to him? Was he going to be beaten? Did the Minjao torture prisoners? What had Mother said about them, and would they kill him if he couldn't meet their expectations?

Kilek dug his nails into his palm.

Calm down.

They wanted soldiers; they wouldn't simply beat him to a pulp for sport... surely.

Someone hauled him to his feet – and he had to recognise their efficiency; his capture spoke of a competence so ingrained it seemed casual.

A soldier stepped into view. The man appeared somewhat weary but his dark eyes locked with Kilek's and then he lifted his sword, the blue-tint to the blade gleaming. Next, the soldier pointed to Kilek, then back to the blade, shaking his head.

Kilek nodded.

The message was clear – do not try to escape.

"*Bao nan*," the man said, then sheathed his blade and turned to leave.

The other westerner gave Kilek a shove. He stumbled forward, managing to keep his feet, then followed the first soldier. The leader, if that's who he was, had already started to shove his way through the wood.

And there, the trail of broken branches, scraped bark and trampled plants Kilek had made offered a painfully obvious trail for the Minjao to follow... his hiding place had always been a terrible one. Fool.

Kilek scanned his surrounds as he walked; just dark tree trunks, serrated leaves and the scent of churned earth and flowering shrubs, it should have been pleasant. No sign of other Minjao nor his friends – though they must have been close by, Paxoph at least had been captured within earshot.

Only after his captors had broken free of the trees, climbed the hill and then descended into the camp, did Kilek get his answer.

At least, some of it.

Pax and Alira sat in the dirt between two dark, canvas tents at the edge of the camp, hands bound. Paxoph bled from a cut on his cheek; he glared at the Minjao where he sat. Alira bore a mark at her throat and her eyes were wide.

He took a step toward them, a reflex.

The soldier jerked him back into line, snarling something. Alira stood. "Kilek!"

"Don't provoke them," he replied. The moment the words left his mouth, one of Alira's guards shoved her back to the ground. Paxoph's jaw was clenched but he didn't move. Good. Pax would keep a level head somehow.

And Kilek had to do the same.

He looked down, staring at the torn grass as he was herded farther into the campsite. Hopefully Mathi, Tyar and Florique remained free. At least then, escape would remain possible. For it seemed that new 'recruits' were to be separated. Did that mean finding anyone from home just became that much harder?

Kilek's captor led him to a huge, bearded man who sat at a long table, his chair nothing more than cut log. Large Beard handed over a green tunic and sturdy-looking, if somewhat worn, boots. He then waved a hand in dismissal.

Nearby, a second soldier waited, his armour bearing a crane in flight; clearly marking him as someone important. This soldier wrote in a ledger. He glanced up at Kilek, narrowing his eyes a moment. "Where are you from, little mouse?" His accent was slight.

"Hasere."

"Ah, you are some distance from home, I see." The man made a mark in one of the columns – the symbols he used flowing like water.

"Why are you doing this?" Kilek asked.

"Tell me, boy. Have you heard of the Song of Silver?"

"No."

"Very well. What of the Night Thorn? I believe it is

sometimes known as the Mad King's Needle?"

He had; it was a legend he'd read many times. "It's probably only a fairy tale... sir." And a typically dark one at that. Why did the Minjao care about such a story?

He nodded, as though he was well-aware. "Please, tell me this fairy tale."

"The Night Thorn is supposed to be a mighty rose bush that King Isidon planted beneath his daughter's window to prevent suitors calling upon her." Kilek paused. "Ah... when one of them was caught nevertheless, the King had the man executed and his body thrown upon the rose bush as a warning."

"After which the daughter supposedly cursed her father and the rose – it never bloomed again and each year the thorns grew longer and sharper."

"Yes, sir. The story usually ends when she drives him into one of the thorns, years later."

"Correct. Now, have you ever seen anything like this?" The officer held up a ring of gold, engraved with an odd symbol that appeared somewhere between sun and spider.

Kilek frowned. Why were they interested in such things? "No, sir."

"Very well. You will be taken to be fed then we will break camp – and do not slow us down or you will be whipped."

Before Kilek could ask another question, he was hauled away, prodded toward a group of unarmed but green-clad people surrounded by the Minjao – Luargot conscripts. Once more, Kilek's captor shoved him forward, this time hard enough that his knees hit the earth. He swallowed a curse then straightened, keeping still as the soldier cut his bindings free and left without another word.

Kilek searched the faces of his fellow prisoners; there was a chance he'd seen someone from the village...

Yet none were familiar. Most expressions were dull as they started back, more than a few bright with fear. All had the look of villagers or farmers, something that he couldn't pinpoint, yet it was clear that all men and women before him were out of place in a war camp. Few approached him and no-one spoke too loudly.

It seemed most of the conscripts came from the southern villages and smaller towns.

And no-one really knew why they had been conscripted.

"Did they ask you about the Mad King Isidon too?" Kilek asked the younger fellow who'd sat beside him after the others moved back to their own small groups.

"Yeah. Makes no sense, right?"

"It doesn't," Kilek agreed. "What about the south? Isn't King Hadeon doing something about the Minjao?"

"Who knows?" the man, Laceon, said with a shrug. "Doubt it'd make any difference to us, we'll be long gone by then, fighting somewhere in the west."

"But why?"

"Something about a great war that all must engage in."

"Between who?"

"Well, old Feloise was the one that heard them mention it. They don't know he can understand a little Minjao but he was moved to another group."

Kilek frowned. "Here?"

"I think they do it to make sure we can't get too friendly with each other and plan something," he said. "So if you've got any ideas about escape, best to forget them, friend."

Chapter 10.

The only chance Kilek found to speak with Pax and Alira over the next few days was for a bare moment while filling their flasks at a stream. They'd been asked the same questions about fairy tales and had not been mistreated. Neither had caught even a glimpse of the others. And all too soon their respective minders sent them back to their place in the march.

Conscripts and Minjao soldiers alike continued west through the hills at a steady pace, moving deep into each evening, steering clear of bigger towns. It was a long and tedious march in many ways: wake, eat a serviceable stew, break camp then march until the process repeated itself in the growing darkness. The only time he was given to himself was sleep or visits to the latrines, great stinking pits that weren't always dug far enough from the camp itself for his comfort... but nor did he grow sick as he'd first feared.

Only one break in the routine existed – he was allowed to train with a wooden practice sword. And while they *were* teaching him how to fight, the purpose seemed equally to humiliate him and the other villagers.

His teacher was one of the only enemy soldiers who spoke Luargot, a large fellow called Souan, whose size concealed great speed – he did not ever lumber, though his voice did boom. The man's black hair had been tied into a long plait that he tucked within his breastplate when he sparred.

Though 'sparred' was being generous; it was more of a swift thumping whenever they faced each other one-on-one.

Even now, as Kilek swung the heavy wood in unison with the other conscripts, their grunts of effort echoing among the trees, it was hard not to imagine a disapproving expression on their instructor's face.

And despite the resentment that grew with each passing day, resentment that he couldn't help sending out in every direction; toward Florique for seemingly abandoning them, King Hadeon for being so oblivious to what was happening in his own kingdom, to the Minjao for everything they'd done – useless though such feelings were – Kilek actually looked forward to the brief training sessions.

After all, the Goddess has given him nothing; learning the sword was something he might one day use.

If he survived.

He swung an overhead blow now, trying to mirror the movements of the man in the green tunic before him. Each day brought them closer to the border… where further north waited Sassehim, and to the west the barren Wickerlands. Once within, if that was their path, the Minjao would be even harder to catch.

Was that where the rest of Hasere had been taken? There was still a chance *someone* from home travelled with him, wasn't there? Only being permitted to move to and from his tent, to the cauldron for food and to the latrines hardly allowed the chance for exploration. The few times he'd tried to approach another group of conscripts he'd been turned away by a guard – the first time with stern words he couldn't understand, and after that with a swift blow.

"You!"

Kilek looked up from the nearest conscript's back.

Souan snapped his fingers as he pointed. Kilek hurried from the line, trying to ignore the eyes that followed him. Though a mere dozen men and a few guards only, the weight of their gaze seemed like an entire town square. A twinge of tenderness in his forearm reminded him of his last sparring session as he gripped the haft.

The large man waved a hand. "Stance."

Kilek spread his feet the width of his shoulders and squared his leading foot with his opponent, as he'd been taught. Next, he gripped the handle with both hands, one close to the hilt and the other lower. Was that everything? Best to hurry, Souan didn't like to wait.

"Your wrists are too open," the man said.

Kilek adjusted and then the westerner nodded, lifting his staff. As usual, he didn't even bother with a practice sword. What mere conscript could challenge him?

A whistle rang out.

Kilek sprang back. The staff whistled through the space where his sword had been. But the Minjao soldier had not stopped his attack – the end of his weapon shot forward. Kilek twisted but a second jab struck his ribs. Pain spread through his torso and laughter echoed from the watching soldiers. Kilek fell to one knee but swiped his blade at where he sensed the man approaching.

A clack of wood was his only reward.

Before he could stand, something crashed across his back and he hit the dirt with a grunt.

More snickering and chuckles filled the clearing. Kilek ground his teeth.

Heavy footfalls neared and a shadow loomed over him. "Good."

Kilek blinked.

"Get up."

He found his feet, wincing at the tenderness in his side. Souan stood with arms folded, staff resting against him as he addressed the small crowd. "Take note. Despite his obvious failure, Kilek did not give up – you must do the same if you want to survive in the west."

"Yes, *hovar*," the farmers and villagers answered.

"Return to your other duties."

Kilek hesitated.

Souan glared down at him. "What is it?"

"*Hovar*, I want to learn more."

The man raised his eyebrows.

"Just now, it was mostly a reflex but I think–"

"You will never be a master swordsman, boy, but you might be able to learn enough to live. Be glad of that much."

Kilek flushed.

"Off with you."

Kilek strode from the man with clenched hands, laughter and jeers from the other soldiers ringing behind him, but he did not turn back. The Westerners' words were empty of meaning but he could guess easily enough.

Still, he would prove each and every one of them wrong.

Chapter 11.

Days of travel through the green hills with their sparse woods and old, half-buried stone fences, and still no rescue. Not even a *sign* that suggested the others had escaped and were following. Were they even now being taken west by a different enemy force?

One thought dominated all others: why was King Hadeon doing absolutely nothing to prevent his own people from being marched to their deaths in a distant war? Surely, the king was aware by now?

No rescue attempts had been made; their path always avoided towns with garrisons.

Before the young man, Laceon, had been moved to another group within the camp, he'd given Kilek his views on the matter. "The King has been reducing the numbers in each garrison for years, so exactly who is around to send word south? When was the last time anyone from the Knighthood visited your village?"

"I cannot remember." Not since he'd been a boy, back when Mother and Father had been alive.

"Exactly," Laceon had said with a nod, as if the matter had been settled.

"But word must be spreading *somehow*. Someone must have escaped capture – we did, for a time."

"Perhaps. But let's say that's true and our troops are out there, I suspect that if they actually do draw near, they will still fail to find us. Remember the man who asked about the Night Thorn?"

"What of him?"

"He is a *menbiya*."

"Like a mage?"

"Yes, supposedly the name for western mages that deal in illusion. He is hiding us."

"But how can you be sure?"

He shrugged. "Can't. But it's better than believing the king doesn't care at all, right?"

"Yes... but I think you already believe that."

Laceon smiled then and the expression seemed to draw attention to a flatness in his gaze. "You don't?"

Kilek didn't have an answer at the time and nor did he now – days since Laceon had been moved. It became clear that while people *had* formed bonds, they couldn't risk being seen speaking with any one person too often.

The farther north-west they travelled, the fewer towns or homes appeared beyond the roads, and the faster the leaders pushed everyone. They did not stop to drag more villagers into their ranks either, as if rushing to meet a deadline. Or perhaps the king's forces were closing in... but it hardly seemed likely.

He had to save himself.

Kilek's feet ached, as did his shoulders and arms, his

entire torso, and while he grew calluses on his hands from the wooden training sword, he did not seem to grow more skilled. Nor did he have a chance to speak to Pax or Alira again and his own ridiculous plans for escape hit the same walls each time. Even if he could steal a weapon and sneak past the sentries of a night, how could he abandon his friends?

If he tried, he would fail.

Yet one morning, a week after being captured, it seemed something was about to change.

A second group of Minjao soldiers, merely a dozen in number, waited at the Pale Gates, their horses grazing beneath the crooked stone pillars. Here, where the juniper and elms thinned and the hills fell away, was a former passage to the Wickerlands – or the Herismeda as it was known before the war, before the land itself had died and its people scattered.

The Minjao mage met the new soldiers as their march came to a halt in the middle of the road, responding as one to a shouted command from the nearest soldier. Kilek moved between those with craned necks who peered to the newcomers. For once, no nearby soldier frowned at him or shoved him back, most had removed their winged helms to lift their swords aloft, many with faint smiles upon their lips.

One of the new Minjao soldiers, his armour covered by a green and black tunic, strode forward and raised his voice. At his words all soldiers took a knee, Souan hissing at the conscripts.

Kilek obeyed; frowning at the stony earth... whoever had been waiting at the Pale Gates was obviously important. Could it be... the Minjao prince? Had 'Yan' been mentioned?

Hard to be sure. His time in the western camp was not enough to become familiar with many words at all, though he knew a handful of basic terms.

Footfalls approached, pausing at regular intervals where a few words were spoken, requests to rise, and then the figure drew nearer still.

"Stand and join the others by the Prince's tent." It was the mage.

Kilek hesitated. Was the man speaking to him?

"Hurry."

He lifted his head. The mage was nodding down at him. Kilek leapt to his feet then started toward the pavilion-like tent beyond the unfamiliar soldiers. It stood tall, a black peak with green birds in flight sewn into the tent flaps.

There, four other conscripts stood before a pair of heavily armed Minjao guards – these men also wearing similar uniforms, these of black and green instead of green and white. Their swords were sheathed but both men actually held long knives, handles facing out where they rested at their sides.

Kilek swallowed as he joined the line. Why had he been singled out? Had he done something wrong? The other villagers, two older men and a young woman, seemed just as confused, one trembled and the other had clenched both hands.

None spoke.

A soldier parted the tent flaps and pointed to the man beside Kilek. "You."

The conscript strode forward with a stiffness to his posture that suggested he fought to keep his fear under control as he entered the tent.

Kilek leant forward as he waited, straining his ears, yet no shouts or screams issued forth, only the low sounds of conversation – the words unclear, but not raised in anger at least. And soon enough the man was released, sent back to his position in the line of conscripts, just as another farmer joined the line.

The soldier who'd chosen the first man pointed to Kilek next. "Now you."

Kilek approached the tent, his apprehension easing, though confusion had taken its place. Just what did the prince want?

Inside, the guard ordered Kilek to kneel before a man seated at a folding wooden desk. Flaps had been rolled up on the sides of the tent to create windows but a single lamp also burned, further illuminating weapons and stands of armour.

A heavy hand fell upon Kilek's shoulder and the chill of steel came to rest against his neck. It did not yet touch him, did not draw blood, but the nearness prevented him from daring to even swallow while he waited for the prince to speak.

The Minjao royal wore a black tunic over what seemed to be a breastplate, with the green worked into the symbol of a crane upon his chest. When he tapped his fingers upon the table, twin tattoos were visible on the backs of his hands, both spirals of silver. Was it a sign of magic? The symbol gleamed even in the dim light of the tent.

"You are Kilek of Hasere?" The man's voice was deep and held within the expectation of an instant response.

"Yes... My Lord," Kilek said, adding an honorific at a squeeze from the guard holding him, hoping it would be enough.

"Tell me of the Rose of King Isidon," the prince asked, his dark eyes intent.

Kilek repeated the myth.

"Is that all?"

He hesitated. "Well, sometimes my grandmother had more to say."

"Go on."

"She said that the tree was burned to ash but seven thorns supposedly survived."

"And tell me of them, what else did she say, young Kilek?"

"That the princess' suitors took and carried them across the lands... as ah, partners in their grief, I think it went."

"Very good, Kilek of Hasere. Now, can you recall where?"

"I believe Torze Kebet and Jasoria. I think others were taken to the eastern islands."

At mention of Jasoria, the Prince raised an eyebrow. "You are sure one of them went to Jasoria?"

"That is how the story was always told to me, My Lord."

"Good. That is enough for now." The prince waved his hand. Kilek was hauled to his feet then pushed toward the tent flap. He looked back; Prince Yan watched without expression.

"Why are you doing this?"

Kilek blinked. The sharp words had fallen from his tongue.

The guard cuffed him across the back of the head and he pitched forward. A boot slammed into his ribs and he bunched into a ball as the pain rattled his torso.

The unmistakable sound of an order came from the table.

Booted footsteps crossed the rug and stopped near Kilek,

who blinked up at the prince. "To protect my people," the man replied.

"By throwing us upon your enemy's swords?"

Prince Yan shook his head. "You will see the truth all too soon."

Again the man made a gesture of dismissal and Kilek was dragged up and out of the tent. Outside, he squinted against the comparative brightness as he was pushed away from the row of people waiting to speak to the prince.

Kilek frowned back at the tent as he stumbled to his position in the line.

Chapter 12.

Kilek woke.

Darkness covered the camp, though a riot of stars joined the moon in blazing overhead, gleaming on the treetops – and he blinked. Wait, the tent... where had... Kilek sat up; there it was, right beside him. "Right." The tent had been given over to a soldier, one of the prince's men. Kilek shook his head and shifted in his bedroll, eyelids quite heavy.

He flinched.

A dark figure loomed over him and his pulse doubled. The shape blocked part of his view, leaning closer to speak softly. "We're leaving now, Kilek." A familiar voice.

He let out a shaky breath. "Florique?"

"Without a word," the mage said.

Kilek rose silently and followed Florique, holding his breath as the man threaded his way through sleeping bodies, taking care with each step. If anyone woke it would mean... Kilek slowed. Within a nearby pool of light, a sentry lay slumped upon the ground. Yet there was no hint of blood, nor did he seem harmed. Only slumbering. Had Florique put everyone to sleep?

And what about Pax and Alira, and the rest of the conscripts?

But Kilek didn't call to the mage, who had already drawn away, out of reach. Better to ask when they cleared the camp. Which did not take long – they were soon circling a pair of the larger tents used by more of the prince's men, heading into the thin trees to safety, where Florique knelt a moment, raising his hand.

Kilek tensed.

Was it too soon to relax after all?

But the man soon shrugged and moved on, more swiftly toward the Pale Stones, which were almost luminescent beneath the moon. Like beacons of hope. Kilek quickened his own step. Before reaching the stones, Florique pointed off to the side – and there, four dark shapes waited.

Familiar ones!

Kilek dashed forward and found the smiling faces of his friends, but they did not dare speak; still, he was grinning like a fool. They would finally escape! Everyone was just as happy it seemed; darkness no doubt hid whatever small signs of fear that might have remained.

A voice shouted from within the camp.

Kilek spun.

Prince Yan charged from his tent, blades in hand, the blue steel gleaming beneath the moon. But it was the twin tattoos on the backs of his hands that drew the eye; they were far too bright to be reflecting light from the sky. The Minjao leader bent by the nearest guard before rising to stare across the camp, straightening when his gaze seemed to pierce the trees to their hiding place beside the Pale Stones.

"What a strong fellow," Florique said.

Kilek blinked. "Florique?"

The mage sighed. "Everyone, into the Wickerlands; go, I will hold him off."

Tyar stepped forward. "But where do we go then?"

"And what about everyone else?" Mathi added.

The mage offered no response – instead, he ran into the open, arms spread wide. Then, he swung them together. A booming clap rang across the night. The wave of sound cast the prince into the air. He crashed into his own tent... and after only a moment, rose.

Then Yan leapt forth, swinging his blades in an almost cyclonic pattern.

Thin, almost ghostly streaks of light grew, following the blades.

They flashed forth.

Florique whipped something from a pouch and threw it into the air before him, moving in one motion. Sparkling dust rained down and absorbed the light from the prince's blade. Yet Yan did not stop and each strike now drove Florique back a step.

Kilek started forward.

Something caught his arm. "Hurry." Mathi, her frown sharp.

"But–"

"You think *we* can help him? Come on."

The others were already fleeing. Mathi dragged Kilek into a run. He tripped on a tree root almost instantly but managed to keep his feet. Even with the moonlight, obstacles loomed so quickly – he crashed through a screen of branches at the edge of the trees, winning a long scratch on his forearm for his efforts, then burst onto the hard-packed earth of the road and kept running.

Light flashed behind but he did not turn.

Instead, he kept his eyes on Mathi's back and pumped his arms, breathing hard. The Pale Gates flashed by, stone as silent as the camp.

The highway sloped down before them, leading to the vast, flat expanse of the Wickerlands. Once a land of forest and lakes, it was now equal parts blackened marsh choked with rotting reeds and barren stretches of leeched wood, decaying willows and other plants that strangled one another in a greying tangle.

At least, so it appeared during the day – of a night, the stars gleamed in distant pools and vanished within the dark clumps of wood and decay.

"Where are we going?" Kilek called.

"Florique said he'll find us if we hid somewhere inside."

"But where?" Kilek asked. The roads within the Wickerlands were often broken, sunken or simply lost – and only by skirting the northern edges did most travellers – if they dared – ever traverse the place.

"When we stop," she said.

They'd reached level ground now and it seemed softer beneath his boots. Dust stirred too as the thin stands of dead trees rose around them in ghostly shapes. Little changed while they ran... though for Kilek, too soon it became a mere jog, but he kept the others within sight at least, and managed to drag himself up to his friends when they finally stopped.

Mathi had taken them off the road to take cover behind a low stone wall where several of the slender, still-dead trees had fallen against the stone.

"This will have to do for now," she panted as she stared back at the now distant tree line and the Minjao camp, where light no longer bloomed.

Kilek followed her gaze. Had Florique defeated the prince? Or did Yan even now prepare search parties? Would he bother for a mere five people, villagers who were untrained, untested in war... although, soldiers had been sent after the *two* who fled near the Crioise River.

He glanced at his friends then; they were focused on sucking in lungfuls of air. Mathi and Tyar leant against the stone, Alira knelt in the dust and Pax bent over his knees. The realisation triggered a tiny rush of satisfaction – perhaps he wasn't so weak after all?

Tyar eventually stood and slapped Kilek on the back, even as he grinned at Pax and Alira. "I bet you knew we'd come for you right?"

"Took a little longer than I'd hoped," Kilek said.

Tyar snorted.

"So you weren't caught then?" Alira asked as she too rose.

"No. I don't think Mathi and I were even chased at first; we kept out of sight but followed you for the first two days, trying to come up with something," he said. "It wasn't until Florique found us that we thought of this."

"This?" Paxoph asked. He was now staring up along their back trail.

"We had to wait until you were closer to the border, so we could escape and go into hiding. Once Florique catches up with us then we plan a proper ambush," Mathi said. "This is the path the Minjao have been taking west; it's got to be how they slipped into Luargot in the first place."

"We're still only six against hundreds. And the prince," Kilek said. "I met him; he's no push over, you all saw what he could do."

"We did," Tyar said.

"Well, if we can somehow rescue the conscripts, we'll have a better chance of freeing everyone else," Mathi said.

Paxoph nodded slowly. "Will that be enough?"

"I don't know." She frowned, and even in her expression of worry she remained beautiful – the moonlight somehow softening her features. Kilek frowned at himself, a stupid time to notice such things. "But whatever we decide, if Florique doesn't return by dawn we leave," Mathi continued. "The camp wouldn't wake before then – that's what he told us."

"But the prince did," Tyar said.

"Can he wake the others?" Alira asked.

Mathi shook her head. "I have no idea. If Florique defeated Yan then we should be safe enough. If he didn't, I don't know."

Silence.

"So... should we look for a good hiding place?" Kilek asked.

Mathila shrugged. "Maybe we should. Let's head west for as long as possible – that's where the rest of the village has to be, so that's where we'd go with or without Florique, I suppose."

Paxoph still hadn't turned from where he gazed up to the Pale Gates. "What about the prince, Mathi?"

She joined him, placing a hand on his shoulder as she looked to the camp. There, the man who'd ordered the attack on Hasere might still live... and Kilek blinked when he realised what Paxoph was asking, and Mathi was suggesting. She was giving up a chance to avenge her parents – and she'd done the same thing by not helping Florique, by instead, pulling Kilek away from the battle. Maybe it had been a slim chance, maybe not. With Florique, she would have fared better than if she'd tried alone, or even with everyone else at her side, that much was obvious.

But she had given it away to help her friends. "Let's get moving, find somewhere to rest," she said.

Chapter 13.

No Minjao soldiers in their green and white had appeared on the dusty road by the time dawn arrived. Kilek turned from his watch and started back to their cold camp; a stump-lined hollow not too far from the forgotten highway. Within, his friends were already stretching where they lay on their bedrolls or cloaks. A dark fire pit rested in the centre and the edges were lined with the stolen supplies, traveller's bread, flasks, assorted pieces of armour and some daggers.

Not much, but better than nothing at all.

"Anything?" Mathi asked as she joined him. Her expression was one of weariness and her hair a mess behind her headband, but she still wore the leather armour and rested one hand on the hilt of her blade – her own sword, since she and Tyar had managed to keep all of their possessions. Her jaw was set; she stood ready for whatever was to come.

"No." And it didn't make sense – if Florique had put a stop to the prince, why hadn't he returned? If the mage had failed, then why hadn't Yan sent out soldiers?

"Then we'll leave – we've waited too long."

"What about the other conscripts?"

"So long as they're here instead of in Minjao, they're safe enough," she said.

Kilek shook his head.

"You have a better idea?"

"I know we can't free them, but–"

"Then let's find Pax's uncle," she said, gripping him by the shoulders as her voice wavered. "Alira's father and Ganoit too – you and I have no-one to rescue, so we have to help our friends, right?"

He opened his mouth to reply – to tell her, who knew if they were even heading in the right direction... but what was the point? Mathi understood. The rest of his friends understood and more, he couldn't forget that Mathi was giving up her chance at Prince Yan.

The image of her father covered in blood and her mother beside him came unbidden.

"Right."

She nodded. "Good."

Tyar approached, munching on a piece of flat bread. "This isn't so different to before, is it?" he asked. Compared to Mathi, it seemed he'd slept a lot better, since no dark circles ringed his eyes.

"We can catch anyone who's ahead of us, especially in a place like this, since a large force can't travel very fast," Mathi said with a nod. She looked around the small circle that had formed before her as Alira and Paxoph joined. "I've only heard stories about this place; any of you spent any real time here? I don't imagine food and water will be easy to come by."

Heads turned to Paxoph.

The man scratched at his beard, which was far messier than when he'd first been transformed. "Uncle Orasef and I have travelled parts of the Wickerlands before... but we never went too deep. We usually visited Sassehim via the northern edge, a few times we had to detour border disputes but I'm no expert."

"You know more than I – all I have is the stories they tell, about the mud-wraiths and the tainted water."

"I don't think the wraiths are real," Alira said. "But I've been thinking about the water... I might be able to purify it."

"How?" Tyar asked.

"Florique showed me a few things. I would like to try them," she said, though she lowered her voice, her gaze drawn to their back trail. Alira too, seemed to be wondering if the man would return.

Tyar frowned. "Is that safe?"

"Do you think Yan will sense it?" she asked.

"Maybe. I guess we don't know either."

"Well, we'll need water sooner or later," Mathi said. "What about food? There's not much left in mine and Ty's packs. Pax?"

"There are some lizards but you have to be careful, most are diseased in some way – we'd better boil the meat to be sure."

Tyar sighed. "I can live with that, I suppose."

"Then let's get moving."

They set off at a brisk walk while the sun continued its rise, adding a little more colour to their surroundings. Pale weeds lined the uneven road, some thin scraps of green still present so close to the border, and equally grey trunks of long-dead willows and oaks lined the path. A foul scent slipped between the trees where the murky tar or marsh and bogs lurked – still not close enough to see.

Several times, when the stands of trees thinned, harder outlines of jumbled ruins appeared in the distance but the band did not approach – the road led directly west, wide enough to allow easy passage for the scores and hundreds who had come before. And based on the trampled earth and weeds, the occasional cast-off item of clothing, the Minjao had moved a lot of people through the Wickerlands.

Just how desperate was Prince Yan?

And how did the fairy tale fit in with conscripting Luargot people to fight in a mysterious war in the west?

By noon, Kilek had not seen a single lizard. They'd stopped to eat a ration of the dried fruit and nuts and share the last of the water, and then it was time to find more – and as they now picked their way through damp earth and patches of rotting plants that somehow managed to cling to life, Kilek found himself watching Alira. Everyone counted on her now, especially if no stream or pool could be found.

Kilek frowned down at the earth when his boot stirred the brown mulch, unleashing a faint cloud of noxious air. How did the place simply continue to devour itself? Centuries since the Herisman War and still it had not completely died nor, it seemed, taken any steps toward recovery.

Was it the taint of forbidden magic used during the battles? How long had the place been the former battlefield of successive wars?

History told of a Herismeda bright with life and exquisite beauty, a harmonious place where people were able to live in peace with plant and animal alike, where the Herisman people could even take on abilities and qualities of the creatures they cared for.

If it had ever been true, there was no evidence of it now. And the surviving stories of their magic offered little in the way of help with traversing the ruin that remained.

"I've found something," Tyar called, waving from nearby.

Kilek joined him. Grey water sat in a hollow between fallen trunks, ancient mud climbing the sides, leaving only a tip of wood visible. Bugs clouded the surface of the water, fragments of skeletal leaves like tiny, abandoned rafts.

"It's better than the black sludge I found farther on," Tyar said.

Alira arrived and knelt by the edge of the pool, Mathi and Paxoph close behind. "No-one thought to take this from me." She was already drawing a pinch of white sand from one of the pouches on her belt. With a slight frown, she sprinkled it across the water, keeping her hand outstretched and splaying her fingers.

"Where did you get that?" Mathi asked.

"Florique." She closed her eyes now and her lips moved but no words were audible. Kilek stared; her expression of concentration transfixing him as much as the promise of magic itself. So like the Alira he knew from home, yet older and prettier, her own excitement revealed a glimpse of the girl she'd been not so long ago.

Time passed and nothing happened. Was there enough sand or was it something else?

Alira's frown deepened.

"Can we help?" Paxoph asked.

"Is it the sand?" Tyar added.

Alira opened her eyes, still facing the water. "No. Florique said I have to see what I want to change. The sand was meant for something else but it *should* work." She glanced around at everyone, lowering her voice. "Could you all perhaps turn your backs... I, I don't know if I can do this while you're watching."

"Of course," Kilek said.

Mathi and Tyar seemed to roll their eyes but still turned away, and Pax smiled down at her. Kilek offered his own smile of encouragement but she had already closed her eyes once more.

Kilek waited. "You can do it, Alira," he breathed.

He shifted his feet, strained his ears. If he took a peek, would that distract her?

"Look!"

He turned. Alira lifted her hand slowly, and strings of mud followed, rising from the water without her needing to touch it. Her eyes were wide now, the disbelief clear.

"It's working," Tyar almost shouted the words.

In the pool, more dirt and leaves, bugs too, all of it sliding toward what seemed to be five invisible strings leading from her hand, and she stood as it grew, until long dark strands of muck and mud were revealed.

Alira cast them aside and they splattered across one of the logs.

Tyar gave a low whistle.

Sparkling clear water lay in the pool. Kilek swallowed just looking at it.

"Fill 'em up!" Mathi laughed. Then she pulled Alira into a hug. "That was amazing, you know."

Alira blushed. "I didn't know if it would work – he taught me a few things but I couldn't really get the hang of this before now."

Kilek grinned as he fumbled through his pack for his stolen flask. When he dunked it coolness enveloped his skin, a welcome sensation. He lifted the flask to his lips and almost before the water reached his tongue the scent of it hit him, so pure. He drank deeply, finishing the flask before letting out a long sigh.

And then he filled it again, drank a little more then topped it up a final time.

Alira hadn't taken a drink yet – she was staring down at her hand now, a small smile on her lips. Her eyes sparkled with joy.

Kilek straightened his shoulders.

Whether it was Florique, the Goddess' gifts or Alira herself or a combination of all three, maybe there was a chance after all.

Chapter 14.

The afternoon swiftly wore down to evening or maybe the listless stretches of the Wickerlands had simply rolled by beyond his notice, due to the new spring to his step. Alira was able to use an unusual magic like Florique – maybe the Goddess had been right about choosing them all... even if she'd given him nothing.

And he said as much to Tyar where they walked rear guard.

"You think the Goddess was right?" Tyar asked, his tone flat.

Kilek looked up to his friend. Where had Tyar's own good mood gone? "Maybe not at first... I mean, I don't know why she chose *me* but together we might be able to–"

Tyar stopped. "I don't know about any of that now."

"What do you mean?"

"Look at us, Kil. She made us older and stronger but what have we achieved so far? Nothing. We were even captured! I have no idea where old Ganoit is and couldn't save him even if I did. We're completely useless without Florique. What kind of gift was that?"

"So you think she made a mistake?"

"Don't you?"

"She's a *Goddess* – how many mistakes do Goddesses even make?"

He shook his head. "Perhaps we're just her first – she'll be full of regret and choose someone else after we're dead."

Kilek blinked. "But you're still searching, like the rest of us."

"Stubborn, aren't I?"

Kilek had to laugh. "Yes, you are. So what are you saying now?"

"That I'll search no matter what."

"Me too."

They continued on in silence then, drawing near another ruin – this one close to the highway, half a stone wall had been repaired with wood and mud. It cast long shadows as the sun dipped closer to the horizon and seemed a fair place to set up camp.

Six figures stepped from behind the building.

All wore swords and green tunics over chain mail... and all were gaunt-looking Luargot men. The lead stranger, a thin fellow whose smile bore a missing tooth, hailed them. "Welcome to the Wickerlands, fellow deserters." Chuckling rose from the others, whose expressions were not as welcoming. In fact, it seemed the men, of varying ages and builds, were eyeing not only the packs and water Mathi and Tyar carried, but Mathi and Alira themselves.

Kilek stared back at them, watching their hands that hung close to their weapons. Unease wormed its way into his own limbs.

"From where do you hail?" Mathi asked, her voice neither cold nor especially warm.

The leader shrugged. "Biranu and Clearwood mostly." Now he turned his head to spit. "Not that there's much to see there now."

Kilek held his breath. His heart began to beat a little faster. The other men were edging closer. Were they truly going to rob – or worse – their own countrymen? Tyar still carried his bow and Mathi her sword but Kilek, like Alira and Paxoph, had only daggers. Unfavourable odds.

"Are you travelling east then?" Paxoph asked. "A large force lies behind us."

"We won't need to go so far," the man replied, and now his smile grew almost feral. "But we will need everything you're carrying." He waved an arm as he charged, his men in tow.

Kilek stumbled back but Mathi cried out as she tore her sword free.

But it was Alira who leapt forward to meet the charge, shouting for everyone to run. She flung her hands up and a great wind roared, casting dust and stone forth. The cloud enveloped the deserters and cries of frustration rose.

Tyar was already sprinting into the Wicker, Mathi and Alira close behind. Paxoph dragged Kilek after and then he was leaping over fallen logs, patches of brambles and mud-choked pools.

"Where are we going?" he shouted ahead.

"Anywhere," Tyar called back. A somewhat shrill note lay in his voice – was it fear or perhaps shock? Maybe it was fear. After all, Tyar and the others only *looked* like adults. Inside, they were just as young as Kilek, and probably feeling the same heart-thumping fear that he currently fought.

A line of trees climbed a hillside in the distance and Tyar had angled toward it. Kilek pounded after his friend, keeping pace with Pax, breath already rasping in his throat. Defensible high ground? Kilek glanced over his shoulder. The bandits had not left the cloud, but how long would that last?

Before they'd crossed half the distance, the deserters were following.

"They're coming," Kilek called.

But the hill was close now.

It rose in a pale, dry slope that crumbled beneath his feet as he climbed. He gripped bases of the trees and pulled himself after his friends, pausing to turn back at the top. The bandits were surging toward the foot of the hill.

"Can you do that again?" Tyar asked Alira. He held his bow once now, arrow set to the string. His face was quite pale.

"I'm not sure – I was trying to do something else, actually."

"What?"

"Florique's trick with his hands but it... came out differently."

"Let's keep moving," Paxoph said. "We have a head start and we're in better shape. I know we have some high ground here but Ty only has three arrows left and we have one sword between the rest of us."

"Not to mention we're no warriors," Tyar added.

Kilek searched the plain... there. A distant cave mouth in a second, taller hillside. He pointed. "We could search that cave?"

"We'd be trapped," Tyar said.

"Maybe it leads somewhere," Mathi replied as she squinted. "It seems to have a very square opening for a cave."

"It's something to put our backs against, at least," Paxoph said.

Alira slid down toward even ground. "Let's reach it first."

Kilek leapt after her just as jeers echoed from behind. He sucked in great lungfuls of the dry air and kept his eyes on the cave mouth, still visible over Pax's shoulder. Uneven earth and clumps of dead grass and stony protrusions slowed him at times but at least it would hamper the deserters too.

The Wickerlands rose as the cave neared and he slowed once more, throat rasping now as he forced his legs to carry him up the final few feet. At the landing before the cave, he blinked – the opening *was* of cut stone. The edges were square and smooth, oddly clean – free of dirt, leaves or webs even.

But no clues as to what lay inside.

"Are we going in?" Kilek asked.

"Let me," Alira said as she strode into the darkness and raised her hand. A pale white glow spiralled out from her palm, wavering before solidifying into the shape of a rose. Kilek drew in a breath – it wasn't just another revelation about the things Florique had managed to teach her in such a short time, but the stone walls that her light revealed.

Intricate patterns of leaves ran deeper into the broad passage, the veins of each leaf aglow as if in response, faintly green. Tyar reached out, eyes alight. "I think these are jewels."

"Leave them for now," Mathi said, pulling Alira deeper into the tunnel.

Kilek looked back – the deserters were bearing down on them still. He charged after Pax, whose larger frame blocked much of Alira's light. Yet it was enough to follow, enough to see dust stirred by their feet as they thundered along the passage. It led straight, soon sloping downward.

Footsteps echoed behind.

Kilek glanced over his shoulder. Dark shapes blocked light from the opening, still distant – for now. "They've followed us," Kilek panted.

"There's something ahead," Alira called back, her voice echoing.

And then Kilek's feet thumped onto level ground, the steps echoing.

A large chamber, circular walls arranged with more leaves and twisting vines. Some different plants now but the faint thread of emerald ran through still, responding to Alira's rose it seemed. Yet what the light failed to reveal were any exits.

"We're trapped," Tyar said flatly.

"Spread out," Mathi said. "No use bunching together now."

A scream echoed from the passage.

Kilek froze.

The crunching of bones followed. Then more screaming, joined by a... wet hissing? Kilek took a step back.

The horrible sounds continued to filter down. Another sharp crack split the air and now Kilek gripped his dagger. What had found the deserters in the passage? Thumping footfalls approached, joined by a rasping hiss.

"Any weapon you can find," Mathi shouted, sword held before her.

The hissing and thumping drew nearer still, a vague shape in the tunnel only.

And then it entered the chamber.

Soft-seeming scales of ruby covered the body of a bull-sized, lizard-like creature – only the red faded to pink then white at the joints of legs, feet and face. And despite the fresh blood that dripped from crooked fangs, the creature moved slowly now, each step deliberate. Talons glistened with blood and gore too.

The thing did not move too far into the room; instead blocking escape. It seemed content to wait, as though well-aware that it had everyone cornered.

"What is that?" Tyar's voice was almost a shriek, even boyish.

The head lay flatter than most lizards, and the eyes were dark slits that did not seem able to fully open. Yet when Kilek took another step back the creature tracked his movement. The hissing grew and its chest heaved, rib cage clearly visible. Was it too old to fight in an open space? The jaws were clearly large enough to snap limbs...

"Whatever it is, we have to stop it," Mathi said as she stepped forward; though her eyes were wide and her knuckles were white around her weapon.

"How?" Pax demanded.

"I don't know – but we have to try something. Alira?"

Alira was breathing heavily. "If I try something else, I might lose the light."

"Right." Mathi glanced around the room, half her attention still upon the lizard. "Any ideas?"

Kilek swore. He had nothing. Just as the Goddess apparently intended.

"Fine."

Mathi charged.

"No!" Tyar reached after her but she was too fast.

The lizard braced itself at her approach. She swung her sword at its head. A claw flashed, deflecting the blade. Mathi skipped aside – only to fling herself down to the floor as the creature's tail lashed out. The tail still caught her side, glancing-only, yet the strike sent her rolling into the wall with a grunt. Her sword scattered across the floor.

Kilek gasped. "Mathila."

Tyar leapt forward as Alira called out strange words, the light flaring.

It was enough; the beast scrambled back, crashing into the wall. Hunks of stone broke free and tumbled down, but the lizard did not collapse. Tyar had a hand on Mathi's shoulder, she was moving but didn't seem well enough to escape on her own.

"Shoot it, Ty!" Kilek shouted.

Tyar ripped an arrow free as he rose to one knee. He set it to his string and fired, the motion smooth. The arrow flashed across the room.

It pierced one of the black eyes.

The lizard reared back with a hiss. Its tail thrashed, smashing more of the leaf-patterned wall. Tyar was gaping at the beast – it had been a stunningly unlikely shot. Yet the creature started forward once more, bearing down on Tyar and Mathi. Pax snatched up Mathi's sword and Alira flared her light once more. Tyar drew another arrow – his second last – and released with a shout.

The shaft flew true, plunging into the lizard's second eye.

Its hiss became a screech.

Another impossible shot!

But Kilek still cursed – what could he do to help? Was

there anything he could use as a weapon? There! He circled to the rubble and lifted the heaviest hunk of rock he could find. The lizard had fallen down now, and Pax and Alira were keeping their distance as it thrashed about, thumping its tail onto the stony floor.

"Now!" Tyar called as he half-dragged, half-carried Mathila back.

Kilek stumbled forward and heaved the stone. The rock struck with a sharp crack, caving the lizard's ribcage. The beast thrashed with another screech as blood spurted from its jaws. Crimson pooled beneath its torso too as its breathing became laboured.

Still Kilek did not approach. The echo of the bones breaking turned his stomach but it was more than that; there was every chance the tail could still lash out.

"Is it finished?" Tyar asked.

"I think so," Paxoph replied, though he did not lower Mathi's sword.

Alira's light grew as her soft footfalls neared, she paused beside Kilek and lifted her arm again, casting a bright glow across the corpse – now it moved no more.

"What was it?" Alira said softly, then looked to Kilek. "Is there anything in the old legends?"

He shook his head. "I've never read about a creature like this."

"Ty, how did you make those shots?" Mathi asked from where she sat against the wall, wincing as she spoke.

Tyar glanced down at the final arrow that he held. His expression was one of confusion – even concern. "I don't know. I'm a good shot... but not that good, nowhere near that good."

"It has to be the Goddess," Mathi said as she pushed herself upright with a grunt of effort.

"Are you all right?" Kilek asked her.

She nodded as she gripped Kilek's outstretched hand, pulling herself from the wall. "Pax?"

"I'm fine." He offered the sword. "What now?"

"Let's keep heading east," she said as she took the blade. "Just, slowly for a while."

"I agree," Tyar said. He strode to the beast and pulled his arrows free, glancing them over. "We probably haven't lost too much time so I doubt Prince Yan will have closed much ground if he follows."

"Let me lead again," Alira said as she lifted the glowing rose of light.

They started up the slope, only to find the passage cluttered with... body parts. Kilek reached for the wall when his boots slipped in blood from the deserters. Once, his boot hit a limb or part of a torso – thankfully Alira's light didn't reach the floor too well from a distance, and with everyone else partially blocking his view, the body parts were vague.

"Wait. There's no light ahead," Alira said.

Tyar swore, then footsteps rushed further along the passage. Smacking sounds followed, then another curse. "There's no opening anymore."

"Is there a switch or lever?" Paxoph asked.

"Nothing I can find."

"Do you need more light?" Alira asked. "I think I can manage but I'm getting tired, to be honest."

"I'll keep looking but I don't think we're going to find anything – it's just a damn wall now, nothing else."

Kilek joined them, frowning at the walls – the pattern

of leaves terminating at blank stone where the opening had once rested. Had the creature somehow sealed the tunnel? Or, was something – or someone – else still lurking within the strange underground?

Chapter 15.

Back in the circular chamber Kilek stood before a narrow opening in the wall – an opening that had not been visible earlier. It looked as though it had been cut cleanly, though the carved leaves and vines revealed no hint of damage beneath his fingertips. At present, only darkness lay beyond the slender opening, but if the door could be slid further, they might escape after all... and yet, how could they be sure it was safe? "This wasn't here before."

"Perhaps the lizard shook it open," Paxoph said. "It was no light-weight creature and it hit the wall pretty hard, more than once."

"Either way, it's our only choice, isn't it?" Alira asked, her voice soft with weariness. The light still hovered above her hand.

"Probably," Pax agreed. He gave her a look. "Can you go on? I don't think I have anything to make a light."

She nodded. "I can last."

"What if there's more of those things in here?" Tyar asked. "Or something worse? We still don't know how or even *if* it sealed the entrance to begin with. I mean, has anyone even *heard* of such a thing? What was it? Kilek – are you sure there's nothing in your stories?"

He shook his head. "They've never mentioned a thing like that."

"Then we have to be ready," Mathi said.

"How?" Tyar asked, his voice a little terse.

She folded her arms. "I don't know. Same way we dealt with the lizard, I suppose."

Tyar threw his hands in the air.

"Let's go then," Mathi said.

"Right." Pax strode to the opening and braced himself against the edge, then pulled. The stone slid silently into the wall, revealing only more darkness. Alira joined him, her light dimmer now, but she led the way without complaint.

"I'll take rear guard," Kilek said, letting Tyar and Mathi precede him – one supporting the other.

She nodded.

"I'm going to try something," Alira said, her voice echoing.

Her light moved to one side of the passage and then stopped. Kilek shifted to glance around Mathi and there, Alira had placed both hands against the green carvings. She whispered beneath her breath and after a few moments, fell back with a gasp. "It worked!"

A faint green glow spread across the walls, running with the vines and leaping through the veins within each leaf. Soon enough, the entire corridor stood aglow with enough of the pale green luminosity to see clearly.

"That's amazing. How did you do that?" Kilek asked, everyone else adding their agreement.

"I... I don't know. Florique told me that light can respond

to all sorts of things but I think it's more this place. It feels like old magic is here."

"Do you sense any danger?" Tyar asked.

"No."

"Well, there's another chamber ahead," Paxoph said. "Let's keep going."

Kilek followed his friends into the room; it was identical to the last save for three openings – one, another passage heading in the same direction, the second a set of stairs leading up and the third, which Paxoph had already approached, appeared to be a large adjoining room. It featured a tall, broad window – empty of glass or curtain, and beyond were featureless walls.

But it was the lizard corpse Paxoph aimed for. Both spine and skull protruded from the room, pale white scales still clinging to the bones in places.

"Let's look around a little – be on your guard," Mathi said as she drew her sword with a wince. But she waved off Tyar's concern as she moved.

Kilek joined Pax while the others searched the remaining openings. He knelt at the skull as Paxoph stepped over the thing's body and into the room. The lizard-creature's eye-sockets were narrow, empty. No clues as to how it died; the remains of the body were in dust and decay, the surface of each bone pitted.

"Anything inside?" Kilek asked.

"Just more bones."

"Human?"

Paxoph nodded, his expression sombre. "I think we're lucky to have survived back there."

"Thanks to the Goddess, I suppose."

"Alira's magic and Tyar's shooting?"

"Right."

He folded his arms. "It could be so – but that still leaves you, me and Mathi to manifest something, doesn't it?"

Kilek shrugged. "You and Mathi, perhaps."

Paxoph put a hand on his shoulder. "Are you so sure there's been no gift for you too?"

"Of course." He couldn't keep the bitterness from his voice.

Before Pax could answer, Tyar called from across the room. "The stair leads to a cave-in. I think we'll have to continue forward."

"So be it," Mathi said from where she and Alira were returning from that very passage. "There's more rooms and more dead bodies this way."

"Lizards?" Paxoph asked.

"And people." She waved everyone after her, starting back up the passage. Kilek hurried after them before Paxoph could ask another question. It wasn't that the questions were unwelcome; it was more not wanting to inflict his bitterness upon his friends – and especially not Pax, who was always careful and considerate.

In the next three chambers they found just one doorway each and similar scenes – only worse. The lizard creatures lay in heaps now, along with the bones of the human inhabitants of the strange, underground... city? Who had they been? Herisman? Westerners or Luargot? Without weapons or clothing it was impossible to tell... and even had there been such clues, there was so little information on the Herisman, he'd hardly be able to tell for sure. Maybe Servant Bastiem would know, though Kilek had read every book in the man's small library and few mentioned the Herisman.

"I don't remember reading anything about a war that used creatures," Mathi said as they passed yet another room. "Kilek?"

"No. Father Bastiem never mentioned anything like this and there's nothing in his history books either."

"I still want to know how that thing survived," Tyar said.

"By luring travellers within?" Alira suggested.

Tyar still held an arrow set to the string of his bow. "Makes sense. I hope it really was the last one"

"Let's get out of here before we need to find out," Mathi said.

The floor in the next chamber lay littered with more human than lizard bones, scores more than the previous room. Kilek found himself grimacing as he walked – it was near impossible to place a foot without crunching over old bones. Many cracked. A few gave muted crunches too, as though they'd been moments away from turning to dust.

Such was the care he took, that Kilek found himself slipping behind.

The others were already halfway down the next passage but Kilek slowed; something gleamed between the ribs of a long-dead lizard. The ribcage stood significantly larger than the other beasts, reaching his chin when he paused before it with a shiver.

Just how large had it been? The base of each rib was nearly wide enough to...

He knelt.

Human bones lay within the cage, as though the creature had swallowed an entire torso – which, no doubt, it had. The victim's skull and spine rested near a smaller set of ribs; hips or leg bones nowhere to be seen. But what did catch his eye was a gleaming pendant on a silver chain.

He reached in and lifted it free.

Shaped vaguely as a heart, it bore a faint engraving – a raven perched upon a branch. The jewellery rested cold in his palm, more so than seemed natural. Yet a sense of a vast... otherworldliness was clear too. Almost as though it carried something vital beneath its smooth surface.

"Kilek, hurry it up!" Mathi called.

Kilek glanced to the opening – no-one had come to check on him but they were no doubt waiting. He glanced at the pendant. Was there really any need to tell them about it? They had their own gifts from the Goddess after all. Perhaps this piece of jewellery was valuable or special in some way. "Maybe this should just be for me."

"What's keeping you?" Now it was Tyar shouting.

"Coming." Kilek slipped the pendant over his head. The silver chain lay chill against his neck, the pendant almost icy, but he tucked it beneath his tunic and started after his friends.

Chapter 16.

Finally, they had found a stair that was not overflowing with rubble or barred by stone doors, a real chance at escape – a prospect that now seemed more likely.

"There's still the possibility that *someone* is here," Paxoph said in response to Kilek's observation. "We still don't know how or *if* the lizard was able to seal the entrance."

"It had legs," Alira offered. "Enough to work a simple lever, surely."

"Which ascribes a level of intelligence to the thing I suppose we shouldn't be dismissive of," he replied. "But I want to believe we are alone now."

"Maybe we should stop on the landing," Alira said, pointing a few steps ahead.

"Anyone want to guess at the time?" Mathila asked as she reached the platform, then tossed her pack onto the stone.

"Time to eat, I hope," Tyar grumbled.

"Let's finish the food and get out of here then," she said.

Kilek dug into his pack and pulled forth the last of his rations, more travel bread; the texture hard and the flavour...

lacking. And while he had plenty of water, it seemed food would become the new concern in the next few days.

They soon started climbing again but before too long, Alira stopped before him. "Do you hear that?"

Kilek paused, one foot suspended as he strained his ears. Nothing. "No. What is it?"

"Like a distant song."

"I can't either," Tyar said.

"Keep going. And listening," Mathi said as she resumed the climb, her sword ready. She was breathing hard and sweat had formed upon her brow, but she didn't complain despite the obvious pain from her injury.

The steps continued and several times Alira hesitated, but it wasn't until the third time that Kilek caught a hint of song, faint as though it passed through the walls. It was fleet, even bright and joyful, composed of flute or pipes.

"There," Alira said.

Kilek glanced at his friends – everyone had stopped this time, apprehension upon their faces, except for Alira: she was calm, she seemed to be enjoying the music.

"Then we are not alone here after all," Mathi whispered.

Paxoph frowned. "So whoever is here is both a musician and a murderer who used that lizard to kill those he lured into this place?"

"Doesn't make a lot of sense, does it?" Tyar asked.

"No."

"Keep your weapons ready," Mathi said as she returned to the climb once more.

The song grew louder, an open doorway revealing a small room with an oddly shaped... instrument; steel and copper piping that disappeared up and into the wall behind the device. Yet the face of the thing included open tubing of various sizes and shapes, creating the music.

"What is this?" Alira asked, moving forward with a hand outstretched.

Tyar peered behind the thing. "How does it play?"

"The wind outside?" Paxoph suggested.

Kilek nodded slowly. Perhaps that did explain it – another Herisman mystery. "This has to be made by the Herisman."

"But what for?" Tyar asked. "Just to have music while walking up and down the stairs?"

"I suppose so."

"Impressive as this is, we should keep moving, just in case," Mathi said.

They resumed their climb and soon light appeared from ahead.

Everyone moved a little quicker now, urged upward by the faint sense of moving air – and when Kilek finally reached the opening and stepped out to a rocky plateau, empty of trees, it was with a sigh of relief. After a moment to simply stand in the air, Kilek shaded his eyes and looked east from the hilltop. No smoke from Prince Yan's camp, nor any sign of soldiers upon the road. Was no-one coming to chase them? Perhaps Florique *had* put a stop to them and freed the conscripts.

But the same question returned to nag at him – why hadn't Florique rejoined them if he'd succeeded?

"No sign of them then?"

Mathi approached, still moving gingerly. He shook his head, even as his heart skipped a beat. With Tyar helping the others set up camp, there was a chance to simply enjoy being with her – yet he chose not to ask how she was;

Mathila could be a little touchy when it came to admitting weakness or asking for help.

"I've been thinking, Mathi."

"Oh?" She slapped him on the back with a grin. "I didn't know you could."

He laughed. "You're in a good mood."

"Well, it's nice to get out of there – I don't like being underground. Or lizards, anymore."

"What do you think it was?"

"Something from long ago... maybe something to do with the Herisman as you suspect, but you know, I came to ask you a question."

He met her gaze, which was serious once more. "You did?"

"Yes. Tell me something about the prince's camp – we watched it while we were waiting for the right time to strike, and I came away with an impression but I want to see if you agree."

"About?"

"Whether you think the Westerners consider the conscripts to be disposable."

Kilek shook his head once more; it was an easy question, though he would have given a different one standing in the wreckage of Hasere. "No. They were training us to fight – they want us to reach the West at the least. That's what I think."

"That's what I'd hoped you would say." She ran a thumb over the lion's head upon her sword where it was belted at her waist. "And what I feared."

"Feared?"

She swallowed. "Because I think I have to face something I don't want to face."

Kilek waited.

"We can't do this alone, even with whatever the Goddess has given us."

He nodded. "I was thinking about King Hadeon a lot in the Minjao camp. About why he hasn't come – and one of the other prisoners said that the Westerners were hiding themselves with magic."

"It makes sense if it's true. I still think word would have reached the south by now. If it hasn't, maybe we're supposed to make that happen ourselves. Maybe that's part of our purpose, to bring the army back."

Kilek nodded, though he glanced back at their friends. Easy to see why Mathi had come to him first. "Do we have the right to ask that of them?"

"I know. It feels like I'd be asking them to give up," she said.

"Maybe tomorrow?" Kilek suggested. "Maybe we just rest tonight, try and eat a hot meal and get some sleep before we decide our next step."

"Good idea." Mathi smiled again. "You know, I'm glad I asked you about this, Kilek."

Kilek raised an eyebrow. "You are?"

"I am. More often than not, you know the right thing to say. Like the time none of us could figure out why little Tian was upset that day at the stream. You were the one who reminded us that no-one had offered to help her."

"Is that the same?"

"It is – you usually think of others, you know."

"Hey, you two, stop slacking off and find us some more wood," Tyar called from the camp.

Chapter 17.

The now slumbering fire had been dug into a pit and surrounded with stones in an attempt to hide the light, but some warmth still rose from the embers and the rock-lizard it had boiled was a warm memory in Kilek's stomach while he sat with his back to his friends, keeping watch upon the road beneath the hillside.

At regular intervals he completed a circuit of their open camp almost as an afterthought, in case Yan had sent someone to circle their position... though how the Prince would have tracked them he couldn't say. Their underground trek had put them some distance deeper into the Wickerlands and in a different direction – unless the man's magic extended beyond what they'd seen.

And again, that was all assuming the prince cared enough to follow. It seemed he had the information he sought.

And more, it assumed Yan lived.

Either way, a change in direction was surely the best course of action. Still, he couldn't help pacing the nearer dawn came. How would everyone react?

By the time the sky lightened enough to break fast – nought but water now – Kilek was unable to keep a frown from his face, part due to the growing ache in his stomach and from what was to come.

"We need to talk about our next move," Mathi said once everyone stood together. Then she hesitated, glancing to Kilek before continuing. "I think it's clear that we need help. More help than what the Goddess gave us and probably more than even Florique can offer."

Tyar nodded slowly. "I agree, but what can we do?"

"Well…"

Kilek stepped a little closer, words tumbling out despite a tightness in his throat. "What if we turned south and brought back the army? I know it would mean leaving the trail and I know that it's not fair for me to suggest that but Mathi and I wanted you to decide."

Tyar shrugged. "I don't know anymore."

Paxoph and Alira looked to each other, both expressions sombre. Alira moved to Mathi and took her hand. "If we go south you might be giving something up should Yan live – the chance to have justice."

Mathi smiled, though it seemed fragile. "Are you sure? This is hard for you too."

"I know but and it's only 'given up' if we fail."

Paxoph sighed. "I don't mean this to be cruel, but for you and I, and Tyar… well, for me I need more than justice. I need to know that my uncle is safe." He raised a hand when Kilek opened his mouth. "But no matter what happens, even if I learn the worst, I will support you all."

Silence filled the camp after his words.

"So what now?" Tyar eventually said. "Do we vote…?"

"I don't want to turn back," Alira finally said softly. "I'm worried about Father... but we barely survived that lizard creature below and without Florique I think we *do* need help."

Mathi looked to Tyar. "Ty?"

He kicked at a stone, facing away as he folded his arms. "It's probably no surprise to anyone, since I've complained loudly enough about it, but I think the Goddess was wrong. If we can get through to the royal city, maybe we've got a real chance – even if it feels wrong to turn back. We were stupid to try this by ourselves."

"Even after the shots you made down there?" Kilek asked.

"That wasn't me alone, I know that. But it's not enough to take on a whole army, is it?"

Kilek frowned. Even with all the evidence before him, Tyar still didn't believe... which was somehow insulting. He'd actually been given *something* at least, why couldn't he accept it? But even so, his friend was right; unnatural skill with a bow wasn't enough. "No."

"Pax?" Mathi asked.

"We move as one."

Alira rested a hand on his arm. "You're sure?"

He nodded, though his gaze turned west but for a moment, and then he lifted the weathered stick he'd found for walking. "Let's not waste the daylight – how does this look?" He drew a circle in the shallow dirt, though it was legible. "Here's our hills." Then, he drew a line west and south. "This way will eventually exit the Wickerlands but into Minjao, and we don't know if more conscriptors are in these areas or not. It obviously puts us further from the capital."

"And if we simply go east from here?" Mathi asked.

Pax drew another line – this one sharply east. "Back inland, where we could turn south toward Alaycron. But if the soldiers have been sweeping east, rather than south, to keep themselves hidden, then we might run into bigger forces or at least, an increased number of *returning* Minjao."

"We can't be sure though. How long have they been here? It might be easier than turning west."

"Agreed. Both paths have their risks."

"Then let's try circling to the west a little before we turn south," Kilek said, tapping a finger in the dirt. "We can see where Yan's forces lie and change course if we need to. If they're looking for us, I don't think they'll expect us to do that. I think they'll head north or follow this road. It'll also be better because the only Minjao heading west will be those who've *finished* conscripting people at that point. We only have to expect soldiers to appear from one direction; it'll make them easier to predict."

"I like it," Mathi said, "but who knows if any are still sneaking *in* to the country? Still, it's probably the best choice."

"And we'll be in the Wickerlands for at least some of the journey," Alira added. "We'll be harder to find."

"We still have to keep our eyes open," Paxoph said. "Uncle and I saw some strange things to the north. I'm sure the southern part of this place is no different."

"Like what?" Tyar asked. "Worse than what you told me that time we fished the Mintwood Falls?"

He clapped Tyar on the shoulder. "I'll tell you on the way."

Chapter 18.

As the sun climbed, Pax led them across the uneven, blasted terrain, telling tales of mud-wraiths and their underground tunnels, the poison pink-fly and boiling tar pits as he took them west around the hill and deeper into the Wickerlands.

The stony earth had given way to crumbling clay and in the depths of shallow ravines, mud that clung to Kilek's boots. The deeper patches created a chorus of squelching as they trudged onward.

"Are you sure this is the best path?" Tyar called from the rear.

Pax paused to turn back. "Not as sure as I was a little while ago."

"We're still shielded from view in here at least," Mathi said. "Let's keep going and see what the bottom is like – I see the sun on water, maybe there's something we can drink."

"Only if Alira uses her magic first," Tyar said.

Alira smiled. "I will."

Kilek hauled his knees up as they continued, licking dry lips. More water, a wonderful idea. Yet the hole chewing its way through his stomach wasn't going to be sated. Food had to follow water. He sighed. How delicate had he become that he couldn't stand to miss a few meals?

"Something wrong?" Paxoph asked from where he forged ahead.

"Just complaining to myself I suppose," he replied. "Think any fish live in the water? And if so, are they edible?"

"Maybe if we boil them or use Alira's magic," he said. "We might be better off looking for the roots of the thorn leaf; it grows to the north, but I'm not sure about here."

"What's it look like?"

"Thin, almost star-shaped. They have pale leaves somewhere between grey and blue and very sharp thorns. They work in a stew. Bitter but edible too."

"I'll take either."

Kilek's calves ached by the time they reached the bottom. The mud spread across a stony patch of land that opened up as the ravine walls fell away, revealing a glittering pool that was no mere pond but nor a lake. Islands of sludge and even more sturdy-looking plots of leeched grass and weathered shrubs floated within. Beyond, more marshland and a haze of green on the horizon.

But something smaller caught his eye – a clump of rag and bone; a skeleton.

Kilek knelt before it.

Yellowed bone and rags, perhaps a cloak or tunic, and it, like the grass, leeched of colour. Gnaw-marks scored the bones too. More than a few were simply missing. But the skull stared up from the pile, eye-sockets deep and dark.

Who had died here? The skeleton rested alone, and certainly more recent than anything they'd found in the

Herisman caves – but it was no deserter. Few people travelled so deep into the Wickerlands, unless out of desperation.

"How deep is the water?" Mathi asked after examining the skeleton herself.

Paxoph lifted his staff and prodded the depths, taking a few steps into the dark water. It reached his shin only and further out, not much higher up the staff. "We could walk the borders easily enough, I think."

Tyar was casting looks of suspicion at the water. "Are we sure there's nothing in there?"

"Hard to know." It seemed Pax was holding back a smile.

"That's not funny, you know. I'm just thinking of what happened back there."

"We could turn back but we might lose the light *and* we'd be that much longer in this place," Kilek said.

Tyar sighed. "Good point – let's get this over with."

They splashed along in single-file, Kilek following Alira, stirring mud as they kept close to the water's edge where it lapped against jagged rocks, letting Paxoph lead with his staff. Dry land – or damp land, at least – was not too far away. Beyond waited another pool, and then another. The murk of the water stretched, a stagnant scent rising as they pushed further into the Wickerlands.

Noon came and they paused upon a patch of land so Alira could work her magic, purifying water collected in puddles and gathered in their single pot. And then it was back to the trek, feet squelching, blisters forming.

Yet the slog was not for nothing – dusk had not even fallen when they sighted smoke above trees, visible beyond a long stretch of barren land.

"What place is that?" Tyar asked as he leapt from the

water and onto the dry earth with a shudder. "I've lost track of where we're supposed to be."

Paxoph scratched at his beard. "This far south west, what looks like a large forest – it has to be Trisoma, right? I can't think of that many places that are basically within the Wickerlands."

"Perfect," Tyar said as he set off at a pace. "They'll have inns and decent food and a damnable real bed – I'll lead!"

"We still need to be careful," Mathi called after him.

"I know, I know."

Kilek quickened his own step, as did the others, and they bore down on the tree line with a mix of determination and anticipation – his mouth began to water at the thought of real meat and sweet breads.

The hunger carried him into the trunks and along the leaf-strewn road, shade from the oak and elms above most welcome, past stone markers and winding minor trails, until finally they stood before Trisoma.

The large town had been walled by stone built up between massive trunks, making each tree a part of the town's walls. Green leaves drifted down as a breeze swirled overhead. The wall was not so tall that it came at all close to the canopy of green, but it looked solid enough, though Mathi didn't think too much of it.

"You have to admit, it's still impressive," Kilek said.

Trisoma had been too far from home that he'd ever needed to visit, and despite the still-hovering threat of the Minjao, despite the urgency of their task, a new tension seemed to energise his limbs – excitement mixed in with the anticipation of food and comfort.

"I'll reserve judgement until we visit one of their inns,"

Tyar said. "I need something to get rid of the taste of those filthy lizards – I'd settle for vegetables at this point. Raw ones, even."

"It doesn't look like the Minjao have been here," Paxoph said, gesturing to the gate that stood closed, unmarred by evidence of ram or fire. Nor did the road leading to the smaller door bear the scars of hooves or the ravages of boots.

"Perhaps the southern gate was attacked?" Mathi said. "Or they didn't actually sack Trisoma, only took the people?"

"Either way, we should still be wary." Alira had quickened her step as they neared the gates, as if in contradiction of her words.

Tyar rapped upon the stout door within the gate.

Chains rattled and a hatch opened, revealing a frowning face. An older man in a polished helm. "I suppose you'll be wanting to enter the town then?"

"Ah, we would, yes," Tyar replied.

"Fine then. Just be quick about it, you never know whether them Western scum might return." The fellow closed the hatch then the sound of bolts being slid free followed. The door swung inward then to reveal the man, still wearing a dark expression but also a breastplate and a brown cloak to go with it.

"Have they attacked before?" Mathi asked.

"Aye. We turned them back though. Wasn't much of a battle to be honest. They weren't a giant force and our archers sent them off with tails between their legs," he said, then shook his head. "Later heard they took some from the surrounding villages instead."

"Have you seen them since?"

"No. You?"

"Further north," Mathi replied. "Some of us managed to escape but they seemed to be heading home with those they'd conscripted."

"Hmmm. Maybe King Hadeon's finally driving the bastards out."

"You've heard from the king?" Kilek asked.

The guard cleared his throat, then paused to cough into a kerchief. "No, but I assume one of our messengers found their way south, lad. Why else would the Westerners be leaving as you said? They haven't returned here yet, either."

"I hope you're right," Mathi said.

"Well, why don't you head for the Lumina Inn near the Lord Darges Fountain and get something to eat, Petra makes the best roast in Trisoma." He chuckled. "Of course, only one other inn to compete with but Petra's meals have always been my favourite."

Mathi thanked him and led everyone into a wide street lined with trees. The stones bore wagon ruts but aside from the lower storeys of some bigger buildings, most of the town had been built of wood and every other shop boasted the best furniture or carpentry tools in town. Several times he paused to look at a particularly fine-looking chisel set but did not want to slow everyone. Yet, the others were also distracted – at one point, Alira stepped away to examine a merchant's window full of different herbs. She stretched to the tips of her toes to look with a smile, and it seemed a girlish gesture somehow; a reminder that she was younger than her appearance.

Other buildings had placed saplings or flowers in their windows; it seemed a lovely place to Kilek, who still kept an eye out for the town's soldiers but found few who might have been Trisoma's protectors.

It did not stop him seeking – and finally, he did find something.

Movement from within the canopy; a glint of steel in one of the trees that made up the wall. He missed a step. Did the archers hide there? If so, had they marked Kilek's own progress to the town, drawn a bead on him? After all, he still wore the green of the Minjao.

Though surely all could see he was an escaped conscript?

Most people who went about their business were clearly Luargot with their generally fair hair and complexions. Few gave Kilek a second look, most seemed to be heading home with baskets of food or strolling toward the hum of nearby market squares, most small but lively with musicians and children urging folks to enter, but Kilek also saw the shaven heads of the Prisawi, folk from the southernmost land.

One, a woman in dark wrappings, smiled at him and he flushed, glancing away – he'd been staring like a fool. But her dark eyes had held him; her graceful movements too, somehow it was almost a shock that her close-shaven hair did not detract from her beauty.

A stupid thought – what did hair have to do with beauty?

Yet he couldn't help glancing at Mathi's golden curls.

"You're lucky she wasn't offended," Paxoph said with a chuckle as they neared the entry to the market.

"Huh?"

"The young woman from Prisawi."

"What do you mean?"

"See her belt?"

A yellow sash hung from her hips. There, a pair of circular blades with gleaming edges and strange symbols swung as she crossed to a medicine vendor. They did appear to have grips but surely, they'd be equally dangerous to wielder and foe?

"They can be thrown some distance you know – cut through armour and bone alike."

Kilek swallowed, then looked up to Pax. "Are you making that up?"

"What do you think?"

Kilek looked back over his shoulder, as the market began to recede. Her arms were bare, the muscles clearly defined beneath the now setting sun. "That you're not lying."

Paxoph chuckled.

"But are the Prisawi people really so quick to fury?"

"I doubt it," Pax said. "I've only met one man from Prisawa and I seriously doubt everyone there is like him."

Kilek nodded. "Well, I don't think we'll be meeting anyone from Prisawi tonight, we have more important things to do, right?"

"The first of which is the meal we've been promised," Paxoph said. "Ever since that guard mentioned the roast, my mouth has been watering."

"Then let's find the fountain," Kilek said, then paused. "Actually, how are we going to pay for everything?"

"Mathi and Tyar weren't robbed by the Minjao."

"But will it be enough to cover us all?"

"Hmmm." Pax hesitated. "If it isn't, we might have to come up with something creative."

"Meaning?"

He spread his hands. "I don't know – I think we'd better start thinking."

Chapter 19.

The Lumina Inn spread along a corner, facing two streets rather than climbing up into multiple storeys like many inns, but what seemed to be a large garden out the back did peek over the thatched roofing. Snorting came from beyond the wooden walls – a stable, obviously – which hopefully meant travellers resided within.

And if so, maybe that meant they'd have news from the south.

Or home.

The gate guard's claim that messengers had already been sent to the capital... had it worked? Unlikely the man had lied but surely if anyone had reached the royal city, the king would have sent his troops north already.

Men and women were passing through the door to take tables, visible through the windows, lamplight not making much of an impact in the street while the sunset lingered. Most folk appeared to work with timber by the sawdust that fell from their overalls, but a fair number of the customers seemed to be finely dressed – rich merchants perhaps? The town was not so large as Kilek imagined a true city to be, so few nobles would live within; but Trisoma certainly put Hasere to shame in sheer size, along with Birnvile or Clearwood, which was probably only half so large as the forest town.

And up until today, Clearwood had been the biggest place he'd visited.

If only his reasons for arriving in Trisoma had been better. "Kilek?"

He glanced to Mathi – she was looking at him expectantly, along with everyone else. "Yes?"

"How does that sound?"

"Ah..." What had everyone been talking about? Bartering for a room and meal?

She sighed. "Pay attention, will you? We'll offer what money we can and our own labour, but you might be better in the kitchen or stables."

He shrugged. Maybe they were right – everyone was stronger and food was more important than his battered pride now. "No objections from me."

"Good. Let's see if we can't convince the lady of the manor then," Tyar said as he strode toward the door.

"Then let me or Mathi lead," Alira said with a laugh. "Or Pax. Or Kilek."

Tyar affected an expression of hurt. "I see what I'm worth now."

"Good." Mathi pushed passed him and opened the door.

Inside, an already full room; few tables empty and serving girls moving between them, patrons calling from their benches. Small flowerpots hung from chains secured to the ceiling, their scents lost but the colour welcome. A few folk from Paxoph's homeland of Sassehim sat mixed in with the locals, most of whom were more interested in their drinks or the serving girls to do more than glance at Kilek and his friends when they entered.

But a thin woman in an apron, whose face was vaguely frog-like, smiled at them. "Welcome to the Lumina Inn, travellers," she said, and her voice was warm and comforting – the kind of voice Camilea should have had, instead of a drunken slur or a growl. "We have both clean rooms and fine meals, if you are seeking either."

"We would love both," Mathi replied. "Are your rooms large enough that three might sleep in one?"

The woman lowered her voice. "Hard times? I see from your clothing that you have no doubt run into trouble with the Westerners."

"We have."

She gestured to the bar then led them to one end, some distance from a pair of men who drank and talked softly opposite. The bar itself was a long bench with carvings protected by a thick piece of glass. Kilek reached out almost impulsively, since he would not be able to reach the actual wood, to the carving – that of the mythical wood dragon Melis, curled sleeping around a giant elm. "It's beautiful, isn't it?" the woman said to him. "Made by the master Bernoit himself it was, back in my grandfather's time. Now, I'm Petra and this is my inn, so I'll hear you out. Room and meal is five silver pigs," she said, using the informal name for the round, snubbed coins. "Two rooms and meals for five would be twenty, or a half gold if you want us to care for mounts."

Kilek looked to Mathi; did they have enough? Mathi

produced four silver pieces. "This is all we carry." It was barely enough for one night alone.

Petra rubbed her chin. "I see."

"Would you be open to barter, ma'am?" Paxoph asked.

"Possibly. What are you offering?"

"Labour, if you need it."

"And I can sew and cook. I know a little herb lore too," Alira added.

Tyar nodded. "I worked the inn back home, so I know my way around the job, ma'am."

"Well, I have a full staff but as it so happens Jili is going to have her babe soon so she'll be home for a time." She chuckled. "And there's always firewood to collect and other tasks – very well, we'll work out the details later. Why don't you take a seat and I'll have Jili bring you something."

"Thank you for your generosity," Mathi said.

Petra scooped up the coins and slipped them into an apron pocket. "No trouble, just know that you'll have earned that other room when I'm done with you."

"We'll be in your debt even after, I'm sure," Paxoph said.

Petra reached up to pat his cheek. "Aren't you a charmer? Get yourself to the table by the window then."

The table she'd sent them to occupy was near a closed door that presumably led to the other 'half' of the inn, the part that ran down the second street, but whether it led to rooms or something else, Kilek couldn't be sure.

His muscles relaxed into the bench – finally, a moment to rest, to be still. And so much the better that it was a cosy place, surrounded by voices and light. Here, the threat of the Minjao receded.

Jili arrived shortly, white apron straining over her

pregnant stomach. She smiled, but her voice was a little strained, as though she neared exhaustion. "Ale for everyone save for the young master?"

Tyar and Mathi shared a glance, fighting back foolish grins.

"Actually, milk for me," Alira said before Kilek could protest.

But did it really matter? He was far hungrier than thirsty for ale in any event. And by the time their meals had arrived; a mix of buttery steak and greens, he had found water to be more than satisfactory.

Between mouthfuls and the clink of cutlery, they decided what else to offer Petra, who eventually joined them near the end. And while Alira had been taken up on her offer to sew, Mathi had been pressed into service as a serving girl with her first shift due to begin once they finished eating. Pax and Tyar were sent to split wood in the stable yard and to Kilek, she offered a few pieces of silver and a list.

"Here you go. I'd like the items back here as soon as you can. Use the market near the Cat Trunk."

"Right." Kilek took the money and the list, then stood to leave, unable to prevent a grin from forming – exploring the town sounded far better than splitting wood.

Outside, he started along the busy street, passing men and women in thick, plain tunics, many of them also bearing traces of sawdust or sometimes sap. Other folk appeared more typical of merchants, dressed in more than one colour and trailed by younger servants or labourers with sacks of produce or crates.

He kept the silver Petra had given him clenched in one fist so the coins didn't jingle from his belt as he walked, and by the time he reached the Cat Trunk – a tall, empty tree trunk whose branches and openings were home to a dozen cats of all colours, the coins felt sweaty.

In the market, haggling and calls for attention rang bright and sharp in the warm air. Everywhere he looked, something new – colourful bracelets of amber hanging from hooks on wooden boards, toy carts and horses, boats and little soldiers with tiny blades of steel, to heaps of berries and vivid apples, rows of ripe pears... though he had been sent for vegetables and meat only.

And his next task was doubtless far more tedious – the stables perhaps? And it would be the same tomorrow and the next day too, maybe longer, if they wanted to earn enough for supplies. Far, far longer if they wanted new weapons and horses, which was a problem no-one had been able to solve just yet. And so taking a little time was a welcome thought, despite Petra's insistence on speed.

Which meant he probably shouldn't stop to look at the many carvings on display, but nearby, an old man with a white beard and bald head sat whittling at the bench in his stall. The displays and stands were covered in charms and pendants of steel, stone and sometimes bone or feathers, many set with tiny jewels. A sign hung over the man's head 'Herisman Artefacts Sought and Appraised' and Kilek slowed.

Could the man know something about the raven pendant?

Kilek approached.

"Greetings, young master."

"Good morning," Kilek said as he pocketed the silver then reached into his shirt to pull the pendant free, letting it rest within his palm. "I noticed your sign and hoped you could help me with this?"

The old fellow straightened as he lowered his carving. "I might indeed."

"Then it is a Herisman artefact?"

"Even at a glance I believe so – but I would need to examine it."

Kilek hesitated.

"No charge for that, young man," he said, misunderstanding Kilek's reluctance. "Though I might offer to buy it from you if it truly is what I believe."

"Well..." Kilek removed the pendant and held it before the man, letting it dangle on the silver chain. "Ah, I hope you can forgive my manner but I tend to worry; I don't mean to imply that you aren't trustworthy."

A chuckle. "I can make do." He leant a little closer and squinted. "It certainly looks authentic."

"How can you be sure?"

"The shape and the pose of the raven are two signs. It would no doubt feature certain tool marks if they had not worn away."

"The raven means something?"

"Yes," he said, leaning closer still, his breath brushing Kilek's hand. "I believe it is Idakov, the Echelon of War according to the Herisman – rare indeed. Where did you find this?"

"In the Wickerlands," Kilek said. And he'd heard of the Echelons, though never read of a specific name. But the Echelons were supposedly between God and Man, according to the Herisman legends.

The old shopkeeper murmured something to himself then

leant back with an expression of awe. "Yet more evidence. I think you *do* have something important that once belonged to the Herisman."

"Do you know its purpose?"

"Not without long examination, and even then I might not learn the truth. In all my years here, I have only come across four items from the Great Ones. Two fertility charms, a Hawks' Eye and now your piece." He met Kilek's gaze. "As I said, it is rare thing, young man so I do not hesitate to make this offer – but if I were to confirm its authenticity beyond doubt, as I am confident I would be able, I can offer fifty gold marks."

Kilek gaped. Fifty? It was enough to buy Ganoit's inn, surely? No-one in the village had ever owned even close to that much money.

The man smiled now. "However, I would not be able to gather such an amount today. Will you be in Trisoma tomorrow?"

"Ah, I'm not–"

"I will give you one hundred, right now," said a new voice. A man in a knee-length coat of orange stood beside them, circular blades half-visible where they hung from his dark pants. His clipped accent, dark skin and shaven head placed him from the same land as the woman from the other market – Prisawi.

Yet just as surprising was the man's offer.

"What do you say, lad?" the stranger asked. He detached a heavy purse from his belt and held it up. "This is but part of what I might offer, for I do not like to carry too much money upon my person." To the shopkeeper, he flashed a smile that was not... predatory, so much as excited. At the prospect of bargaining or at the Herisman pendant? Did the man even know that was where the raven stone came from?

Surely he did, else why offer so much gold?

"I apologise for my interruption, good merchant. I would like to give you the opportunity to respond in kind."

The fellow shook his white head. "I could not best, let alone match such an offer."

Kilek tucked the pendant back into his shirt. "No thank you, sir, but I'd like to keep it, since the pendant has sentimental value."

"Truly? Then why have it appraised?" The man smiled again. "I see you are no stranger to the bargaining game. One hundred and fifty pieces."

Kilek closed his mouth as, once more he found himself somewhat slack-jawed at the amount. But still he shook his head – something about the pendant *was* special despite a lack of obvious uses or power, and something about the Prisawi man seemed untrustworthy. "Even if you offered two hundred, I don't think so."

The stranger leant closer, his eyes straying to the neck of Kilek's tunic. "I could offer even more than that, my boy."

Kilek took a step back now, narrowing his eyes. Was he in danger? Here, about to be robbed in the middle of the square? In the light of day? "No thank you." Kilek turned to the shopkeeper. "Thank you for the information and goodbye to you both," he said and hurried away.

He strode to the opposite end of the square, pushing his way through more bodies dressed in brown and green, their faces indistinct, murmuring apologies as he did, and began collecting the food he'd been sent to purchase, glancing back toward the appraiser often.

Yet the man in orange had not followed; he was still speaking to the old shopkeeper. Nor did he look after Kilek – it was hard to tell from a distance, but the Prisawi man appeared well enough at ease. Was that the end of it then?

Safe now?

Or had the danger been an exaggeration-only? There was a chance the fellow was simply some overzealous collector. Kilek collected the last of the food and left the square at a jog, the cheer of the place now tainted.

Chapter 20.

Ahead, the Lumina Inn waited at the end of the street – its open doors inviting, the sense of shelter so close that tension crept into his limbs as he hurried onward. Once there, he'd be able to deliver the supplies to Petra and warn the others about the Prisawi man. It meant revealing that he'd found the pendant, but if the man followed and proved dangerous then it was better to have–

"Excuse me?" A hand fell on his shoulder.

Kilek jumped.

He spun, reaching for the useless belt knife... and found himself face to face with the Prisawi woman who'd smiled at him upon arriving in Trisoma. Up close, a brooch of pinkish red, shaped as a swan, was visible where it hung from her neck.

She smiled and he lowered his hand; how soothing her expression. "Forgive me for startling you, I am only seeking help. I'm somewhat lost. Do you know your way around Tirsoma perhaps?"

"I'm a traveller," he said, the words difficult to speak.

"Oh, then perhaps we could help each other?" She reached out to take his hand. Her skin was warm and smooth and when her fingertips brushed the inside of his wrist a moment of dizziness overcame him.

"I can try." It was important to help her.

"Well, I am searching for the town's famous fountain because there is a market nearby that sells fine jewellery. Do you know it?"

Did he? "I'm not sure." But disappointing her was not good. "I can help."

"Wonderful! I'm hoping to find a particular piece of jewellery there, perhaps something new to wear around my neck?"

"Like a pendant?" he said, looking up into her dark eyes.

"Yes indeed, that would be perfect, Kilek. Do you have one?"

Beneath the pleasant haze a bee buzzed – it was trying to tell him something, to warn him... but he couldn't lock on to the words at first, and when he did, the questions it asked just didn't make sense – how did the woman know his name? Wasn't she looking for a jeweller? And didn't she know the town already, she was familiar somehow...

The beautiful stranger leant closer, reaching out to brush a hand against his cheek. "Maybe you have something lovely that you could show me?"

Making her happy was important.

"I do, but I keep it out of sight because it might be made by the Herisman." He drew the pendant from beneath his tunic and held it up before her. "Someone offered me two hundred..." A Prisawi man in an orange coat. Maybe she knew him? The bees buzzed louder.

"Kilek." She breathed his name and he shivered in response. "That might be just perfect, you know. Would you like to give it to me?" Her voice was so reasonable, her tone kindly. She knew what was best; it was important he offer his assistance, to make her happy.

And yet could he really part with the pendant?

"I'm not sure." The bee was awfully loud.

"Ah," she purred. Now she gave his hand a slight squeeze. "You mentioned gold. If it is gold you need, I have plenty at my room, if you would like to come with me? The inn is not very far at all. Let's just go for a walk together, just you and I, Kilek."

The bee receded.

How generous she was, offering to accompany him to her inn. Letting him walk beside her – even, beyond all reason, holding his hand! "I'd like that, My Lady."

Kilek trailed her back along the street – it seemed to be the wrong direction, but then, she knew best – and swatted at his ear with his free hand. Where was the bee, why did it bother him? The wooden buildings, the passing people, receding music, it was all muffled somewhere in the background; only the woman mattered.

"Not much further now," she glanced down at him and smiled once more – this time it made his heart flutter; she *had* to stay happy, the warmth of her smile *had* to fall upon him again. Maybe the pendant wasn't that important after all? She seemed to need it. When they arrived at her inn, he would give it to her.

It was the best thing to do.

"Kilek of Hasere?"

A tall figure in armour stood before him, one gauntlet

resting upon a longsword. The man's black tabard featured a yellow outline of three poplars, not unlike spears. His shield featured the same design – Knight of Alaycron! The knight's expression was stern, a long moustache touched with grey adding to the stoic visage.

"I am," Kilek replied with a touch of awe – to meet an actual knight of the kingdom!

"How can we help you, My Lord?" the woman asked, her words falling across Kilek's own response.

"King's business, I am afraid, daughter of Prisawi." He held out a steel-encased hand to Kilek. "And quite urgent, so I must insist that I relieve you of your duty as... guide?" His expression was not so warm as his words and Kilek tilted his head at a faint return of the buzzing, as though from a vast distance.

What was the king's business? It seemed important. Perhaps after it was done, he could find her and offer the pendant.

"My business is urgent too." Her own voice had lost some of its soothing qualities.

"Then perhaps whatever business the two of you have can be continued at a later date – I am His Majesty's vessel in this matter, one of great importance to the people. I trust a visitor to the great land of Luargot would be more than happy to cooperate most attentively."

The woman's eyes narrowed but she only released Kilek with a bow. "Of course."

The knight took Kilek and started back along the way, pulling him along at a clinking stride. Kilek looked over his shoulder; the woman stared after them, pleasant expression that she'd worn before now vanished.

"You've been bewitched, lad," the knight said. "It will pass, but for now you are extremely suggestible, so we'll be returning to your inn."

"That sounds like a good idea," Kilek said with a nod. The man seemed trustworthy; and why wouldn't a Knight of Alaycron be true? "I'm happy to help the king if I can."

"In due time, you will."

The Lumina Inn appeared swiftly, the knight pushing through the door and then passing the quiet common room and heading for the rooms out back, where the stern-faced man showed Kilek to a bed – his bed, in the room he shared with Pax and Tyar? As Kilek lay back, letting his head sink into the cool pillow, he looked up to the knight. Somehow, the man's face blurred into a memory of father's dark hair and short beard, but the image fled as swiftly as it came.

"Rest here. When you wake, join us downstairs," the knight said. His eyes were a cold blue, though his tone had not been harsh.

"Yes, sir."

And though he didn't really feel tired, Kilek closed his eyes.

***

Kilek woke with a flinch.

He sat up, blinking at an orange haze – the colour soon spread into browns and the deep blue of the curtains in his room, yet all warmed by the sunset. A warm, sweet breeze entered through the open window, stirring the curtains, bringing the scent of jasmine.

"How did…"

The woman!

Kilek swung his legs from the bed and stood. Where was she now? He clawed at his throat – the pendant remained. Relief flooded his limbs. He reached for a cup of water and drank deeply. His memory was still hazy. There had been a knight too... The man saved him from the Prisawi woman... she'd used some manner of magic? And there had been the Prisawi man too, in the market... when money hadn't worked it seemed they moved on to magic.

How far had the two been from trying murder, if her enchantment had failed?

He shivered.

At least he seemed to suffer no lasting after-effects from her magic.

Kilek strode from the room and headed along the passage, passing paintings of forest scenes and then a young couple in travel-stained clothes heading for their own room. He had to thank the knight, but where was the man? The now bustling room was full of locals and a few travellers, but there in the far corner, standing by the door leading to the other half of the inn, was the only person in armour – the knight.

When the older man saw Kilek, he motioned him closer.

Kilek started to cross the room – only to find himself face to face with one of the serving girls hurrying toward the kitchen.

"I'm sorry..."

Mathi stood frowning at him, a tray of empty mugs in hand. Her blonde hair fell down to her shoulders and she wore an apron that hugged her hips and breasts; he looked away. Had he been staring like a fool?

"Move it, Kil."

He stepped aside. "Petra has you waiting tables tonight too?"

"Yes – but it doesn't matter." She nodded toward the knight. "Just get in there and tell them what you can; they've already spoken to us. And we didn't mention the Goddess, by the way."

"Tell *who* what?" he asked. It was not a story just anyone would accept.

"The king's men about the Minjao, obviously," she said, lowering her voice before continuing on toward the kitchen. The kitchen... he glanced back up to his room – had he delivered the goods Petra wanted? He'd have to check later.

For now, Kilek hurried across the room, slipping on spilt ale as he did. He managed to keep his feet, and shrugged off laughter from some patrons as he came to a halt before the knight. As before, the man's expression was unyielding but he nodded down at Kilek. "I trust you feel more in control of yourself now?"

"Yes, thank you, sir..."

"Venostac."

"I am deeply in your debt, Sir Venostac."

A faint smile may have graced his lips. "I suspect it is the Gods themselves that you are indebted to."

"I am?"

"Yes, for you surely have her luck, considering that I found you in time."

Kilek nodded slowly. "You were looking for me because of the Minjao?"

"We were – we have been speaking to any and all who have encountered the Western forces, and when your friends mentioned you had spoken directly to the prince, I sought you in the market. Now come, Kilek, I would hear your story."

"I don't know much, truly."

"I suspect it will be as or more interesting than the tale your friends shared – you have faced considerable hardships with no small measure of tenacity, it seems."

"Ah, thank you, Sir Venostac."

The man pushed the door open and ushered Kilek within, to a long room with high windows and a dining table that near stretched its length. Yet all chairs bar one were empty, another knight occupied one to the left of the head. He too, wore tabard and longsword, though no gauntlets and only mail.

Nevertheless, he looked the part – though this man was somewhat younger than Venostac, his short hair was blonde and his moustache thinner, smooth skin giving him the look of nobility.

"Welcome, Kilek," the waiting knight said. "I am Sir Filen, Knight of Spring. I hope old Veno hasn't been too much his usual dour self?"

Sir Venostac grunted but did not answer as he took the seat at the head of the table.

"Ah, he saved me," Kilek replied after a moment's hesitation.

Sir Filen laughed. "So I hear. Well, we have heard reports of her attempting to rob innocent travellers but she and her accomplice will be sent on their way or imprisoned, so please tell us – in brief – of how you came to meet Prince Yan of the West."

Kilek explained as best he could, trying to keep to the

relevant details but leaving out exactly who they came across beneath the temple. By the nods from both knights, they were familiar with the story and it wasn't until he reached the Minjao questioning that they slowed him down.

"Wonderful, Kilek," Sir Filen said. "Now, can you share, as close as you can recall, what the prince's man and also the prince himself said?"

"I'll try, Sir." Kilek frowned as he struggled for the exact words. Focusing on the mage's almost bored expression and the prince's deep, commanding voice helped. "I think he was the mage in the camp and he asked if I had heard of the Song of Silver but I hadn't."

"I see. What then?" Venostac asked.

"He wanted to know about the Night Thorn – and I did know that. He also knew it as the Mad King's Needle."

"And you shared the tale?"

Kilek nodded. "But I think he already knew the story; he mentioned the curse and the way the rose never bloomed again."

"What of the aftermath?" Sir Filen asked, leaning closer. "The rest of the fairy tale."

"It was the Prince who asked about the Thorns and the seven suitors. I had heard the tale mention them fleeing to Jasoria and also the eastern islands."

"And what followed?"

"Is there more?"

Sir Filen glanced to the older Knight, who shook his head slightly. "Well, we will say only that one part of the story does not end there, precisely. Was there anything else?"

"Actually, yes. The mage – he showed me a gold ring with a strange symbol. I couldn't tell if it was meant to be a spider or the rays of the sun."

Again, both knights shared a look, this time one that appeared more troubled, but did not explain. "Thank you, Kilek. Can you describe it further?"

"He never let me hold it," he said with a shrug. "It was gold; it seemed quite old. I don't think anyone was wearing it."

"Anything else?"

Kilek frowned. "Not really, My Lord."

"Is there something wrong?" Sir Venostac asked.

The room grew quiet. Kilek looked down at his hands where he'd laced his fingers upon the tabletop. The question was almost too obvious – so little about the last few weeks was 'right'. And yet, would they throw him in some dungeon if he spoke his mind? The men were waiting. "Yes... but I do not know how to say it to a pair of knights."

"You think we are wasting time with these questions," Sir Filen said.

"Well, I had wondered why you aren't asking me about troop numbers or their movements. About Prince Yan's magic or the mage, the one we think is hiding the raiding parties, that sort of thing. Isn't that why King Hadeon sent you here?"

"So he did," Sir Filen said, then leant back in his chair. "Kilek, we are part of a large force that is even now camped outside the walls. The king is moving, but our task is important too, though it is not for either of us to explain precisely why."

Kilek swallowed his disagreement; King Hadeon had not moved swiftly enough by far – but the mention of the army, even part of it, waiting outside *did* ease some of the resentment. "Then you're going to rescue the people of Hasere? And the other villages and towns?"

"That is not our remit, lad," Sir Venostac replied. "However, I am sure Duke Tireste will fight for that worthy goal without us. Sir Filen and I are trying to learn the reasons behind the raids."

"The Night Thorn and that ring? Prince Yan mentioned Minjao being under attack."

"And the truth of that we must also discover, and so we are following his trail. Yet with but two of us at work, we are tasked with observing and reporting only."

Kilek gripped the table. "I understand, but what should my friends and I do?"

Sir Venostac stood. "I believe it best if you take word of what you heard from Prince Yan to the royal city – we would provide an escort, horses and provisions, of course."

Kilek inhaled. "To Alaycron?"

Sir Filen chuckled as he circled the table to ruffle Kilek's hair. "Right. You'll love it, Kilek. A thousand sights, pretty girls, stunning food; it is truly the Autumn Jewel of the South."

"There is danger too, Sir Filen," Sir Venostac said.

"Always and everywhere – but that's what the escort is for, and the pigeons, so there's no need to worry. Besides, Kilek's friends seem capable enough of looking after him."

"That we could debate; they are untried."

"So were we all once."

Kilek stood. It was important to do something – anything that might make a difference, no matter how small. "We may not be knights but you can trust us to deliver word, My Lords."

Chapter 21.

"The royal city," Tyar said, a smile in his voice where he stood before the window, facing a breaking dawn that was largely colourless. "I'm *almost* looking forward to it."

"I would have been thrilled too," Alira said softly.

Kilek didn't agree aloud, but his own excitement was mixed in with left over guilt from having to turn from their original path, and the urge to convince the king that his subjects needed rescue.

Like everyone else, he wore new clothes now, a comforting leather jerkin and a black cloak, which bore twin poplars of white; mark of a squire or maybe a supporting force. It was no realisation of a dream but was a little closer than he'd ever truly believed he'd come. Just wearing a cloak with a certain stitching seemed to let him hold his head a little higher.

Mathila especially seemed to be smiling to herself as often as not, glancing down at the poplars on her own clothing.

He carried a sword again too, not that he knew how to use it truly, the weight of it odd upon his hip. Still, the garments were of a sturdy cut, perfect for travel. Even the boots were impressive, far softer within than anything he'd worn, yet durable on the outside.

Tyar still had his bow and quiver, but a long hunting knife now hung from his belt too. Pax stood at the door, pack slung across one shoulder. He, too, carried a new weapon – a long-handled hatchet, which had been also provided by the Knights of Alaycron. Alira wore a new bow and knife, Mathi a fine spear.

One of the knights intended to give her a sword too but upon seeing the lion's head blade, urged her to take care of the weapon, proclaiming it the equal to anything he had.

They'd also been provided with food; enough rations for the weeks to the capital. Now it was simply time to wait for enough light to meet the escort downstairs – someone sent by Sir Filen and Sir Venostac.

A knock came upon the door.

Paxoph straightened. "Yes?"

"It is Sir Venostac."

Pax opened the door to reveal the knight, who stood in full armour. "Please, come in, My Lord."

"I appreciate the offer of hospitality but I wish to speak with Kilek – swiftly before we leave."

"Of course, Sir." Kilek moved to join the man outside.

Sir Venostac closed the door gently, then lowered his voice. "About your pedant."

"Yes?" Kilek reached up to his throat, a half-realised motion. He'd assumed the knights had not been aware of it or considered his misfortune to be random.

"The Prisawi cannot be found but I spoke to a certain stallholder. If what he tells me is true, you may hold quite the treasure indeed. I urge you to keep it hidden, Kilek of Hasere."

"Why?"

"Obviously to avoid similar problems occurring in the future... but also because such objects can be dangerous if their purpose is unknown."

He nodded slowly. "I understand."

"Good lad. If you should ever desire more information on it, seek out a sage in Alaycron by the name of Coranet. She may be able to help you."

"Thank you." Relief must have flowed into his voice at the realisation that the knight did not seek to take the pendant, for the older man smiled.

"I will let your escort know you are ready to depart," Sir Venostac said, then bade him farewell; heading for the common room.

Kilek returned to his friends.

"What was that about?" Tyar asked.

"He wanted to know about what that mage asked us again," Kilek said. Then he shrugged. "The escort is here too."

Mathi rose from where she'd been sitting on Tyar's bed. "Well, let's get going. We have the knights' letter and we've got a job to do anyway."

"First-hand reports are always better," Paxoph added.

Yet no-one added that taking the message guaranteed little, and that if anyone had a chance at making a difference, it would be the force outside the walls who were even now readying to leave.

Tyar turned back to the window. "Think the king's men will be able to figure out what Yan is really looking for?"

"They've got to be better than us," Mathi replied.

Silence fell across the group.

It *did* still feel wrong to turn away from the search again… but truly, what could they hope to achieve alone? Everything came back to that simple and obvious point.

"Come on," Mathi said once more.

Kilek lifted his own pack and followed her into the empty passage and to the common room where Petra spoke with a new knight who stood in full armour. The innkeeper held a parcel of something she'd baked, the fresh scent was wonderful, but the escort had folded her arms, brow furrowed in a sign of impatience. Her age seemed to lie somewhere between Kilek's own and the age his friends only *appeared* to be, though a wariness to her cool blue gaze gave him pause.

"Here," Petra said as she handed the parcel to Kilek with a smile. "They're still warm. Safe travels to you all. And don't worry about anything outstanding on your bill, you've worked enough and the knighthood is covering the rest."

"Thank you, ma'am," Kilek replied, his voice echoed by the others.

"I am Clara," the Knight said as she gestured. "Follow me to the stables, if you please."

Kilek fell into step behind her, the clink of her armour loud in the hush. Few patrons had risen to leave, yet any travellers wouldn't be so far behind, as the sun was climbing swiftly enough when they met their mounts in the cool stable yard.

Lady Clara began un-tethering the reins of several horses, which had been tied to what appeared to be her own mount, its bridle bearing a scorched version of the Knighthood's symbol. "Do you each know how to ride?"

"We do," Mathi said.

"Then mount up; I want to cover a lot of ground today," she said as she swung into her saddle with a frown.

Kilek exchanged a glance with Tyar, who'd raised an eyebrow. The implied question was clear – what was wrong with Lady Clara? But neither answered, instead, transferring their packs to their mounts before climbing into the saddles. Lady Clara was already nodding to the stable hand as she passed through the gate, her mount's hooves clacking on stone.

Kilek murmured to his horse as he took the reins, one hand reaching down to stroke the animal's neck. It had been a while since he'd ridden, but the different view was welcome; he didn't feel so small compared to his friends anymore.

"Our escort seems quite unpleasant, doesn't she?" Tyar asked, lowering his voice.

"Maybe she'll relax a little once we get on the road," Mathi said with a shrug.

Tyar muttered to himself and Kilek nodded along, though again, he said nothing. Neither Paxoph nor Alira spoke either, they simply rode after the knight. Kilek took the rear position, patting his horse's neck again as they clopped down the street.

Lady Clara was staring back toward them from the corner. "Hurry it along, people."

The town of Trisoma was still abed for the most part, many windows with the warm glow of lamp or candle but none of the occupants seemed in a hurry to leave their homes. Those who had started their days already were mostly merchants and stall holders heading for their markets, passing between the striped shadows cast by surrounding buildings.

At the gate, a man with wild hair and a patch-work cloak hauled himself up from the wall to limp forth. When he neared Lady Clara, he lifted a wooden bowl. "Your charity would mean much, Lady Knight."

A pair of gate guards approached, but she raised a hand, stalling them. "It is no trouble." She leant over her pommel. "Of course." The dull clink of coins striking the bowl followed and then Lady Clara started toward the shadowy wood beyond the walls. The beggar limped back toward the wall and slunk into shadows cast from one of the mighty oak trees that made up the wall.

"Hmmm." Tyar frowned after the man.

"What is it?" Alira asked.

"Some towns like to chase beggars away – it's cruel, I know, but I've heard of it plenty. Remember that man who had been injured in some old war, the spring when the stream broke the banks?"

"I do."

"Well, we welcomed him and he said, other places had turned him away, especially if he was near a place where visitors might notice. The guards went to intervene just now but Lady Clara stopped them."

"So?"

"So, like I said – many towns don't want visitors to see the beggars upon arrival. Is Lady Clara truly so kind?"

"We've only just met her. You don't know what she's like."

"I know, but that man didn't ask any of us for charity. Only her."

Kilek had found himself half-convinced that Tyar was simply looking for reasons to dislike Lady Clara... until his friend's last point.

"He's obviously an informant," Mathi said. "Left behind by the army."

Kilek glanced ahead to where Lady Clara had stopped, and once more raised her voice. "Don't fall behind. I can't protect you if you dawdle."

Kilek tapped his horse's flanks and his friends joined him, it did not take long to catch up to the knight. "Forgive us," he said. "It's been a while since we've ridden."

She only gestured to the trees. "Be watchful now. The Minjao may not dare travel so far south but ambush from brigands is always a risk."

"Ah, right," Kilek said. "We will."

And he did, staring at the shadows and twisting his head at any movement within the trunks, but after an entire morning of doing so and noting only birds or small animals, it seemed a pointless endeavour, especially so close to Trisoma. Yet Lady Clara continued to watch, while still appearing at ease – it was clearly a habit for her.

Leaves were fluttering down to the earth as a breeze picked up around noon, and Lady Clara called for a halt in a small clearing set off the road. A grassy space, quite level with a cold fire pit; it seemed ideal, especially with the sound of running water not too far distant.

Yet when Kilek dismounted his joints cried out in protest, muscles afire. "Gods be damned," he hissed. The others didn't seem to be in quite as much discomfort, so he curtailed his complaints as he tied his mount to a branch. The horse snorted and started on the grass.

From afar, the sound of axes striking wood echoed; the people of Trisoma at work.

"Eat swiftly, as we're moving on soon," Lady Clara said as

she started between the trees, toward the stream.

Kilek rifled through his pack, removing the sweet breads from Petra and sharing them around.

"How long do we have to travel with her?" Tyar asked around a mouthful.

"The whole time if we want them to take us seriously at the city," Mathi said. "Even with Sir Venostac's letter – they'll probably think we stole it if we turn up alone."

"You sure of that?" Tyar asked as he plucked at his tabard.

"I'm sure we don't need to risk it," she replied.

He grinned. "Well, how about this then, how long to Alaycron from here?"

"I think at least two weeks."

"How... wonderful," he said, and slumped back down to the log to continue eating.

"So long as she gets us there, it doesn't matter that she's unwelcoming," Mathi replied.

"Right," Alira agreed.

Tyar took a final bite, then licked his fingers.

"I, too, am becoming worried about our own reception in Alaycron," Paxoph said. He stood with folded arms, staring into the trees.

"But Sir Venostac is part of a group trying to find out why Yan is seeking myths," Kilek said.

"I know, Kil. But I wouldn't be surprised if they take our report and then put us somewhere out of the way. They aren't going to ask us to join the forces chasing the Minjao, are they?"

Another hush fell across the group.

What Pax described wasn't an unlikely scenario by any stretch. Kilek tapped his fingers upon the log.

"Mount up, everyone," Lady Clara said from the trees, appearing, water flasks in hand. Her expression gave no indication that she'd heard their conversation.

Kilek took a drink from his own flask then hurried toward his horse. Perhaps they'd been lucky and she truly hadn't heard, but taking better care wouldn't hurt – Lady Clara didn't seem the type to take criticism kindly.

Chapter 22.

Nothing had changed by nightfall but their camp was well-ordered and more – Lady Clara had set trip wires around the clearing. She also required a watch, the firelight reflecting in her eyes when she paired everyone up.

No-one complained, though Tyar frowned into his meal.

Kilek had drawn the final watch – paired with Lady Clara herself. It might have been insulting, not to be trusted, and perhaps it was all a little excessive... but once he finished his meal and sought the bedroll within his tent, a sense of calm fell across him. He closed his eyes and steadied his breathing – it all seemed a little easier now, having a true adult along.

And he slept well enough, despite waking once in the night at what he thought had been a muffled groan, but the camp was silent and no more sounds followed. He rolled onto his side and closed his eyes once more.

"Wake."

Kilek sighed, sleep still weighing heavily. How long had it been since he'd last stirred?

Something nudged his back. "Come on, boy."

Lady Clara's voice.

Kilek rose, rubbing at his eyes, which were slow to adjust to the scant light of embers beyond the tent flap. The knight waved him into the cool dark. "Bring your sword," she said.

"Right." He snatched it up, stepped into his boots and threw his cloak on as he followed her to the edge of the camp. There Lady Clara stood, staring down the smudge of somewhat paler road, the ghosts of tree trunks looming around.

In the silence between them his breathing seemed too loud.

Eventually, he spoke. "Did anyone report any danger?"

She shook her head.

"Ah, is there a threat I should be watching for, Lady Clara?"

"None in particular, boy. We simply watch."

"My name is Kilek," he said with a smile. "I am from a village in the north, Hasere."

"That I know."

Kilek fell silent once more. The knight was clearly not willing to talk, and her sour nature did not encourage him to try harder. Did something trouble her or was she simply an unpleasant person? In the dark, it was impossible to tell. Instead, he turned away, to stare down the other end of the road, listening to the woods at night, tiny shuffling sounds or the flap of wings as some night bird took flight.

His feet then legs ached and he shifted often until Lady Clara ordered him to complete a circuit of the camp.

On his walk, he kept clear of the lines Lady Clara had set, and the tents, managing not to crash into any low-hanging branches. On his second passage, he paused at an odd sound from the water – a tiny splash?

He froze, breath stuck in his throat.

Time crept by and the sound did not repeat itself. Had it been a splash at all? Had he imagined the damn sound? Kilek stared into the darkened trees, hand on his hilt, but nothing moved, nothing appeared and no more sounds followed.

Just a small animal?

Something from one of the sleeping horses?

Lady Clara was not so distant that he couldn't get her attention... if there was even a problem. And so he waited and still no more similar sounds. Either he'd imagined it or something harmless had fallen into the water.

By dawn, it was clear there had been nothing to fear and the blushing light eased the remaining tension in his muscles. He started on the fire while Lady Clara woke the others, handing out tasks again. This time, even Mathi seemed to resent being told what to do if her glower was any indication – rising early was not something she enjoyed.

Kilek ate his cheese and bread slowly but soon found himself in his saddle again, as though his limbs had moved of their own accord after breaking camp. Somehow, the weariness of the watch lingered, though he found himself increasingly sure there had been nothing to the sound.

The morning grew warmer as the trees thinned and still no attack came, nothing to even catch his attention; just the jingle of harness and tack, a few bird calls and the scrambling of tiny claws from the dark green undergrowth, tiny white and blue flowers twitching.

Twice they passed wagons laden with green vegetables

and once a line of horses carrying bags of wool, a harried-looking merchant leading, his whip cracking long after he passed. Lady Clara signalled for everyone to be ready but the man's haste was not due to any pursuit.

When the trees finally gave way it was to stretching green and gold farmland, roads and lanes cutting cleanly and straight. Between, most of the land had already been hewn and sown – wheat already grew. In the distance, a caravan headed east, doubtless toward Jecomar, considering that the capital was far too distant to reach by nightfall.

In the open now, they rode on at a brisk canter, Lady Clara leading.

Behind him, Paxoph and Mathi were discussing the distance and time to camp, trying to estimate where that would be, their voices raised enough to carry over the clap of hooves and rush of a breeze across Kilek's face.

But another sound soon filtered its way down – a buzzing from above.

Kilek twisted in his saddle.

Twin shapes of darkness bore down on the group from the sky, black and purple glinting in the afternoon light. A wave of nausea stirred Kilek's gut and he swayed in the saddle, gripping the reins. The things drew closer and the buzzing rose in pitch, like a pair of endless shrieks. Was it... *Cabeku?*

"Tyar!"

"I see them." He was struggling to unsling his bow, using his knees to grip his mount. Yet his horse seemed to be missing every other step. Were the insects truly so powerful? Alira had not drawn her own bow, she had both hands full with her mare.

Kilek coughed back bile, even as he fumbled for his sword. Thankfully, his horse handled his unsteady movements well enough, despite her own snorts of agitation.

"Shoot!"

It was Lady Clara.

Tyar's horse was slowing – yet it allowed him to take aim. Tyar drew the arrow back and released the shaft. Black feathers shot forth.

The Cabeku tilted its translucent wings.

The arrow flew wide by a narrow margin.

"Bah." Tyar fired again but missed a second time, and worse, he was falling behind as his horse faltered. The insects swooped lower now; one aiming for Lady Clara and the second bearing down on Alira. Kilek angled his mount toward her, sword raised – and an arrow tore through the creature.

It dropped to the ground with a thud.

Steel flashed as Lady Clara swung her blade. The insect's legs clattered with each blow where it hovered above her, pale purple ichor dripping from its mouth. The drops sprayed but she caught the hissing liquid on her shield each time.

A piercing cry cut through the clamour.

Something streaked down to slam into the Cabeku. Kilek straightened in his saddle – it was a hawk, feathers of orange and gold ablaze in the light. The bird was larger than natural and its powerful talons tore the insect in half with a mere twitch, scattering the pieces as the great bird ascended.

Too soon, the hawk was a dot in the sky.

Kilek stared after it. *Where* had the bird come from?

He slowed his mare, then turned to the others – most

of whom were riding back to Lady Clara with pallid expressions, though Tyar led his gelding up the road at a jog.

The knight had dismounted to kneel over the insect Tyar shot down. Kilek joined her, wrinkling his nose at the acrid scent that rose from the segmented body, strongest where the ichor still pumped forth. The translucent black wings were bent and broken and the bulging eyes dull.

Tyar's arrowhead had already turned black from the acid, the shaft broken in two. The jagged legs twitched as it died.

"What is this abomination?" Lady Clara breathed. She reached out to prod it with her sword, overturning it to reveal the slick underside.

Kilek opened his mouth but Mathi shot him a look.

The knight still stared at the Cabeku corpse. "I need an old cloak."

"Won't the blood burn through?" Alira asked as she pulled her old cloak from one of her saddlebags. She held it out.

Lady Clara nodded as she accepted the cloth. "Hopefully not once it's dry." She looked to Tyar. "A fine shot."

"Ah, thank you," he replied.

"What about the bird?" Paxoph asked. "Are hawks so large to the south?"

Lady Clara was still frowning at the insect. Her icy gaze revealed some concern, but whether about the insect, the hawk or both, it was impossible to say. "Not that I have noticed, no. But it seems we are fortunate that it happened upon us." Her voice held some suspicion, but who exactly it was directed at remained just as unclear.

"What if more come?" Mathi asked.

"We seek cover. Failing that, we protect your archer so he can protect us," she said as she kicked dirt over the still-glistening ichor. Then she wrapped the insect in the cloak, affixed it to her saddlebags and mounted up. "Onward now."

Kilek checked on his horse, her eyes seemed calm enough. No sign of distress. Good. His own nausea had vanished too. He swung into the saddle and glanced up to the sky. No more birds or insects. Why had they come? Were the Cabeku acting as spies? And if so, who was seeking them? Javoteth? Or one of his surrogates?

"Let's keep going," Paxoph said as he rode by.

Kilek nodded, then drew level with Alira. She rode with her reins in one hand only, the other held a brilliant feather of gold, tipped with fiery orange. Her expression was one of awe, green eyes bright with joy.

"Alira?"

She glanced away, and for a second, she didn't seem to truly see him. Then, she smiled. "I'm fine, Kilek."

"It's a beautiful feather."

She nodded, then lowered her voice. "Share the watch with me tonight."

"Ah, I'll try," he said. "Won't Lady Clara decide again?"

"She'll appreciate us taking initiative."

Kilek nodded slowly. "I can see that... but why?"

"I have to share a message but Lady Clara doesn't need to hear it – we'll need to tell the others, too."

He leaned a little closer. "Tell them what? And who is the message from?"

"Avendria."

Chapter 23.

Lady Clara accepted their offer to take first watch, just as Alira predicted, and so after a stew of salted pork and carrot, which Kilek ate quickly, he found himself sitting upon a log beside her, facing the darkness.

Night cloaked their camp, which was nothing more than a depression beside the road. Again, the weather was mild enough that there was no real problem. At their backs, beyond the tents, wheat stalks rustled softly in a warm breeze and before them, an empty line of hard-packed dirt that represented the road.

"What did Avendria say?" Kilek finally asked softly, once he was sure the others were asleep. His impatience was tempered somewhat by a reluctance to hear any more from the Goddess. After all, what could she say that would help at this point? "Did she... appear within the feather?"

Alira shook her head. "No, I heard her voice."

"And?"

"She said that we need to find *Daciael*. Do you know it?"

He scratched at his head. Daciael *was* familiar, why?

"I think so. Isn't that a valley above the fields of Jecomar? Supposedly the old kings used to vacation there."

"Then there must be something in the valley we need to see or do or find."

"It's a little vague, isn't it?"

"Right. But she must know something, Kilek – she's a Goddess."

Kilek lowered his voice even further. "True enough. But doesn't this mean she is helping us directly? I thought that was against the rules – can't our enemy do the same now?"

"What if that already happened, and her sending us a message, even a vague one now – and the hawk for that matter – was a *response* to something another surrogate received from Javoteth?"

That was entirely possible. He exhaled. "Well, whichever it was, I think we need to be even more watchful now, in case there's something following those two insects."

"I agree." She glanced down to the feather, which even at night did not seem dim, not the way Alira's or his own clothes did, the twin spear points on their cloaks hardly visible beneath the stars.

"What about the others?"

"I'll tell them. Like this, or maybe when some chore takes us out of earshot."

"Good idea." He glanced back over his shoulder to where Lady Clara's tent stood beyond the embers, sealed for now. "But how do we convince Lady Clara?"

"I don't know."

"She wouldn't believe us about any of this – who would?"

"So maybe we need to appeal to her sense of the practical. Perhaps logistically the place could be of use?"

"It's a detour... and I think it's clear Lady Clara wants to be done with us."

"Of course, that's silly of me," Alira said, lowering her head.

"No, I didn't mean it like that," Kilek said quickly, adding a smile that he hoped came through in his voice. "We'll come up with something – we still have to reach Jecomar."

Alira nodded. "So what of you, Kilek?"

"Me?"

"Do you still think about the Goddess' gift?"

What gift? "I try not to," he said after a moment.

"You know, I think it's cruel too but I also think she must have a plan. A purpose, at least."

Kilek laughed softly. "It's really nice to hear someone agree that it's cruel."

She put her arm around him and pulled him close. "I know we're all wrapped up in our own changes... and everything, but I believe in Avendria; she's seen something in you and when it finally becomes clear, things will be better. In the meantime, I can listen, you know?"

"Thank you." And he did take comfort in her words; words Alira would have used before the change but they seemed somehow more mature now. Was that part of what the Goddess had given them?

"It's nothing – you were the only one who used to listen to me when I mentioned my... feelings back home. It meant a lot, not to be ridiculed."

"Well, I've always known you're not a liar."

She smiled.

"Do you sense anything now? Has learning things from Florique helped?"

"Actually, I haven't felt much since. I didn't sense the Cabeku or that damn lizard... I feel like I should have been able." She shrugged. "But it was never predictable anyway."

Before Kilek could reply, Alira stood.

"What's wrong?"

She pointed beyond the road. "Look!"

A soft pink glow wove its way between the trunks. It moved at a steady pace, pausing here and there as it approached. Kilek stood, a hand on his sword but he did not draw it yet. The glow illuminated little; a white robe and a pair of hands it seemed – but still the figure was not close enough for many more details.

"Is it a spectre?" he breathed.

"Should we wake the others?"

The glow drew nearer then paused – changing direction, moving parallel with the camp now, at a steadier speed and then angling away, into the darkness until it disappeared. Kilek stared after it, eyes wide. He shook his head after it seemed clear the light was not returning. "I think so; I don't want to follow it alone."

"Me either."

Kilek hurried into the camp. Who or what had approached them in the night, carrying what could not have been a lantern? Was it related to the sound he'd heard on his first watch? Or the Cabeku somehow?

At Lady Clara's tent, he hesitated. How should he wake her? Would she be angry – even though it was important? Alira was already rousing the others. He knelt by the opening. "Lady Clara?"

No answer. He raised his voice and called her name again. Behind him, Alira was explaining what they'd seen as Tyar built up the dull embers. Still no stirring from within the tent. "Lady Clara? Something has happened."

Silence.

Kilek turned to the others. "I can't wake her."

"I don't hear snoring, so she's not exactly a heavy sleeper," Mathi said.

"Is she even within?" Tyar asked. "Maybe she's on watch herself, since she barely trusts us to buckle our own boots."

Kilek waved his hands for Tyar to stop, but still, there was no response from Lady Clara.

Paxoph joined him before the tent, raising his own deep voice. "Lady?"

"Just open the tent already," Mathi said.

Yet no sooner had she spoken when the tent flap parted. Lady Clara frowned up at them, light from the fire revealing more detail; wisps of her blonde hair escaping the plait. "Why open my tent?"

Kilek blinked. "We saw something."

Lady Clara stood, opening her cloak to free her sword in hand as she scanned trees. "Then tell me what – are we under attack?"

"No. Alira and I saw a figure in the trees – it was robed in white and it carried a glowing pink light."

She raised an eyebrow. "You say 'it' – are you telling me you believe you saw a spirit? Are you sure you didn't drift off and mix dream and the night, boy?"

"No," Kilek said, raising his voice, feeling his face flush.

Lady Clara sheathed her blade. "I see nothing now."

Alira straightened. "It was no ghost – unless you believe Kilek and I imagined the same thing at exactly the same time? We don't know what or who it was. It approached, then veered away when we noticed it. We thought everyone should be aware."

The knight sighed.

"Thank you, both," Paxoph said. "I will be extra wary when it is my watch."

"Me too," Tyar added.

"Fine," Lady Clara said. "We all watch until you are satisfied that there is no threat. Then, back to regular shifts." She moved to the fire and sat with her back to the growing flames, facing the tree line.

Kilek moved to the opposite side of the camp. He folded his arms, jaw clenched. Lady Clara was wrong... but whether she believed them or not, why bother belittling him? Gods, no-one else was any older, truly! If she knew, would she be calling Alira 'girl' and doubting her story?

He sucked in a deep breath and exhaled slowly; he had to stay in control of his emotions. The strange figure might still be out there and more, his friends had spoken for him. Especially Alira.

Yet even so, he couldn't help an irrational desire pushing through – if only the strange figure would return, then Lady Clara would know she was wrong.

Chapter 24.

"I still don't understand why it took so long for her to wake," Tyar said where he rode beside Kilek at the rear of the line. The sun pummelled them as it drew high overhead, making the dust of the road sizzle – or so it seemed as the sweat poured down Kilek's back.

"I know." The top and throat of his tabard clung to his skin and he had to wipe sweat from his brow and beneath his eyes all too often. His friends seemed to be equally uncomfortable, especially Mathi who was muttering to herself, but Lady Clara bore it stoically – as did the green fields they continued to ride through. Other travellers were few and far between, though one middle-aged man stopped to speak with Clara, sharing news of the road ahead – and it seemed to contain no apparitions, enemy soldiers or large insects.

So they could expect a trip just as uneventful as the rest of last night's watch.

When the traveller passed the end of their line, he nodded to Kilek and Tyar.

Kilek returned the greeting, then glanced after the fellow. The traveller carried a sword and worn pack, his cloak as plain as the rest of his clothes. A patch covered one eye. Had the man lost his sight in a battle?

"That might have been my future, you know," Kilek told Tyar.

"Huh?"

He gestured behind them. "That traveller's face. If the Minjao had taken us to the west, and you hadn't saved us, who knows how we'd have been hurt? Or how quickly we'd have been killed."

"Well, that's not on the cards anymore, thankfully," Tyar said with a chuckle. "Instead, we have to tell our story and hope people with more might than us can get the job done."

Kilek nodded slowly. "But don't you still want to find Gan yourself?"

"I do."

"But?"

"Right, there's always a 'but'. And it's like this, nothing's changed from before – we're still not enough, Goddess or no. I mean, I still want to do it myself but I have to face the truth."

Kilek had no answer and they rode on in silence until smudges of smoke appeared ahead; Jecomar. Beyond it, in time, they would reach the capital where they would do their best to help unravel Yan's purpose.

In the meantime, the town of Jecomar waited upon a hill that overlooked the fields – it was a large, walled city that dwarfed Trisoma.

He let his horse slow to a halt.

A trail of smoke, thicker than any chimney, rose from

somewhere in the city. Even as they watched, it thinned out, as though whatever fire had been ablaze was now dealt with or perhaps a distant wind taken the smoke. The walls were just as tall as those back in the forest town but much longer, and the towers and spires rose in stone too, these flying blue pennants but unlike the drawings of Alaycron he'd seen, where the buildings seemed more ordered, Jecomar was somehow uneven.

Its size remained impressive enough but near half the stone was of a greyish blue, whereas other buildings and spires appeared paler, like sandstone – and while the grey towers had peaks of black tile, the paler structures were thatched or sometimes featured flat rooves. As though two builders had set to work without speaking to one another.

"No-one ever talks about that," he said to Tyar, pointing.

"Supposedly King Netau started the city and King Gilio expanded it," he replied.

Kilek glanced at his friend. "How did you know that?"

"Gan's family is from Jecomar – but it's not exactly a secret, either. I thought you'd know that."

"Well, maybe I do but I didn't remember..."

Tyar chuckled. "You know more about myths and legends and dragons than the present day."

At the towering gates, a pair of guards in breastplates and blue and black tabards paused from where they were inspecting a merchant's wagons to wave Lady Clara through, obviously having noted her status.

Her presence did offer some convenience at least.

Inside, people crowded the streets. Not just the locals in their typical Luargot tunic and pants but also a few folk from the deepest south; the land of Gywthar. These were merchants mostly with their large, bird-drawn wagons. Or at least, the bird-like *Collara* – it was only the second time Kilek had ever seen one of the creatures, dark feathers and heavy hind legs with large, cloven hooves. Their eyes were large and moved slowly upon long, muscular necks, as though eternally calm.

But he could not look for long, since unlike in Trisoma, moving became more difficult as Lady Clara led them up and away from the poorer buildings nearest the gate, their horses' hooves lost in the clamour. Most were warehouses and smaller homes, but the taverns all bore the same notice pinned to the wall beside the door.

While waiting at an intersection as a caravan of lumber and stone rumbled by, Kilek stepped close enough to read one of the notices.

"'Be Warned: Patrons of any establishment within Jecomar caught using counterfeit coins will be imprisoned without delay'."

He glanced to Paxoph, who'd joined him. "That's troubling."

"Let's move," Lady Clara called.

They climbed on, circling up toward cleaner, quieter parts of the city. Here Kilek had to pull his mount away from sunflowers that grew at the edges of small parks, the lush grass and sparkling fountains just as enticing for him – to dunk his head but once would have been enough.

But even if Lady Clara had been likely to wait, most of the fountains were already full of children and folks a little older – people his own age, laughing and splashing each other. At one park, a man in the blue of a city guardsman chased some children from the fountain, club swinging from his belt, but his expression suggested he did not much care to bother.

Once, a child dressed in a ragged hood approached Mathi with wide eyes. "Ma'am, if you seek fine lodgings, my cousin runs the finest inn in the city. I can take you there."

"Ah, not today," she replied.

He smiled. "But wait until you see the rooms!"

Lady Clara stopped. "If you seek an easy mark, look elsewhere, boy. If you seek charity, know that the Knights will care for you."

He flinched back, his smile vanished. "You think I'm stupid, bitch?"

She did not respond.

The boy spat onto the cobblestones then fled.

Lady Clara rode on and Kilek once again found himself exchanging glances with Paxoph, noting the others appeared equally surprised. Was something afoot in Jecomar with the knights? Or did the child know Lady Clara personally? The latter didn't seem likely, which was probably more troubling.

Here, where the sandstone dominated and the warehouses had long disappeared, the Luargot nobility appeared to be more common, whether eating on balconies of upper storeys or strutting about, servants trailing them in muted colours and with arms laden. The nobles' dress was of a far finer cut, blushing silks or patterned cloth, the leather on their boots supple and their hands near dripping with rings.

Many of the ladies walked the street in form-hugging dresses with servants holding umbrellas to shade them from the sun, their pale skin almost corpse-like at times. Yet where their complexion appeared almost unhealthy, the jewellery at their necks more than made up for it with glittering displays of excess.

Tyar whistled to himself as a particularly striking woman rode by in a white carriage, who despite her pale countenance, leaned out the window, peering from between maroon curtains with a dull expression. Yet the topaz at her neck was certainly vibrant enough to catch the eye.

Mathi narrowed her eyes at Tyar but said nothing, and he didn't seem to notice. Yet Kilek felt a stab of jealousy. It was ridiculous, but he found himself craving even such negative attention from Mathila. Paxoph had groaned at Tyar's response to the noblewoman and Alira made her sniff of derision quite loud.

"That's enough of that," Tyar said with a weary tone. "I was looking at her *jewellery*. Can you imagine the kind of place we could stay at if we sold her necklace?"

"We will be staying at the Knight's quarters," Lady Clara interrupted. "You will find them serviceable and clean."

"Would some luxury kill us, My Lady?" Tyar asked.

"Unlikely, but too much will certainly turn you into something vapid and empty. I assume you actually noticed her eyes? She is a husk."

Tyar opened his mouth to reply but it seemed he was at a loss for words – and Kilek didn't blame him, the knight had hardly been forthcoming about anything during their travels, almost every word she spoke was a command.

Ahead, a stern shape rose up, the building resting directly before an intersection of streets.

Like those around it, the knight's lodgings were several storeys tall, though the building was one of the few made from bluestone. Narrow slits stood in for windows and the gate was large, sturdy oak banded with steel; clearly a military building. What appeared to be a lookout's post rested atop the building, where a figure in breastplate and helm watched them approach.

"Welcome to the Jecomar Post. We will stay here tonight, long enough to resupply in the morning, and then we head on toward Alaycron," Lady Clara said when she stopped before the gate. "While we are here, you will address the knights as 'sir' or 'my lord' and 'lady' as you have done so with me. After the ninth bell, guests must stay within their rooms, do you understand?"

"No, we do not," Mathi said, folding her arms. "Aren't you meant to be our escort, not our jailor?"

The knight nodded. "And I am. But this is not a frivolous place and that is the rule of the Knighthood."

"Then we'll be exploring the city before nightfall, My Lady," Mathi said.

Lady Clara gestured back to the street. "Of course, but be sure at least one of you survives to travel on to Alaycron tomorrow, otherwise this trip will have been for naught."

"Are we in danger here?" Paxoph asked.

"No more than in any other city."

"We'll be just fine, My Lady," Tyar said with a smile devoid of cheer. "I think we'll dump our packs inside then take a look around."

Lady Clara did not reply, only knocking upon the gate. After a short time, the rattle of locks being opened came, then the creak of hinges as half the gate swung inward. Two knights were revealed, one with greying hair and the other far younger – but both nodded to Lady Clara without speaking, ushering her within and motioning for everyone to follow.

The younger knight took everyone's horses as the older man led them immediately into what seemed to be a guard house with chairs, table and hearth, with barely a glance at the sunny courtyard. Instead, it was following the knight in his clinking armour down a dim corridor of stone, one that seemed to be circling half the building.

When the knight stopped it was to unlock a steel door, revealing an antechamber and another corridor, this one with rows of cells – or tiny rooms not unlike a barracks. Which was hardly surprising.

"Take any room that is free," he said. "Meals are served two bells after sundown and the doors are locked by the ninth of the day."

Then he left them standing in the hall.

Kilek glanced into the nearest room. It was austere; a cot, shelf and window. Nothing else – but at least it was cool here out of the sun. Hopefully the night wouldn't be unbearable. At least prior to taking his rest, there was something to look forward to – and not just exploring the city but spending time away from Lady Clara.

He placed his saddlebags within and then checked on the others – everyone had dumped their own belongings and now gathered together, Tyar grinning like a fool and even Mathi smiling with the others. Beyond them, Lady Clara had chosen a room and was even now closing the door.

"Good," Kilek muttered.

"Come on, Kil," Tyar said as he started back down the corridor, nearly bounding along.

Kilek had to laugh – it was nice to see everyone in high spirits, for what seemed like the first time since they'd left home, and it banished his darkening mood.

Chapter 25.

Kilek knelt before a fountain they'd passed on their way to the Knight's Post and splashed his face with the water. A ripple of coolness spread across his skin, running down his chest. He sighed, a smile upon his face now. He scooped more water up and used it to rub at the sweat on the back of his neck.

In this particular park there were no children, just an elderly couple dressed in the dark blue of the city livery, who trimmed the roses that ran along the borders. The relative quiet left a lot of room for Kilek and his friends, half of whom had joined Kilek at the fountain, this being a statue of a serpent curled around a sword, the water pouring out from between its fangs.

"How are we going to convince Lady Clara that we need to visit Daciael?" Kilek asked.

Tyar sighed where he lay sprawled across the nearby grass. "I don't know if we can."

"But we have to try," Alira said. She sat not too far away, upon one of the stone benches. "I don't think the Goddess sent us that message for nothing."

"She still wants us to save the lands, right?" Tyar said.

"Of course."

"Well, whatever it is, I hope it's big because we all know just how outnumbered we are."

Paxoph rose from the fountain, shaking drops of water from his hands. "Let's try to figure something out at an inn," he said. "I'm feeling a little hungry, aren't you?"

"An outstanding idea," Tyar said as he sat up.

"Should we save what money we have?" Kilek asked.

"Perhaps not while the Knighthood is paying," Paxoph replied, then frowned. "But now that I've said it, let's hold back a little."

Mathi flicked water at him. "Whatever you say, Grandfather – let's get going."

The streets beyond the park were just as busy as before. Kilek noticed more nobility out and about, many giving him looks of disapproval due to his half-soaked appearance, but such censure didn't bother him and they soon found a suitable inn several blocks across from the park; the Two Kings.

"We have to go in here," Tyar said. "They clearly have a sense of humour."

Two storeys tall, the bottom half was bluestone while the upper sandstone. The commitment to the idea didn't end there either; the inn bore rows of tall, narrow windows with stained glass, the colours alternating between deep blue and rich amber.

Inside, the light played out exactly as Kilek had imagined it would; striped swathes of colour crossed the tables and benches, back to the bar and its shelves of liquor. The common room seemed between meals as few people lingered, talking softly, but the innkeeper moved from a blue patch with a smile.

"Welcome, travellers, to the Two Kings." He nodded to Tyar, his red beard, which was large enough to make up for the hair missing from his head, shifting against his apron. "I am Oderra and I'm happy to offer meal or room."

"Thank you, Oderra," Tyar said. "We'd love to eat if your cook is willing?"

Oderra's laugh rumbled. "Always! Let's find you a table then."

Once he'd taken them to seating that fell mostly in an 'amber' section and taken their order, the innkeeper headed for the kitchen.

"So... does anyone have any ideas?" Alira asked.

"To convince Lady Clara about Daciael?" Mathi asked.

Alira nodded.

Paxoph shrugged. "We have no reason for such a detour, short though it would seem to be."

A long moment of silence passed.

Kilek tapped his finger on the table until Mathi frowned at him. He tapped harder a moment, then stopped, leaning back in his chair. It was impossible, surely? Lady Clara would not accept any reason.

"Can we say that we saw that spectre again and we want to investigate?" Tyar finally suggested.

Mathi leant forward. "No – but maybe any lie is as good as another, why don't we just go there ourselves?"

"What?" Tyar asked. "Do you mean, we eat now and then just take off?"

"Exactly. It's not so far. We could be there and back before the Post locks up."

He was grinning now. "Even on foot?"

"I think so – and I doubt we'd be able to convince her of anything if we were caught in the stable."

Paxoph was nodding slowly. "According to the map I received from Sir Venostac, the valley is within walking distance, though it's rarely visited to hear Uncle tell it."

"He's been there?" Kilek asked.

"A long time ago. He only mentioned it once... I think he said, it was like an overgrown garden that had once maybe been magnificent."

Tyar slapped the table. "Then that settles it – once we're finished here, we're going for a walk."

A serving girl approached the table, arms laden with trays of steaming food. She handed out drinks too – and once again Kilek was given water without being offered a choice. And while his friends ate and drank, perhaps a little too much based on their raised voices and slightly flushed faces, Kilek focused on the meal that was well worth the wait: peppery meat and fluffy potatoes, both slathered in rich gravy.

Before they finished eating, a thin man dressed in grey overcoat and pants, silver trim at the cuffs, approached the table. He was flanked by two of the city guard who held their cudgels; both weapons were steel-tipped.

"If you would set your cutlery down and accompany me to the prison offices, I would appreciate that."

Tyar burst into laughter, squinting up at the man. "You want us to what?"

Mathi laughed too, her face as flushed as Tyar's – the fools were drunk.

The stranger's expression grew hard. "You are accused of passing counterfeit coins, so it is best not to test the Duke's patience."

"That's not true," Mathi cried, speaking over Tyar, who was spluttering now.

Kilek lowered his fork. The man's claim made no sense – they didn't even *have* any coin from the city, only what had been provided by the Knighthood or what came from Hasere.

"Then I am sure that, after you answer my questions you will be set free but it is my duty to treat every report seriously."

Paxoph stood slowly, keeping his hands raised. "We are travellers only arrived in the city today and so we carry only coin from the north."

"You will have a chance to explain yourselves, that I can promise."

The innkeeper approached with a frown on his face. "Inspector Quiselie, I doubt they even knew the difference. You have the coins now – what harm?"

"Oderra my good man, consider your establishment's reputation... and while you are doing so, allow me to complete my work."

Oderra gave a short bow then stood back. "Of course, Inspector."

"Will you walk or be carried forth, perhaps?" Quiselie asked.

"We will walk," Paxoph said, raising an arm to deter Tyar. Mathi too, glared at the man. "If you would also send someone to the Knight's Post and ask for Lady Clara, I am sure she will vouch for us."

The inspector gave a sharp nod. "Very well – let's go."

***

The dim room was little more than bare stone enclosing a table and chair, damp where they'd descended beneath the exceptionally plain building the Inspector had taken them to, quickly splitting them up once inside.

Two coins rested on a table before Kilek, gleaming beneath the lamplight.

At a glance, neither appeared false. Both were silver, the visible side bearing old King Raquan's stern face and bald head. The year of his coronation sat beneath his name and on the other side, would be the outline of a stag.

Inspector Quiselie gestured to the table. "Please, pick them up if you so desire."

"Where are my friends?" Kilek asked, keeping his hands rested on the table before him. He tried to glare at the man but it probably wasn't much in the way of an act; his defiance was more loosely contained desperation – he was alone, Lady Clara had not appeared and the Inspector would not listen to reason.

"As I have told you, they are safe, boy – providing they cooperate, as you must."

Despite his worry, Kilek frowned at being called a 'boy' once more – why did everyone have to continually refer to him that way? Each time, it was a stinging reminder: the Goddess had overlooked him. "You have already asked me the same questions a dozen times."

"And so I might again – you travelled from the village of Hasere and have important news for the King about the

Minjao; that I have heard. You travel with a knight, Lady Clara, who has yet to vouch for you as promised. You were simply taking a meal at an inn near the Post of the Jecomar Knighthood."

"Yes."

"And here is what I also know. Sometime after arriving in the city you succumbed to temptation and agreed to help circulate the counterfeit coins – it is understandable; you were desperate, having travelled so far with so little. Perhaps you were even afraid of what they might do to you if you refused?"

"What?"

"Or maybe you simply went along with your elders, those who should have taken better care of a young lad such as yourself. You are not to blame, Kilek."

"That's not true."

"Yet when you used such coins to dupe the merchants and in fact, *all* people of Jecomar, you took something from them. You contributed to a lessening of the King's currency with those... things."

"This doesn't make sense – none of those things happened," Kilek said, his voice rising.

Inspector Quiselie sat across from him now. He lifted the coins, showing them to Kilek, stag-side out. The outline showed the stag atop an outcropping, ears standing, antlers proud. "I'm sure you've noticed that one ear is slightly smaller than the other? There are other subtle differences too, aspects the criminals have not been able to replicate yet."

Kilek gripped the table. "What does this have to do with us?"

"I need you to tell me all about the people who hired you,

Kilek of Hasere."

"No-one hired me. I'm just trying to tell the king about Prince Yan of the Minjao – and Lady Clara is helping us. Sir Venostac and Sir Filen sent her."

The Inspector sighed. "A final chance now, to tell me the truth."

"I am!"

"Very well – until you are ready to be honest, you will be taking up new quarters here in Jecomar: Duke Tireste's dungeon, a far less salubrious place than this."

Chapter 26.

The sun had begun to crawl down behind the buildings as he was escorted along the back streets, the cobblestones a more uniform shade best described as 'worn' or 'gritty' but as before, the tall buildings featured masonry of two colours. Thanks to the busier thoroughfares, the backstreets remained near empty. Inspector Quiselie and his two guards led them past refuse or stacks of empty crates as they headed toward the looming wall of the castle, the parapet visible in glimpses between the rooves.

Kilek glanced over his shoulder – his friends followed Quiselie with glares, their own hands now tied like Kilek. Behind them in turn, the two guards walked with sneers in their blue uniforms, ugly-looking cudgels in hand.

"Does Lady Clara know you are taking us to the Duke?" Mathi called to Quiselie.

"She will, once I send another messenger."

Muttering followed his reply, but nothing Kilek could pick up. Before the end of the street, one of the guards snapped at his friends and silence returned. On they walked,

Quiselie avoiding market squares or rows, skirting the parks too. Was it because he didn't want to 'expose' the citizens to such criminals, or because he had something worse in mind?

Kilek frowned at the Inspector's back. Surely the man wasn't planning something violent? Would he risk doing something untoward to anyone associated with the Knighthood? And yet, if the man was truly concerned about criminals devaluing the King's currency, then why didn't he parade the 'counterfeiters' through the main thoroughfares, as an example?

A sharp grunt and a shout echoed from behind.

"Kilek, run!" Mathi shouted.

He spun.

Both guards lay on the cobblestones. One was struggling to his feet – until Paxoph's boot knocked him onto his back. Mathi flew past Kilek, her shoulder lowered. The inspector whirled.

Too slow.

She crashed into his chest and sent the man flying.

"Move," Tyar cried as he sprinted forward.

Kilek charged after them, footfalls thundering along the stones. A pair of wagons appeared ahead, blocking the path, but Mathi angled away from them, finding a narrow side-street. Kilek skidded into the alley and ran harder, hiking his knees as he burst into a broad street.

A woman shrieked, whipping a basket back as he flew by.

Shouts echoed from further behind – and new cries joined as more people within the street objected.

"Where are we going?" Kilek shouted.

"No idea," Mathi called back.

"We need to free our hands," Alira said from where she

ran beside Kilek.

Stacks of timber and stone loomed ahead, dozens of men sitting atop them and talking as they ate their bread and cheese. They rested beneath the frame of what would be a new two-storey building, blackened stone still visible between the fresh timber. Hammers and saw blades glinted in the afternoon light.

Was it the building that had been afire when they first saw the city?

Mathi turned into the shell.

New cries followed, and Kilek glanced over his shoulder – the builders were waving after them, looks of confusion clear. But behind them in turn, the inspector and his thugs had just burst from the back streets.

"Did they see us?" Tyar asked.

"I don't know."

Mathi slid to a halt – the construction was almost complete here, fresh-lain stone blocking access to the next street. Kilek clenched his jaw. It was so damn close, the windows stood empty of glass, the timber sills being installed by a white-haired man in dusty green overalls.

Paxoph jogged back toward the stacks of timber, where a large portion of the labourers approached. "I'll see if –"

"Hold it," one of the builders said, a man with hulking arms and a barrel chest. "What by the gods are you lot doing?"

Kilek exchanged glances with everyone else. What could they say?

The other man gestured back toward the street with his head. "We know it's about the Inspector but we're handling them for the moment – tell us what's happening."

"Why are you helping us?" Paxoph asked.

The bigger man folded his arms. "We don't know if we are yet – still might turn you over."

"We'll hear you out," a new voice announced. It was the older man who'd been working on the windows. "Can't get a fairer deal than that."

"Inspector Quiselie thinks we're spreading fake coins around," Mathi said after a moment's hesitation – then forging ahead when no-one protested. And why not? It was obvious they had to gamble on the builders, since no-one knew what Quiselie really had in mind. "We've escaped. He was trying to take us to the dungeon, but he's wrong. We only arrived in Jecomar earlier today; we're not working for any criminals here."

"Some old, isn't it?" one of the builders asked the bigger man.

But it was the white-haired fellow who answered. "I'd like to believe you folks. Word is spreading that they're rounding citizens up whether it's true or not. People are getting worried. Maybe you're easy targets, being travellers." He shrugged. "But then, you've got some connection to the Knighthood? Or have you stolen that clothing?"

"No. We are travelling with Lady Clara," Paxoph replied. "The inspector claimed he had sent for her but we began to suspect he has lied."

"Especially when he had us slinking through the backstreets, supposedly on the way to the Duke's dungeon," Tyar added.

The older man regarded them a moment longer before nodding. "Parts of your story aren't so different from what I've heard from a few others, to be honest. Very well, I want you inside those cabinets over there – we'll send the Inspector and his men on a merry chase, then you can be on your way."

Paxoph extended his hand. "Thank you...?"

"Ledeuc," the white-haired man replied as he shook Paxoph's hand. "Now quickly, we'll cover you up with a tarp."

Kilek dashed to the nearest, a large cabinet with plain, unvarnished doors. The hinges were bright and new. He opened the door with a frown... it was empty of shelving, still being restored or built it seemed, the lingering scent of ash now seeping into his awareness.

"Hurry lad," one of the builders said.

The first step laid his fears to rest – the base was solid. Kilek pulled the doors closed, the darkness falling over him like a welcome cloak. But would it be enough? And where was the inspector? The builders must have done something impressive to delay them.

A blanket fell across the cabinet, blocking most of the remaining light. Kilek crouched, sucking in a breath as he did – the narrow glimpse revealed little, just a tiny slice of the room and a pair of moving legs.

"Get along then, make it look like they've taken the stairs," Ledeuc said.

"Right," came the reply.

"What about the spiders?" another voice asked. "No-one's been down there for a long while."

Ledeuc snorted. "Just go."

Footsteps and muttering followed, then steps descending – perhaps to a basement and presumably some sort of escape tunnel built in by the original owners? Either way, the trail was lain. Next, the Inspector had to follow it.

From the street, arguing voices approached.

"I'm sorry again, Inspector – it's an unfortunate accident but I'm sure we'll have it cleaned up in no time."

"That I do not care about," snapped Quiselie, his voice drawing near.

"Well, I'm sure your man will regain consciousness soon."

"Enough. Just show me where they could hide." His footfalls came to a halt. "Ledeuc?"

"Inspector." Ledeuc's voice was not particularly welcoming.

"You saw the fugitives, I assume?"

"I did."

A sigh. "Then tell me, old fool. You don't have the Duke's ear now, so don't think you can throw your weight around anymore."

"Tell your man there to take a few steps back, Quiselie, unless you want me to rearrange his head with my hammer."

"Genoi, let's give him some room," the Inspector said. "Now, speak."

"The basement," Ledeuc replied with what sounded like genuine reluctance.

"Better," Inspector Quiselie said. "If you'd only been so cooperative while in Duke Tireste's employ you'd still be there and not reduced to this."

"You'd better hurry, Inspector – I believe there is an escape passage down there, you know, the one the owners used to escape the very fire that gutted this place."

"Bah."

A rush of footsteps followed, echoing downward. Then, only silence. Kilek pressed an eye against the gap in the cabinet doors but he saw nothing. Would it work? And what had occurred between the two men in the past?

"Let's wait a little longer," Ledeuc said.

Kilek shifted as best he could, a cramp forming in his side. He held in a groan. Still, only quiet from the room beyond, and a wordless din of voices from the street.

"All right, on your way, friends."

Kilek pushed the door open, the blanket snagging momentarily, before it slid to the stone floor. He blinked against the light as he straightened. His friends were doing the same and Ledeuc was pointing back toward the street. "Back the way you came, then left and a right at the tailor with the big windows should get you close to the northern gate."

"You think we should leave Jecomar?" Mathi asked. She was attempting to rub at her side, being cramped up can't have been pleasant if she was yet to fully heal from the lizard attack.

Ledeuc motioned for everyone to raise their hands, then began cutting through the ropes with a belt knife. "Might be safest – Quiselie knows you're working with the knighthood, so he'll have someone watching the Post by now."

"Thank you for everything you've done for us, sir," Alira said.

"Well, it was for me just as much as you, folks. Now get moving and good luck."

Kilek found himself nearest the exit, and so he led his friends out and back along the path they'd taken, but not without a glance to the opposite end of the street where he half expected to see the Inspector.

Yet no sign of the man.

Instead, a group of the builders worked to clean up a whole mess of fallen lumber.

Kilek gave them a wave and then it was into the busier streets where the press of moving people slowed them.

"What now?" he asked Mathi. "Should we leave?"

"I think Ledeuc is probably right about the Inspector – and if we mention this to Lady Clara, she'd have us back on the road immediately."

"So we have to decide between heading to Alaycron ourselves or aiming for the valley, it seems," Paxoph said.

"It could be a good place to hide out for a while," Tyar suggested.

Alira nodded. "Maybe whatever the Goddess wants us to find there will help?"

"What about Lady Clara?" Kilek asked. "Once we've been to the valley, should we return here to try and find her?"

"How will we know it's safe?" Alira asked.

"We won't," Mathi replied. "If we decide to travel with her again then it's going to be tough to sneak back in to the Post. And who knows if Quiselie will try to take us on the way out?"

"We don't know enough about who has more authority here," Paxoph added.

"The knighthood, surely?" Kilek asked.

"Maybe not – Quiselie is the Duke's man," Tyar replied.

"Let's start with the valley," Mathi decided. "Part of me wants to go back for my sword, but getting out of this place is the best thing to do now, whether we return or not."

Chapter 27.

The road to the mysterious Daciael and the valley where the old kings had supposedly taken retreats lay overgrown with dirt and spiky grasses, thin nettles and shrubs with broad leaves, the stone cracked underfoot. It did seem that in places, there had been tiers where different plants and trees might have thrived but now it was either bare or overgrown.

Kilek brought up the rear, glancing over his shoulder at regular intervals but no-one followed across the grassy hills. They'd escaped Quiselie and Lady Clara did not know where they were either, which was both welcome news and a troubling thought, considering what lay beyond the Goddess' errand.

But again, that had to wait. So he trudged on, keeping an eye on their surroundings – mostly more grass and rocky mounds topped by deep green shrubs; sweet-voiced Yellowbelles flitting between the branches of bigger trees. The place seemed empty of all else and even the blunted signpost with its rotten panel blended with its surroundings.

But it marked the beginning of the valley, a gentle slope

down toward lush grasses dotted with pink and white flowers. Twin pools of clear water stood at the bottom, cast in shade from the rocky walls that rose up above fir trees lining the valley.

"I don't see anything that looks like a building," Tyar said. "Did the old kings camp?"

Alira chuckled. "Doesn't sound very pampered, does it?"

"Seems like it'll be harder to find what we're looking for too," Kilek added.

Mathi sighed. "Well, we'd better get started anyway."

She led them down into the valley, stirring pollen and bees as she strode forward. The air cooled a little once they reached the shaded bottom but the valley revealed no secrets, not even a trace of the place's former purpose.

No stone, no steel or sawn wood either – at least, nothing above the ground.

"Did the Goddess say exactly what we're looking for?" Paxoph asked.

"Only the word 'Daciael' and that we had to look in the valley above Jecomar."

Kilek pointed to the tree line. "Maybe there's something in there?"

"Good idea," Mathi said and she gave him a bit of a shove. "Let's split into two groups. Whistle if you find anything, you three."

Side by side they climbed through the undergrowth, seeking open spaces, the loam cool here. Kilek took a stick and prodded at any old spot that looked especially flat but there was never any stone beneath, only the earth itself. After a time they reached a rearing rock face. He stopped to lean against it a moment.

Mathi strode to a clump of vivid green toadstools and gave them a kick. "We're going to lose light before too long."

"That'd be just our luck," he said with a sigh.

"You think so?" Mathi asked as she joined him.

He glanced at her; she was suddenly awfully close. "Ah, yeah. What are the chances we'd choose the very inn where counterfeit coins had been used?"

She chuckled. "I was thinking we were incredibly lucky, Kil. I mean, that idiot Quiselie clearly underestimated us. Two guards for five people? I'm only sorry it took me so long to think about escaping."

"Hmmm."

"And then, we stumble across Ledeuc? There were a dozen hiding places I could have tried but that's where we ended up – helped by a man who has a past with the inspector?"

"A lot of people probably know someone like Quiselie."

"No, I think we're getting help even if we can't see it. Different to Alira's bird or us getting strong. It's more specific, like Tyar's skill with the bow."

"From the Goddess?"

She nodded. "Who else?"

Kilek gave a half-hearted shrug. "Maybe we are. It might explain a few things but I wonder if that counts as intervening in the mortal world. She didn't seem to want to do that."

"I agree but that's not quite what I was getting at."

"Huh?"

She smiled at him, a gentler smile than usual. "I have a theory that maybe the Goddess gave you something after all – I think you might be lucky."

He opened his mouth to reply but a sharp whistle from

not too far away cut him off. Mathi pushed from the wall. "Come on, Lucky, you can think about it later."

Kilek followed her between the trunks, pushing branches and soft leaves aside with half-realised movements. Was she right? Had the Goddess somehow given him Luck? Considering all the misfortune that had befallen them, it didn't seem likely... did it?

But why hadn't Avendria *told* him that's what she had done?

Why leave him uncertain?

Yet he didn't dismiss it either – instead, a far better idea would be to watch and see at the least.

Alira and the others stood before a rubble-choked ravine that might have once led up the towering hillside. Now, only pale trunks, broken branches empty of leaves and grey mud mixed in between the jagged heaps of stone, remained.

She held the vibrant orange feather up before the wall with a slight frown upon her lips. "I think this might match one of the grooves on the rock face."

Kilek stepped closer. The stone wall was largely featureless. "One of the grooves?"

"Yes, there's two."

"I can't see anything."

"Neither can we," Tyar said with a shrug. "Maybe it's because she can use magic?"

"Let me try this anyway," Alira said as she held the feather up against the wall. It flared, then dimmed. She removed her hand and the feather remained in place... then it began to sink into the stone until only a deep, warm glow remained. But the outline of the feather remained upon the rock.

"What's supposed to happen?" Mathi asked.

But Alira didn't answer. Her gaze remained fixed on the stone. Eventually, she blinked. "There is a door here," she said. "Avendria says Daciael waits beyond."

"So, what now?" Tyar asked.

"I still need another feather." Alira turned and her eyes widened.

Kilek spun – and gave a little jump.

A blue hawk sat on one of the lower branches, twice the size of a regular bird. It regarded them with dark eyes. Like the hawk from the wheat fields, its feathers spanned a range of hues from a deep blue to a brilliant shade like azure water.

It clicked its beak then launched itself up between the branches, bursting from the canopy in a hail of leaves and small branches. A single blue feather fluttered down with them. Alira stepped closer, reaching up to catch the still-falling feather. "Thank you, Goddess."

She returned to the wall and lifted the feather. The stone drew the blue in, where its glow joined the orange light. Searing bright lines spread up and then out to form wide arches that hit the ground. They then grew dim and cold as the doors swung inward, feathers fluttering to the earth. Alira collected both, tucking them into her belt, then turned to face everyone.

"Here we go, then."

Chapter 28.

"What else can those things do?" Tyar was asking Alira as they walked the passage, heading toward distant light.

"I don't know, yet. Hopefully other things."

The tunnel was wide but a chill from the rough stone walls seemed to reach right into Kilek. Their steps echoed as they approached the rectangle of light. He did his best to listen for anything unusual; being unarmed in such a place brought unpleasant memories of the lizard creature rushing back.

The crunch of its jaws.

Yet he had been wondering the same thing as Tyar... and couldn't fend off a troubling thought; if the Goddess offered such gifts, what equivalency had their enemy given *his* Surrogates? Part of him wished she'd never mentioned the arrangement; he'd have been able to continue on thinking she was simply helping, not potentially endangering them.

"Like what?" Tyar asked. "Do you think they could be used as weapons or something?"

"I'm not sure," Alira said. "But I know they are precious

gifts... She doesn't want me to lose them."

"And she had nothing more on the mysterious Daciael?" Paxoph's deep voice almost boomed in the tunnel.

"No. But we're close."

"Good," Mathi said as they reached the light. "I want to get this done before dark."

"Why?" Tyar said with a snicker. "Do you have plans for this evening?"

A soft thump filled the passage.

"Hey!" Tyar said. "Careful now, that's my drawing arm."

"Look ahead, fool," she said, but there was a fair amount of fondness in her tone.

Kilek squinted against the brightness... and gasped.

A swan-like bridge of glittering white, half in shadow, half-bathed in the sun's rays, stood before them. It spanned a steep ravine, leading to stone steps that climbed up to what might have been a grassy hilltop.

It all rested beneath a massive opening above; its curved walls sloped down in long ridges... as if a giant had bent to scoop the earth up and away. It left the blue sky and a mountainous cloudbank of white and wisps of grey visible; the bank's movement slow but still he stared at the beautiful if vague shapes within.

"Does anyone else see a problem?" Tyar asked.

He was pointing to the bridge.

Holes were visible in the stonework, both on the walkway and the rails; the images of birds in flight crumbling, scrollwork that seemed to represent the wind just as damaged. Farther along, an entire section had fallen. Far too wide to leap across, there was a large support column that still stood between parts of the span and someone had lashed thick ropes and boards to create a makeshift bridge.

Nearer the steps on the other side, another large swathe of stone had fallen away, and there, only a jagged section ran with the rail. Was it possible to creep along it with care?

Kilek approached the edge.

Failure meant a long fall – enough to break limbs, or worse, for it was no calm pool below, just the stony earth. He narrowed his eyes. And bones. Animal or human, he couldn't quite be sure.

"Well, we don't have a choice," Mathi said, striding forward.

Tyar caught her arm. "Hold on. How do we know the bridge is safe? Can't we... test it first somehow?"

"How?"

"I don't know. Pax?"

He shook his head. "Nothing I can come up with – not without actually attempting to cross it."

"That's my problem. Alira, can those birds fly us over?"

"They're big but not that big," she said, her own eyes troubled.

Tyar nodded but his jaw was clenched. "Yeah, you're right." He took a few steps closer, stomping on the white stone at the very beginning of the span.

"You scared of falling?" Mathi asked, her tone expressing surprise.

"No, I'm scared of landing. Some of the rocks down there look very sharp."

"Then don't fall," she said as she started across.

"Wonderful advice," Tyar muttered, remaining motionless as Pax and Alira passed. Kilek joined them, the stone firm beneath his boots. For now, at least. Yet no footsteps followed him; he glanced over his shoulder and Tyar was beating at his thigh with a fist, mouth moving but no words audible. He'd always been uneasy with heights, rarely climbing too high in trees as a boy.

"Want to do it together?" Kilek asked.

His friend shook his head. "No, I can manage." His voice was quiet. He stepped forward then, his footfalls smacked on the bridge as he caught up. Together, they detoured the holes and gaps, Tyar's jaw clenched tight.

But when they reached the rope bridge, Tyar faltered.

Mathi and Paxoph had already crossed; now Alira was taking her own first steps onto the boards, her hands clinging to the thinner rope rails as she moved. It swayed and creaked a little but held steady. It all seemed strong enough, it was weathered but the twined rope looked thick at least.

"You think it'll hold for us?" Tyar asked.

Kilek nodded. "Now that I've seen it up close."

"It seems a little old."

"Each strand is twice as thick as your arm," Kilek pointed out.

"Right, yeah."

Kilek placed a foot upon the boards, one hand hovering over the rail, and when he took it the rope was firm. It swayed a little with his weight, but he did not look around or down, instead he stared to his friends on the other side and kept walking. And soon enough, he was halfway across, pausing once more.

Tyar held both rails and had taken only one step across, his eyes wide.

Kilek turned back and stopped before his friend. "I can help if you want?"

"No, I can handle this," he said, then took another step, exhaling as he did.

Then another and Kilek backed up to give him room. His friend was starting to sweat but he kept walking, one deliberate step at a time, until finally, Tyar leapt to solid ground upon the other side.

"Great work," Kilek said, slapping his friend on the shoulder.

Tyar laughed, his voice still unsteady, but followed Kilek along the ledge and then up the stairs – they were no challenge after the bridge. Kilek took them two at a time to catch up to the others, leaping the final few to land on a grassy knoll.

Here, moss covered the earth, spreading between clumps of grass like an expensive velvet blanket – like the one Father Bastiem kept hidden away in his old chest. It climbed the fallen logs and surviving, broad trunks, darkening in the shade. Leaves of blue-green had fallen yet did not seem to be decomposing and little white blooms filled the hilltop with a sweet scent.

"Look," Alira said.

In the centre of the hilltop glade something shimmered in the air.

A silvery cloud, quite large... indistinct yet clearly present in the world too, as though it *resisted* the eye, as though it had a purpose and that was to remain hidden.

"What is it?" Kilek asked.

"I believe what the Goddess wanted us to see," she said as she approached, stretching out her hand. "We just have to remove the cloak."

She pulled.

The shimmering disturbance spun away beneath her grip but Kilek did not see where or if the fluttering shape landed.

An enormous skull now sat upon the earth.

Moss covered the base but the open jaws and their forearm-length fangs were white and smooth, as though they had been well cared for. Heavy brows covered the eye-sockets; these were dark despite bone visible within. How large had the creature once been? He could have stood within the mouth and not reached the roof at a stretch.

A dragon.

An actual dragon-skull, here, concealed within the very hill. Kilek shivered, his voice disappeared in the awe that held him but he was smiling too.

"Is this..." Tyar trailed off as he stepped forward.

Mathi's eyes were a little wide. "I thought dragons had been gone a long time – centuries."

"Me too," Tyar said.

"So who's been cleaning the teeth? Who hid it?"

"The Goddess, surely," Alira said, but she did not seem sure as she crept forward.

Kilek finally joined her with Mathi and Pax too, neither of whom seemed willing to draw too near but by their expressions, it seemed a similar awe urged them forward, almost against a certain tension in their bodies.

Up close, runes covered the bone. Somehow, they did not seem man or magic made. More... a *rightness* about the symbols implied they were a natural part of the dragon's skull. Which hardly made sense, yet who was a mere villager to argue with the evidence? Simply because he'd never read anything like it in all the stories about dragons didn't mean much. Most of the symbols bore a purposeful look, as though the swirls, slashes and dots held some clear meaning.

"What are they for?" he asked.

Alira shook her head, tears in her eyes. "I do not know."

Silence fell across the glade.

A sense of vast age, of centuries-old power and majesty now both lost and still somehow lingering, fell over them; it was enough to give everyone pause. For Kilek, it seemed his entire body was trembling ever-so-slightly, in anticipation, in reverence of even such a beautiful creature's *memory*.

Finally, Paxoph spoke. "As wonderful as this moment is, I cannot help but worry. How will the skull of a dragon aid us?"

"There must be a message, must be something," Alira said as she wiped at her eyes. "Why would she send us here otherwise?"

"At last, I have found you all," said a new voice.

Kilek whirled.

A tall man stood at the top of the stair. A sword hung from his belt, his dark leather pants and boots seeming to suck in the fading afternoon light; yet more unusual, the man wore no shirt or tunic, leaving a muscled torso bare. A white collar covered his neck and Kilek noticed fingerless leather gloves when the man drew his weapon.

Ashley Capes

Chapter 29.

"Who are you?" Mathi demanded. Her hands were clenched at her sides.

"I am Nakir, but that is not relevant, truly." He motioned with his blade. "Now you must decide how you will each die – upon your knees? Fighting, perhaps? I hold no grudge against any of you and wish to offer you a choice, grim though it will seem."

"We have no weapons," Alira shouted.

"That I know, yet you can still die with honour," Nakir said.

Alira lifted her hand and light flared… then faded, as though she had wearied herself revealing the dragon's skull.

Nakir barely paused as he neared.

"Run," Mathi cried as she leapt forward.

But Kilek was frozen in place. His heart thundered within his chest – it was madness, she didn't need to sacrifice herself for–

Nakir swung his sword.

Mathi spun. The whistling of the blade missed her

completely.

The strange assassin pulled his weapon up, eyebrow raised. "Interesting." He stepped after her, sword raised again but Mathi had darted closer. She dropped to one knee and swung her fist. The blow smacked into the man's abdomen. Nakir fell back with a grunt.

"What's happening?" Tyar asked.

Kilek had no answer. Mathi was so fast, her movements lithe and compact, flowing and confident, as though the prospect of facing an armed assailant with her bare hands was as nothing.

Even her blue eyes blazed with a light unnatural... Kilek frowned. It was more – her eyes were not simply brighter, but what looked like blue blood had filled them and even now began to seep from the corners.

Mathi's gift?

Nakir lashed out, cutting low and high, in and out of backswings, his own actions fluid.

But Mathi dodged each blow, spinning almost like a dancer.

And whenever she drew close enough, she lashed out with hands or feet, and even once with her knee. But Nakir was just as quick to dodge and she was not able to land another blow. Yet still, she knew when to take her chances, moving up after an overextension from Nakir, slipping within his guard and forcing him to leap back.

Both began to sweat before too long, and still none could land a strike.

Once, when they leapt apart, Nakir paused to smile. Mathi's expression had not changed from furious determination. And each time it seemed there might be a chance to help, Kilek fell back. The two moved too fast, too unpredictably; if he blundered in too close, he'd only get himself or Mathi killed.

Nakir charged Mathi again, lunging when he neared.

She side-stepped.

Yet Nakir had anticipated her move. He twisted his wrists to break the lunge and his attack became a slash.

The blade whistled toward her stomach, moving quicker than Nakir's somewhat awkward adjustment should have allowed.

Mathi clapped her palms together.

The blade flashed to a halt between her hands.

She glared at her enemy, then twisted.

Steel snapped. Fragments scattered across the ground. Nakir blinked, then lashed out with the broken blade. Mathi ducked away and swept Nakir's legs from under him with a kick. He hit the ground and tore the moss.

But he rolled to his feet at once and tossed the broken weapon aside.

"Master cautioned me about you."

"And who would that be?" Mathi demanded, fists still raised, her legs braced for another attack. The unnatural tears of blue blood had spread down to her cheeks.

"Sadly, I think it seems you're in danger of winning this encounter."

A glow spread from the white collar, swiftly enveloping him and then he was gone.

Mathi exhaled, then crumbled to the earth. Tyar dashed to her side and Kilek joined him. She lay in Tyar's arms. The streaks of what seemed like blue blood were already fading... replaced by red. Had she actually been *bleeding* from her eyes while she fought? Gods, was this truly a mark of Avendria? Mathi's gift was clearly that of a warrior but what cost came with it?

"Mathi?" Tyar shook her gently but she did not stir, even when he raised his voice.

Yet she was breathing at least.

"I can't wake her," he cried.

Alira leant closer. "Is she just exhausted?"

"The blood is troubling," Paxoph said.

"Maybe we can take her back to Jecomar? Find a healer?" Tyar suggested.

"Is that safe?" Kilek asked.

"We have to do something," Tyar snapped.

Kilek rose with a glare. "I know that!"

Paxoph leant between them. "We all want to help but we have to think a moment. Can we even carry her across that bridge?"

Tyar's shoulders slumped.

Kilek glanced back toward the steps. Impossible. Few other options remained, however. Who knew if Nakir would return? Turning the glade into a fortifiable campsite would be extremely difficult, and probably a waste of time, with or without the failing light. At least the weather was fine and no-one else knew of the location... hopefully. Nakir may have followed them to the clearing and it seemed his master was powerful enough to offer some sort of magic-travel to the man.

And he had been warned about Mathi, and presumably all of Avendria's surrogates.

"Maybe we should stay here until she wakes," Alira said after a moment.

"Yeah." Tyar stroked Mathi's hair as he nodded.

Kilek turned for the few trees that grew around the perimeter of the clearing. "I'll try and find some staves or something," he said.

"Right," Paxoph replied. "I'm going to look for water. Alira, can you stay with Tyar?"

"Of course."

At the first tree, Kilek paused. Could he find enough suitable branches? He reached up to try one of the lower ones – the spruce was maybe not ideal but if he sharpened the end on a rock at least, it'd make a temporary spear?

Kilek gripped the branch with both hands and wrenched down.

It snapped cleanly, as did the next four he found, though the last tore the trunk's ridge-like bark a little and he frowned. "Sorry."

"Are you apologising to trees now?"

Paxoph stood behind him. He carried the broken blade that Nakir had discarded but by his expression it didn't seem he'd found any water.

"Ah, I guess I am," Kilek said with a chuckle. "Any water?"

"Not without one of us heading across the bridge again it seems; that's what we now have to decide."

"You don't think we should split up?"

"Not truly." He sighed. "I'm sure we could all hold on until dawn, and hopefully Mathi recovers by then."

"And that Nakir stays away."

"Yes."

"Who do you think sent him? Is he one of Javoteth's *Anesca*?"

"Didn't seem to be a Westerner, did he?"

"No, and no accent either. He was clearly Luargot," Kilek replied as he leant against the trunk. Beyond Paxoph's shoulder, Alira and Tyar sat beside the still-unconscious Mathi. "We have to be really vigilant tonight."

"Agreed. Maybe a ring of branches and twigs. In case one of us falls asleep."

Kilek frowned. "Is that directed at me?"

"No, Kilek. We are all weary."

"Right. Sorry."

"You need to find some peace, you know."

"Peace?"

"About the Goddess. She has given you something, I am certain of it but you cannot rush a Goddess and you cannot know her reasons."

"If she told me I would."

"Of course, but she must have a good reason."

"Even if that's true it doesn't really help. I feel useless, Pax. I hate it."

"We don't think that."

"Thank you... but I can't shake the feeling." He shrugged, then glanced up to the darkening sky. "Even so, I want to take the first watch."

Paxoph nodded.

Together, they returned to the others, where Kilek sat nearby and began to whittle the edges of each spear. Not that any of the shafts were truly straight or close to unbreakable but it had to be better than a few belt knives, a broken sword, and nothing.

No-one spoke much as Kilek paced their little camp, positioning himself near the steps several times, the wide starry sky lighting his way just enough. After a time, when the faint snores from Paxoph rose and deep breathing from the others, he started back, stepping over the somewhat clumsy twig alarm.

But he'd barely taken two steps before pausing.

A faint light glowed within the dragon's mouth. Had it been there the whole time? The inside of the skull was empty, surely? He approached slowly, spear held ready but not from any sense that it would actually help.

Kilek paused beside Pax. Should he wake anyone?

What if the light was something reflecting the stars... He shook his head. Fool! Light wouldn't reach the throat of the skull.

He crept closer, peering between the fangs.

The pale glow came from a single sharp tooth set at the back of the jaw. It was broad but not so large as the others, yet what was more noteworthy was its sheen – the surface gleamed like a pearl. Kilek climbed into the maw and knelt before the fang.

Was it actually waiting for him? Was *this* what the Goddess wanted them to see? Not the dragon-skull itself, but the fang? Why? It would not make a weapon.

He reached out and his fingertip brushed the bone...

Chapter 30.

The glade disappeared.

So, too, the dragon-skull.

Day had come and he knelt upon the shores of a glittering lake. The water's surface was golden, as though the sunset were shattering itself over and over, small waves meeting despite the lack of wind.

Above, mountainous white clouds hung frozen in their own majesty.

"Young one."

The voice was a whisper from water.

Kilek peered closer; a figure was ascending from the depths – a man in a black coat with silver buttons, a white scarf at his neck. His long dark hair spread like seaweed as he rose, finally breaking the surface with a smile. The stranger's face was unshaven but he did not seem unkempt; more, his eyes glittered from beneath dark brows.

"Hello?" Kilek rose and stepped back.

When the man reached the shore both his clothing and hair had already dried. The sense of him was a weight upon

Kilek, not unlike facing the Goddess. Not so powerful but it still took Kilek a moment to speak.

"Who are you?" he finally asked.

"Humans called me Daciael." He smiled, revealing fangs. Yet normal teeth seemed to replace them quickly... or had there *never* been fangs in the man's mouth? "You have been sent by Avendria, yes?"

"I have," Kilek said, then hesitated. "Are you the dragon in the glade above Jecamor?"

He nodded. "Though I knew the place as Injemora; it was many moons past now."

"Can you help us?"

"Not I personally, as you might imagine," he said with a small smile, and once again, it seemed fangs lined his mouth. "You speak now to something of an echo, perhaps – but while I have time, I will share what I believe the Great Bird has sent you to hear."

"Thank you."

"To deal with the coming onslaught, seek the Clarion Song and use it to call back my descendants."

Kilek straightened as he stumbled over his next words. "You mean... the dragons have not vanished?"

"Not precisely; though three oceans lie between you and they. It is not a distance humans have managed to travel in perhaps a thousand years now."

"Then this Song will make it possible?"

"Yes. Call and they will return."

"Where can we find it?"

Daciael turned to hold out his hand before the water – the ripples grew still and a vision appeared in the surface, the royal city. Even small as it seemed, as though a bird glanced down from high above, the red rooves, glass skylights and connected walkways were clear and hardly so different from the books in Father Bastiem's shelves.

"Alaycron? The royal city?"

The dragon began to fade. "Yes. The Song was kept by a line of Queens there – we knew a Queen by the name of Liana. Good luck, young man."

"Wait, the current Queen is..." Kilek trailed off.

Daciael was gone.

Darkness returned; Kilek was once more crouched within the dragon-skull, the fang he'd reached for now sat as dull and dark as the others. He exhaled. The return of dragons? *That* was what Avendria wanted from them?

Surely even the Cabeku would stand no chance against them; dragons were able to breathe fire, wield magic and supposedly even stop time. He clenched a hand. There *was* a chance. "Is this what she wants me to do?" Finally, a way to be truly useful.

But doing so meant finding the Queen's ancestor first – or, more likely, records of her song. Assuming the king would even listen to such a request... Still, what choice did they have? If that was what it took to prevent the lands being smothered by the shadow of the Cabeku – and worse – then so be it. He had to be a part of that struggle... and hopefully, such a struggle wouldn't take him so far from home, from the people of Hasere.

Because they deserved help as much as anyone else.

And with dragons on their side, there was nowhere Prince Yan and his men could hide.

Chapter 31.

Kilek woke with a groan; his muscles were so stiff that rolling onto his side took far longer than it should have. But he managed, blinking up at the clear sky. The morning sun was bright, already warming the air despite long shadows from the high walls. An odd feeling lay over him but he could not place it. Had something happened?

Calm voices spoke nearby.

He rubbed at his eyes, then rose with a smile when he saw Mathi. She and Pax sat speaking together, trying to decide their next step it seemed. Her face was clean of blood and she appeared well.

Tyar was nowhere to be seen but Alira knelt nearby, sorting materials into her pouches; sand, dirt and moss. Could she use them all? Florique had taught her a lot in a short span of time, either that or the Goddess was helping.

"Mathi, how do you feel?" Kilek asked.

"A lot better."

"What happened?"

She spread her hands with a chuckle. "If you're Lucky it

looks like I'm Fast, right?"

He blinked – the dragon! Of course, after speaking with Daciael he'd fought the desire to wake everyone, instead letting them rest after the attack, but he'd have to share the news as soon as Tyar returned. "Then it was the Goddess?"

"Who else, right?"

"Yeah, I guess so. But you seemed to bleed a fair amount from your eyes."

She reached up to brush her fingers across her cheeks. "I feel fine now but I don't think I could manage anything like that soon. You know, I don't even know how it happened but it just... I was just suddenly more alive than before. It was like he could hardly make a move that I couldn't anticipate. Well, for the most part, anyway."

Kilek looked to Paxoph. "So we can probably assume you've been given some extra skill or ability too," he said. "Like the way Tyar can shoot now, or the way Alira's magic has grown so fast."

"And you," Pax replied.

"I think he's Lucky," Mathi said. "We've had our share of good fortune."

"Maybe," Kilek said. Bringing dragons back seemed equally likely now, and it wasn't exactly a skill but if that's what he had to do, he'd do it with just his own flesh and bone.

Tyar returned from the trees, his bearing and manner far more relaxed now. He glanced at Kilek but didn't apologise for yesterday and Kilek didn't bother greeting his friend. Would Tyar even believe him? Maybe the news could wait a moment longer... "So, what should we do?"

"If we return to the Post, we're better off doing it at night, aren't we?" Mathi suggested.

Alira turned from her pouches, tying one drawstring. "So, we've ruled out heading directly for Alaycron?"

"We have no weapons or supplies," Paxoph said.

"Right. Well... what about Nakir? And that inspector? Can we find food and water before we head back to the city?"

"That should eat up some time before nightfall," Mathi said. She stood with what seemed to be a frown of surprise.

"What's wrong?" Tyar asked.

"Nothing. I'm tired but I didn't realise my ribs... *everything* feels better than before."

"So, you don't need us to help you walk?" Tyar asked, his brow furrowed.

She shook her head. "I'm fine, let's just get going."

Kilek opened his mouth to speak but hesitated again. Why? He brought good news, and Tyar would be glad of it, poor mood or not. And after all, this was the whole reason they'd come to the valley in the first place.

But Mathi gave him pause now.

Although she'd led them across the mossy earth to the steps, by the time she reached them she was already breathing hard. Yet still she waved off Tyar's supportive arm and started slowly down. Kilek kept a smile to himself, glad he hadn't made his own offer.

The white span, half in ruin, waited for them at the bottom, but the return trip was not so bad, and even Tyar managed it with more grace. Perhaps it was his worry about Mathi but still, they had soon creaked their way across the rope bridge and beyond, passing through the tunnel once more.

Somehow, it seemed a lot longer than a mere day ago that

they'd travelled in the opposite direction, the first crossing, the revelation of the dragon's skull...

Kilek slowed. Now that they were safely past the bridge and Mathi had caught her breath, it was probably time to share what he'd been told. Holding onto the information was just selfishness... even if it did feel nice to receive something that his friends had not.

"Everyone, I have something to tell you, about the dragon," he said. "I know why the Goddess sent us here."

"What?" Tyar glanced over his shoulder.

"I wanted to wait until we'd crossed the bridge," he said. "But Daciael *was* the dragon, I spoke to him last night... it was like a dream."

"That's incredible – what did he say?" Alira asked, her eyes alight.

"That Avendria wants us to find..."

They passed into the light of the woods, where a figure waited for them, arms folded where she stood beside a line of horses.

Lady Clara.

"Mount up," the knight snapped as she climbed into her saddle. "It's likely I was followed here on this fool's errand."

Kilek closed his mouth. The rest of his tale had to wait; it was nothing Lady Clara needed to hear.

Tyar glared at her. "Yes, greetings to you too. You know, if you'd found us sooner, we wouldn't have had to hide here."

She pointed a gauntleted finger at him. "And if you'd stayed in the Post the Inspector would not have found you."

"But we did leave and he did find us – where were you?"

She clenched her teeth. "Gods, are you all children then? Get moving; we have to put some distance between us and them."

"No!" A voice shouted – and dimly, Kilek was aware that it was he who had spoken.

Lady Clara twisted in her saddle to face him, her eyes narrowed. "What?"

But the words burst free. "You're so quick to dismiss us as children, as foolish, aren't you? You repeat the words over and over yet *we* escaped Quiselie, *we* survived this place, and you have not found us so easily, have you? You know what I think? I think this is about you, Lady Clara."

"Boy—"

"You take out your anger on us," Kilek said, folding his arms across his chest, "because you resent the task you have been given – and *that* is truly childish."

She leapt from her horse and before he could react, swung her hand.

Her slap snapped his head to one side.

White light flashed and his ears rang. Blood filled his mouth – he'd bitten his cheek, but he faced her with a sneer. "You prove my point, *My Lady*." He spat blood onto the leaves underfoot.

Silence filled the wood after his words.

Lady Clara glared down at him. "You will not be the cause of my dishonour. Even if you all continue to make my duty to protect you harder than it ought to be." The knight returned to her steed and swung into the saddle once more. "And as for the rest of you, you would do well to keep your charge in line."

Kilek clenched his teeth.

Mathi opened her mouth to reply but the knight continued, raising her voice.

"And if you want to claim that you are each so capable – then forge a path on your own but if you wish to reach Alaycron alive then follow me now." She tapped her horse's sides.

Alira dashed to Kilek's side, the others crowding around behind her. Tyar gave him a nod of approval but did not speak, instead glaring after Lady Clara. "Are you hurt?" Alira asked.

"I'll be fine," he said with a slight shudder. His limbs trembled and he was breathing hard. Where had the outburst come from? And why couldn't he control it once it started? "I didn't realise I was going to say that."

Mathi chuckled. "We noticed."

"So, what are we going to do?" Paxoph asked.

Kilek waited for Mathi to answer but she, like the rest of his friends, was looking to him. "Oh. Uh, she's probably right about things being safer with her."

"Possibly," Tyar said. He gestured to the nearest horse – a bow was strapped to the saddlebags. "We have mounts, supplies and our weapons once more."

Mathi found the lion's head blade and smiled as she strapped the scabbard back on. "For now, let's travel with her. It can't hurt to have her along, especially if Nakir returns. And maybe she knows some short-cuts."

"I suppose."

"Hurry," Lady Clara called back without turning her head.

They mounted up and started after the knight, and when they drew near, she did not speak – which suited Kilek just fine

Maybe *he* had been the one who was unaware of the strength of his own feelings. Being referred to as a child again had set him off, hadn't it?

And still, he could not reveal what he knew about the dragons.

Fool.

Sharing the news right away had been the obvious thing to do and he hadn't.

He tested the depth of the cut in his cheek with his tongue as they rode from the wood then up the valley, flowers bright beneath the warm sun. A slight breeze did cross the road when they exited the valley and started south-east along narrower, less well-maintained trails. They passed farmhouses with their thatched rooves, empty chimneys and neat, fenced yards. More than a few had men and women out planting, young children often at their feet.

The young ones always called and waved, the adults rarely so.

Lady Clara did not engage with them either, picking up the pace where the road allowed and remaining vigilant. When they stopped for a noon meal, she spoke as though the confrontation in the valley had not occurred.

"We will sleep in a Highway Post tonight to be safe. As usual, two will watch, as I still believe the Inspector has sent men after us. I cannot confirm it yet, though I will try to do so this night."

"Do you plan to ambush them?" Paxoph asked when it seemed no-one else was going to speak.

"If necessary."

"Won't that cause friction between the Knighthood and the Duke?"

"Only if my hand is revealed. Something is amiss in Jecomar, according to my superiors at the Post. I have been given full authority to deal with whatever arises on this journey."

"Something more than the counterfeiting?"

"Perhaps." Her cool blue eyes appeared troubled. "Again, I do not know what. But if I can learn the truth I will, though that is second priority."

She started her meal then and offered nothing else, and when she finished, it was back into the saddle to continue east. Here, the roads were smoother and the grains had fallen away. Lady Clara pushed them a little harder across more open ground, checking on the horizon often.

It was still too difficult to share the specific details he'd been given by the dragon, but the news was somehow less urgent, now that they were making progress toward their other goal. At least Kilek assumed his friends agreed. Or maybe it was simply an additional wariness around Lady Clara.

They did not encounter other travellers until reaching the Highway Post as the light began to fall, where a pair of knights were dismounting before the stout gates.

Lady Clara stiffened in her saddle upon seeing them but said nothing.

Kilek exchanged a glance with Paxoph.

What now?

Chapter 32.

The Highway Post was a large enclosure with a stone wall. A small, wooden lookout tower kept watch though it stood empty for now. The tower was half-concealed by shadows from an enormous oak that sent its leaves fluttering into the dusty yard when the wind whipped up.

It tugged at Mathi's hair where it was not constrained by her head band, whereas Lady Clara's braid did not seem much bothered by the wind.

What *did* seem to bother her was the pair of knights who were gathering their possessions. One turned at the sound of hooves, and when he saw Lady Clara he nodded but did not speak, instead leading the horses toward the stable.

The other man, a little younger, approached with a smile. "Little Clara, what brings you west?"

"Duty, Sir Maxime." Her answer was no cooler than usual, yet Kilek had not forgotten her reaction upon sighting the knight.

Sir Maxime was, like Lady Clara, a Knight of Spring by the white poplar on his cloak, but his came with an embellishment, a stripe across the bottom – and by his dismissive glance to Kilek and his friends, it seemed likely that the young man believed such a mark made him better than those around him, whether knight or not. "Nursemaid to recruits? Hmmm. Can't believe you were overlooked for that business with the Minjao."

"And you, Sir Maxime?"

He gestured to the wooden stables and row of cabin-like rooms. "Merely chasing down a fugitive, nothing so interesting."

"Then I wish you good fortune."

Sir Maxime chuckled. "I'll hardly need it but thank you. And I look forward to our next meeting – it's been wonderful catching another glimpse of those destined to complete the truly meaningful work of the Knighthood."

Lady Clara said nothing though her jaw was clenched as she led them to the cabins. "Two per cabin – boy, you are with me."

Kilek opened his mouth to object but stopped. If she'd been angry before, her brush with Sir Maxime had done nothing to ease that ire now.

Instead of joining her or his friends at the fire pit between cabins, however, he volunteered to care for the horses, leading them to the stable. There, he unburdened his mount first, feeding her from the oat bag and lingering within the stall. From his vantage the others were preparing a meal and Lady Clara merely sat silently. It seemed that Paxoph was doing his best to keep polite conversation going, but Kilek couldn't move his feet.

Spending the night in the same room as Lady Clara was going to be difficult enough, no hurry to spend any more time with her.

"You seem young to be recruited already, lad."

Sir Maxime approached from the neighbouring stall. Gone was his mocking tone from moments before; it seemed he was genuinely curious. Kilek was genuinely *wary* as he put on a smile. "Thank you, Sir."

The knight sighed. "It was a question, rather than a compliment. In any event, be careful not to align yourself with Clara Greensborne, even a commoner might bring his name under ill-repute by doing so."

"Ah, I don't understand, sir."

"Just take the warning," Sir Maxime said as he left the stall. "And offer it to your companions if you care."

Kilek stared after the knight with a furrowed brow. "What was that all about?" he whispered to his mare, to 'Fleet', as he'd named her, and patted her strong neck.

Sir Maxime hardly seemed trustworthy, even having spent so little time in the man's company, so what was his word worth? And while Lady Clara was curt at best and even violent, how could she possibly poison anyone's reputation simply by travelling with them? Were the two knights rivals back in the capital?

By the time he finished with the other horses only Tyar remained before the flickering fire – the others seemed to have sought their rest quite swiftly.

Kilek joined his friend on the log. Across the way, nearer the second row of cabins, Sir Maxine and the other knight ate around their own small blaze.

"What do you make of all that?" Tyar asked quietly after a moment. He was chewing on his nails, a habit he'd had as a youth and which now looked odd upon a grown man.

"Something personal," Kilek said. "I hope it doesn't make more trouble. Sir Maxime doesn't like Lady Clara for some reason."

"I'll keep an eye on them for now," Tyar said. He paused, as though he was going to ask something else, perhaps about the dragons, but he glanced back to Lady Clara's cabin and said instead, "I'll wake you for your watch."

"Thanks." Not an apology either, then.

Kilek pushed himself to his feet. Maybe he was still being childish, waiting for an apology that might never come and resenting his friend for it. It had just been words in the heat of a horrible moment.

But Kilek said nothing himself.

Coward.

Instead, he approached the cabin he would share with Lady Clara, pausing a moment before pushing the door open. When he did, he found the knight already lying with her back to the door. Kilek sat upon the opposite cot, then removed his boots, lay down and pulled the blanket across his body.

At least it was dry and out of the wind, even if the even sound of her breathing seemed to be somehow predatory.

And yet, not a single thing he'd informed her during his outburst had been a lie.

He'd done nothing wrong.

Kilek rolled to face the wall and closed his eyes, letting the dark ease his weary limbs into sleep.

***

Sir Maxime was gone when Kilek and his friends followed Lady Clara from the Highway Post the next morning. Last evening's wind had vanished; the leaves it had stripped from trees remained scattered across the Western Highway with its precisely-spaced stone and sign posts, though they did not stay upon it long – quickly switching to another back road.

This ran behind a stretching gully lined with poplars, drooping willows and a twisting stream. It seemed a quiet road; they passed only a woodcutter and his son. At noon, it was another meal of muted conversation and then back into the saddle.

"Where will we sleep tonight?" Mathi asked sometime later, when the afternoon had begun to wear down. The trees now cast long shadows, bringing a chill to a day. It was as though here, summer was waning, despite the season barely having begun.

Lady Clara looked up to the trees. "We will reach a cave before nightfall. I have used it before."

"I notice we are still travelling by back roads," Paxoph said.

"We still may be followed; I have not been able to discover the truth of the matter. I could send you on and lie in wait. If only one or two of the Duke's men follow that would be one thing. But anything else and… I would rather we stay together."

Alira had slowed her mount to draw level with everyone else. "I… I want to ask something, if you don't mind. Something I think we should have asked before."

"Yes?" the knight asked.

"I wondered… do you know why are we being followed

at all? Surely the Duke would not waste men on us. As far as Inspector Quiselie claims, we only *used* counterfeit coins. He did not seem to believe we made them, and it sounded as though he had plenty of leads."

Lady Clara nodded. "That is true..." She trailed off with a frown.

"Lady Clara?"

"I hesitate to give credence to this but after seeing those insect-things – I do not know for sure that who or whatever followed me from the city was actually human."

Alira blinked and Kilek knew his own face would have been a mirror of surprise – and more, of a deep unease.

"Wait, what does that mean?" Tyar asked with a frown.

Mathi had a hand on her sword hilt now.

"Simply what I said," Lady Clara snapped. "At least one of those who followed me seemed... unnatural somehow. I could not put my finger on it." She shrugged. "And perhaps I was wrong. But once more, seeing those insects I have no wish to be caught unprepared."

"You could have told us this earlier," Tyar said.

"And what would you have done had I shared my suspicion – one which is still unfounded, you realise."

"I don't know. Confronted it."

"And there is your answer," she said. "It is too dangerous."

"We can handle ourselves, you should know that."

The knight shook her head. "I see no point in arguing about this. I made my decision and we have kept ahead of any who may follow. You have no need to chase down something that may not exist."

"But you are not sure, yourself, My Lady," Paxoph said.

"No."

"Then why didn't we ask those other two to come with us?" Tyar asked.

Lady Clara rubbed her temples a moment. "So can you handle yourself or not? Which is it?"

"Obviously–"

"Forget about Sir Maxime; he would only be a hindrance."

"Doesn't he outrank you? That means he must have some skill."

She smiled but it lacked warmth, only a weary bitterness. "If you consider being born into the right family a skill, then yes, he has that much. Yet such family connections won't be much use to us if we are attacked by something."

"You said *something*," Alira pressed. "You're sure, aren't you?"

"No. I simply want to be prepared."

Kilek glanced to the sky. Could it be Nakir? The man was certainly unusual... though he did seem human. "We should have talked about this before."

Lady Clara did not answer at first, instead turning to the road and snapping her reins. "I could say that same to each of you."

Kilek kicked at his mare, urging her forward. "What do you mean?"

"Sir Venostac may have missed something about you five but I begin to wonder. Two strange occurrences connected to you is concerning."

"You think we are drawing them?" Mathi asked.

"Perhaps. And perhaps you do not even know why. Either way, I have a duty to fulfil. So let's pick up the pace."

Chapter 33.

The cave admitted them to its bare, dusty interior before full dark.

Yet Kilek was sent out to descend the steep slope in a search for firewood. He bent to scoop up the first few pieces, bark flaking away beneath his grip, then slid down a little further to clamber across a fallen tree. The canopy provided enough shade for thick undergrowth, the branches of some shrubs almost sticky. The moss deep too but most of the shattered branches at the fallen tree had been leeched of colour; more than dry enough to burn.

He tugged at one of the larger pieces then paused.

Distant footfalls echoed from below.

Kilek glanced down the slope. Something tore its way through the dark trees, swatting at low-hanging branches as it climbed. Kilek stumbled back, firewood tumbling free. The figure wore a black or brown cloak and seemed human yet it was moving too fast, surely?

It was already too close.

He ripped his sword free as he gave a shout – part fear,

part warning to the others.

The figure loomed over him, the face grey and *far* too smooth.

Kilek swung his sword.

Something knocked it clear, jarring his wrist. Pressure snapped down around his throat. He kicked out as he was lifted, even as his air was cut off. Blinking through blurred vision, he thrashed hard when he caught a glimpse of eyes as they snapped open.

Wide set, pale, almost lilac in colour, they rested in an unnaturally smooth face of hard angles. And more, they were many-chambered eyes too – inhuman.

Insect like.

And all the more terrifying; the fact that aside from the rigidity and colour, the face could have been human, had it not been distorted just enough to reveal its true nature.

Cabeku.

Kilek clawed at whatever limb held him but his efforts were for naught. Darkness smothered him.

***

Kilek swallowed; his mouth full of tongue – why was it so swollen? Something jolted his whole body and he groaned. In the silent darkness, his head seemed to weigh ten times its usual weight but opening his eyes was impossible for some reason. The jolting continued. A large bump sent a wave of pain coursing through his head.

He groaned again, louder this time.

The jolting stopped.

Silence – everything was so quiet. What was happening?

Something had gone wrong – a stinging liquid coated his tongue, chill and soothing despite the minor discomfort it caused.

And then the darkness returned.

***

Twice more he woke to similar confusion and pain, only to feel the same stinging liquid drive away his wakefulness and plunge him back into nothingness.

Yet each time his mind seemed to bring with it a little more awareness – the thumping seemed to be explained by travel, but from where? And *to* where? It was too hard to put it all back together, especially with his memories so damn hazy.

Each time, he heard nothing, saw nothing. Each time, the pain gradually grew in his head. Yet well before it might have become unbearable, he was sent to sleep once more.

This time was different; he was still... and resting on the ground?

Too hard to tell. All darkness. And his body was both heavy *and* weightless – numb, with no way to know if he was truly at rest or only thought he was. At least now, the pain in his head was easing rather than growing. It seemed light bore down upon him but he could not tell from where.

His tongue was not so dry now either. Did that mean he had not been asleep as long as the last time?

Muted sounds surrounded him yet they remained unclear. They did not fade, instead they grew louder and more insistent. Kilek strained his ears, fought his eyelids but nothing changed. A scream seemed to well up within him yet it, too, was smothered by the inky world that had enslaved him.

The sounds ceased.

Raised voices followed, then they eased too.

***

Light bloomed.

Kilek opened his eyes, then raised a hand to shield them, squeezing his eyelids shut once more. "Where..." He choked on the word.

"Drink this." Cool water touched his lips and he took the mug, drinking deeply.

He opened his eyes again, squinting. "Thank you."

Light and shadow were resolving into shapes; three people bending over him where he lay on the ground and two others behind them. He returned the cup and rubbed at his eyes with a frown. His limbs moved too slowly.

"Kilek, can you still hear us?" A woman's voice – Alira?

"I can." He tried to smile but his face didn't seem to be responding – but he remembered now – the Cabeku had taken him from the wood. "What happened? I remember some... thing attacked me."

"We think it was another insect," Alira said, her voice troubled.

"Only, it was like a man," Mathi added.

Kilek sat up, swallowing back a wave of nausea. Made sense; the thing had no doubt been related to the Cabeku. And drugging him in some manner too, in order to keep him compliant. He winced at the memory of whatever he'd ingested... the thick, unpleasant taste. What was the creature exactly? It had been so fast – and its arms, had it been slicing and smashing a path through the trees?

His vision cleared enough to see everyone properly; the relief on their faces clear. He blinked back tears, suddenly overcome. If they hadn't followed... "Thank you... for saving me."

Tyar put a hand on his shoulder. "We'd do it again."

Kilek smiled.

"Come quickly – you should all see this," Lady Clara said from nearby.

Kilek pulled himself upright, accepting Tyar's arm to help with his balance. He hobbled to where the knight stood; it was a riverbank with yellowed grass beside a dry bed, and the broken shape of the Cabeku. He shuddered. It lay sprawled at Lady Clara's feet, the black cloak open to reveal a human-like body but like the face, only the shape was correct. The texture was smooth and hard, almost like a shell – save for where it had been broken and gouged, purple ichor visible. Beneath the human arms and hands, twin sets of thinner, more mantis-like arms hung, most also broken.

But it was the eyes that Lady Clara had called them over for.

An acrid stench rose from the man-thing's head, steam hissing as the wide orbs melted down into the skull. At first it was slow, but the process soon quickened and then spread – causing the nose, mouth and cheeks to cave in.

"That's quite disgusting," Mathi said.

The forehead and jaw dissolved next and then only a stinking puddle remained, sizzling through the dry grass. Kilek had to fall back, his eyes watering. "How did you kill it?" he asked.

"We mostly hacked it to death," Paxoph said. "It helped that Tyar was able to slow it down."

Tyar grinned. "You wouldn't believe the shots I was able to make."

"What do you mean?"

"I'll tell you later," he said. "It's been a long week; I was thinking we could head on to the city now that Kilek is safe?"

"Wait..." Kilek turned. In one direction, an old trail ran across a grassy plain of withering grass, their horses picketed nearby but appearing generally dissatisfied. In another direction, the empty riverbed, which ended at a range of low hills. The afternoon sun was sinking but the day was not finished – how could it have been an entire week? Hadn't he only been asleep for a day or so?

"The city lies beyond those hills," Lady Clara said. "If we climb them, you will see a marvellous sight, I must admit. But before that, I believe we all must speak about what has happened."

"So... it really carried me a whole week? And you all chased it down? It was so fast."

The knight nodded. "Faster than our horses but not quite as enduring. Now, let us eat while we talk."

Once food from the saddlebags had been passed around, Lady Clara had everyone sit in a circle, then pointed to Kilek. "Tell us what you remember, first."

"Well, I was collecting wood when I heard footsteps approaching. I looked up and saw it coming fast; the trees and undergrowth didn't seem to slow it at all. I'd barely drawn and called out when it knocked my sword aside and caught me by the throat." He reached up to touch the skin but it was not tender.

"We heard your shout," Alira said. "I saw you being carried by that thing – me and Pax chased it but it was too fast."

"But its path was clear," Mathi said. "We followed it most of the night and before we collapsed, Lady Clara noticed a pale light on the plain."

"The ca... creature?" Kilek asked, almost calling it a Cabeku.

"I thought so; it did not seem natural and the light returned each night we followed. I think it may have been rejuvenating but during the day we seemed to gain ground, as though it slept when we did. And so gradually we closed with it until earlier today."

"That's where I came in," Tyar said, still grinning.

"Your bow?" Kilek asked.

"And these," he said, gesturing to his eyes. "I saw it before anyone else and once we were close enough, I feathered the bastard."

Kilek straightened. "You shot at it while it was carrying me?"

"I had to take the risk – besides, I didn't miss. Slowed it down enough that we could catch up and now you're sitting here safe and sound, right?"

Kilek had to laugh. "I suppose I can't argue with that."

Lady Clara nodded, almost to herself. "It was another truly remarkable shot. To be honest, even I had not been able to see the thing and I have excellent vision."

Tyar spread his hands. "So do I, I guess."

"And that leads me to my next question – what are you all hiding?"

Tyar's smile vanished and silence fell across the group.

The knight folded her arms. "This I must know, people of Hasere. It is clear you are not simple villagers bringing news to the king. If you expect me to continue my efforts to ensure your safety, I must know the truth of what is happening." She gestured over her shoulder. "For that abomination should not exist upon these or any lands."

Kilek exchanged a glance with Mathi who seemed to be just as unsure as everyone else. In the silence, tension grew. But did they have a choice anymore? They needed Lady Clara, especially if another of these new, far more disturbing Cabeku appeared.

Still no-one spoke.

"You have been attacked by strange insect creatures twice in a short span of time; that is no accident," Lady Clara snapped. "The first time, you seemed more surprised by the hawk than the creature. And this latest fiend may have been contacting or seeking others, we do not know its purpose in taking one of you," she said, her voice growing sterner. "I do not intend to be unprepared, nor fail in my duty, especially this close to Alaycron."

Kilek sighed. "We first found one of these things beyond our village," he said finally. The tension that had beamed across at him from his friends, the same tension he'd no doubt sent them, seemed to ease a little – as if no-one else had been willing to be the one to actually share their secret. "It had killed the fox that tried to eat it."

Lady Clara nodded. "Continue."

"No-one is lying about wanting to convince the king to send more soldiers after our families," he said. "And we really have come face to face with Prince Yan of Minjao; he was asking the conscripts about Luargot myths and legends."

"Supposedly, he seeks the Night Thorn; Sir Venostac told me."

"We didn't want to hide the truth," said Mathi, "but who would believe us?" She shrugged. "But we couldn't carry any of the insect's body because it dissolved and so we had hoped our word would be enough."

Lady Clara regarded everyone a moment. "Doubtless you would have failed to convince anyone but with the corpse from the fields and now that thing, you will be taken more seriously. However," she said, her gaze flicking to Tyar, "none of that explains your archer's ability. Even if it is not a consistent skill, it is overall, seemingly beyond what even the heroes of Old Deluargot were said to manage." To Mathi she said. "And your ability with a blade is impressive for an untested villager."

"Father trained me since I was a girl," Mathi said with another shrug.

She faced Tyar now. "And you?"

"You could say I've been blessed by the Gods," Tyar replied without a moment's hesitation. "I can't explain it any other way."

Lady Clara heaved a sigh. "Very well, keep the rest of your secrets – for now, but do not seek to lie to the palace, for you will not leave those hallowed halls if you do."

Chapter 34.

Lady Clara pointed down from their vantage upon the barren hill of stone and earth.

The city of Alaycron rested below.

Another warm sunset cast a glow across the stone buildings, whose red-tiled rooves bore what seemed to be a golden trim yet it was, according to his father, but crushed granite affixed to sandstone by the Herisman artisans who helped build the city over five hundred years ago. From above, the colour gave the city's rooftops and skylights the sense of being aflame, yet more of a smouldering effect rather than an inferno.

From four sides where the city rested upon the plain came long, broad roads lined with trees. Each was a mighty thing. Even from a distance their size was impressive, and while the leaves were mostly green now, during the autumn the city would no doubt live up to its name: the Autumn Jewel.

Small figures, some mounted, some with wagons and just as many on foot, approached from the two directions Kilek could see properly.

But something other than the flow of people caught his eye; walkways spanning the buildings. They ran between the round towers, from building to building, some with doors built within and even, it seemed, toll stations? The walkways held their own share of traffic, near equal to that on the cobbled streets below.

And while the walkways seemed to pass through walls, between the treetops of gardens and even split into multiple levels, there was one place they did not travel – two if he counted the towering walls.

The palace.

The grand building boasted its own white walls and beyond, stretching lawns and more rows of trees. These thin poplars led nearly to the palace itself – a collection of stern buildings that might have been part of a fortified keep with its rows of narrow windows and parapets, its dark stone offset only by the red rooves.

But around the central buildings newer stone structures stood. Pale like the walls of the massive compound, these were shaped more like pillars, their purpose unclear. They led to domed structures nestled closer to the keep, these also bearing the red rooves. Spots of green seemed to grow from them, as though trees had been planted within and around.

Paxoph gaped. "How long must it have taken to grow the trees that line the road to the city?" he asked. "And the rows must stretch for a hundred yards."

"Seven generations," Lady Clara said, and she seemed to almost smile as she stared down.

"Impressive."

She nodded. "I will let you enjoy the view a moment –

I'm going to find some more water and start on our meal."

"The riverbed seems quite dry," Alira said. "I might be able to purify any muddy puddles."

"That would be welcome."

"Do we need so much?" Kilek said, glancing at the horses where they grazed below.

"It would be prudent," Lady Clara said. "The creature gave towns and natural waterways clear berth, and so we had little chance to stop."

Kilek nodded slowly. "You risked a lot for me, thank you again."

"Of course," Alira said with a smile, before joining the knight in their descent toward the camp.

Mathi turned to Kilek. "We spoke about that on the chase. Maybe the Cabeku don't like water? We weren't able to test the theory, really." She glanced to where Lady Clara and Alira walked, pausing a moment as if to ensure the knight was out of earshot. "But I think we need to talk about Daciael, finally. We can fill Alira in later. What did the dragon say?"

"And what did it look like?" Tyar asked.

They both wore similar expressions of excitement, and Kilek could almost see the youths they had been. He paused a moment, taken aback by the momentary impression. He'd almost forgotten how they once appeared.

"Ah, like a nobleman in black, only with fangs I think," Kilek said. He explained the water and the other details before moving on to the message. "He told me we need to 'Seek the Clarion Song' and use it to call back his descendants."

Mathi's eyes glittered now. "Call back? You mean,

dragons are not extinct?"

"He said they were three oceans away."

Paxoph murmured his surprise but Tyar slammed a fist into his palm. "This is more like it! With a horde of dragons we could stop the Cabeku with no problems – even those new things."

Kilek had to smile; their high spirits were a welcome reprieve. "I know. Not even insects from a God could stand against dragons."

"Did he share the song?" Paxoph asked.

"No, we have to find it in the city, I think. He said it was held by the line of Queens – but he mentioned Queen *Liana*."

"But Queen Mae reigns in Alaycron."

"Then we'll just have to ask her once we've delivered our news to the king," Mathi said, her expression moving from awe and excitement to determination.

Kilek glanced down. "Wait, I think..." he trailed off.

"What's wrong?" Tyar asked.

"What about everyone's families? If we follow the Goddess' wishes and go searching for the dragons, aren't we abandoning everyone again?"

Mathi slapped him on the shoulder. "Think about it, we're not going to be much use to the army, let alone be allowed to join it, *or* be much help to the village if we're stuck in Alaycron, are we? But with the dragons, we can hunt down Prince Yan if he survived and find Florique and everyone else."

"That makes sense."

"So what will our next steps be?" Paxoph asked. "How do we convince the queen to help us?"

Kilek frowned. "Alira's feathers?"

"Magic, even magic from the Goddess might not be enough."

"What we need is for Avendria to personally vouch for us," he said with a sigh.

"Let's figure that out when we reach the city," Mathi said. "We have Sir Venostac's letter and perhaps we could convince Queen Mae to at least meet with us. If she's at all reasonable, then she'll hear us out."

Chapter 35.

At last they reached the Avenue of Branches that led toward the city's western gate, joining the scores of travellers upon the stone road.

Each tree seemed to be its own giant, broad as two people sleeping end to end and two storeys tall before the lowest branches began, such magnificent oaks. The bark had swirls closer to gold than brown and the sea of green above blocked enough of the hot noon sun to cast shade but not stop the light, so wide was the road.

Beyond the line of trunks, stretching gardens of green where travellers stopped to sit upon the grass and eat, where children ran and chased butterflies while their parents sat close together. People who travelled alone sat too, on the hardwood benches or resting against the scattered stone statues of various heroes and kings – Kilek saw the enormous hammer of Medir the Forger at one point.

And that was only the folk *off* the road.

Those that rode or walked toward the gates were just as plentiful; merchants with all manner of wares, from bright vegetables or salted meats, to bolts of cloth and furniture, or groups of young people bouncing along with great big smiles and cheerful cries, knights in their armour and squires in leathers, nobles in their finery leaving trails of perfume, or, when hidden from view in carriages, only the echo of their laughter from behind the curtains.

And it was not just Luargot people; Kilek also saw men and women from Sassehim in their tan robes and dark sashes at the waist. Folk from Prisawi headed for the city too and Kilek found himself giving many a second glance... but none were those who had attempted to rob him.

People who hailed from the Tirrana Islands in the east also travelled the road. One group of the tanned-women hummed in unison as they strode along in their sandals and knee-length robes of pink and red silks, accompanied by a more warrior-like fellow; taller than the women, he wore boots and a vest of yellow, allowing him to stand out amongst those he travelled with.

And perhaps that was the point; he was noticeable, and not just because of his weapons, but they were plentiful. He carried twin swords across his back, one shorter than the other, both handles wrapped with yellow ribbon. A hatchet hung from his belt too, along with a dagger opposite. Just visible where his vest revealed part of his shoulder, was the ink of tattoos that presumably covered the man's back.

The stories said that such markings had not only important meaning to the people but magical properties, not that Kilek had ever come across a chance to meet and ask anyone from Tirrana.

"I wouldn't stare at him if I were you, Kilek," Tyar said.

"Agreed."

The protector did sweep his gaze across his surroundings, a stern look indeed, but it did not linger long on Kilek or his friends. Because the man didn't see them as a threat? The group soon fell behind as Lady Clara pushed them into a trot.

"Why were the women humming, do you know?" he asked Paxoph. Of all the people from Hasere, Pax and his uncle had travelled the most. "I know everyone wants to buy their spices but not anything about the humming."

"It was lovely, wasn't it?" Alira asked. "It seemed almost like a ritual."

"I believe it is a song for Safe Arrival," Pax said. "Uncle Orasef and I once travelled with a small group before we went north."

"It is rare to see them visit the royal city," Lady Clara said without turning. As ever, her gaze seemed to rove their surroundings.

"Why is that?" Alira asked.

"I am not sure, truly," the knight replied. "It is usually to trade the very best spices directly with the palace – but they carried no wares."

They rode on, drawing nearer the city walls but their pace slowed as the lines of people stopped for checks. Ahead, a dozen knights worked in pairs beneath open gates so large they cast giant shadows. Most travellers the knights simply let pass through the iron gates but merchants had their wagons searched and large groups on horseback tended to face the same scrutiny.

Yet as before, Lady Clara afforded them swift entry by nature of her status. Grumbling rose from behind, but when Kilek glanced back to the lines of people watching beneath the hot sun, he saw no murderous intent.

"We have plenty of time to reach the palace, so we will go there directly," Lady Clara said, a hint of steel in her voice now.

"That would be wonderful," Paxoph said.

Lady Clara nodded then led them into the royal city.

Unlike the other cities Kilek had seen – not that the number was large – the capital did not seem to place its warehouses or inns so close to the gates, or at least, not the western gate. Instead, it was two-storey homes beside the inns, many with broad ground floors and narrower upper storeys to make room for what seemed to be gardens. Many were connected by walkways, and a massive one also ran overhead, following the thoroughfare.

The walkway had regular support columns, which often featured gated spiral steps with serious-looking locks, but the columns appeared few and far between – as though some magic provided strength beyond steel and stone.

And yet that wonder was eclipsed by the underside of the floating bridge.

A fantastic mural, with painted figures revealing a scene of battles where knights fought shadow figures, their blades bright. Other sections showed the Luargot champions pitched against figures in green that may have represented the Minjao, a lush land of tree and flower as the backdrop.

"That is amazing," Kilek said, craning his neck as they rode.

The others offered similar responses, but Lady Clara sniffed. "It is but an attempt to distract those who travel below."

"What do you mean?"

She gestured upwards. "Such walkways are generally reserved for the nobility or very rich commoners, since they are safer. The paintings are a poor concession for those of us below who can be exposed to crime at the worst and sometimes long delays at the best."

If true, it *was* unfair. "But they are still beautiful at least," Kilek said.

"Only compared to a child's scrawling."

He looked away from a knight depicted protecting an ally from a coiled serpent – the green scales were clear, the fangs, the crest of the knight's shield. Maybe the colour of the man's eyes could not be gleaned from below, but it hardly seemed a disaster. "Is it truly so poor?"

She shrugged. "It is the work of Deyasso; a poor student of the master Nicale."

"These are famous painters?" Alira asked.

"Of course. In the palace, if you are lucky perhaps you will see some of Nicale's work and it will become clear."

Kilek returned his gaze to the walkway above. The mural had changed – now that same knight rested against a tree in a sunny glade. Beside him, his shield wore the vestiges of battle and his blade lay across his knees. In the distance, other soldiers took respite too. For the following panels the artist seemed content to continue the theme; the knight fought yet more battles – one at night beneath a silver, blazing moon that was reflected in a raging river.

A shout came from the upper storeys.

Kilek turned – but it was no sign of attack, instead, an old man yelling down to the street from his window. There, a pair of kids ducked in and out of the crowds. The man slammed the shutters. Unlike either Jecomar or Trisome, many of the windows here were protruding, with rounded moulding above the glass, giving the windows four 'sides' from which to peer.

They were similar to the crushed granite look, a picture of wealth; reminder that he now walked the jewel of the south. The beauty and wealth was both dazzling and overwhelming. The city held so much of... everything, and he'd barely stepped within its gates.

From one of the intersections, a song drifted down the street. Three figures dressed in bright blue capes and white tunics performed; two with flutes and one singing. The words seemed to be about current nobles but carried no real meaning to Kilek, though those listening laughed along with the performance.

He once again peered up to the walkway.

Now, the images had changed to much more recent events; the construction of the city itself, the Luargot citizens aided by Herisman, it seemed, considering the unusual look to the folk in the white robes, their skin seemingly tinted with rose.

Other moments were difficult for him to guess at, even with his love of myth and history but several scenes with richly-clothed men and women on thrones appeared to be important proclamations. In one such image, the ruler bestowed a sapphire-lined breastplate upon a kneeling knight.

He dropped his gaze, and the palace lay before him.

Up close, it was not so dissimilar to the other buildings, the same protruding windows, sandstone and red tiles but the palace held peaked towers and its own grid of walkways, these often arranged with hanging plants. Most plants were dotted with red and pink flowers like teardrops, softening the look of the keep. In autumn, no doubt the leaves would match the roof but for now they made for pleasant green splashes against the stone.

So too, they contrasted the yellow and orange flags and giant, wall draping that proclaimed the poplars of the Knighthood on one side of the giant doors, and the King's Stag opposite. Somehow, the colours had not faded and more, the wind did not seem to have ripped the draping either. Perhaps it was replaced regularly.

They dismounted before a short flight of steps and climbed to great double doors that lay open. Inside, a large antechamber lined with mirrors, fig trees and a pair of sculptures in white marble – one a deer skewering a wolf on its antlers, the other a less unusual choice – Fiana the Goddess of Prosperity, standing tall in her furs.

A pair of unsmiling knights met them, their gleaming breastplates featuring tri-coloured stripes on their poplars.

"State your name and purpose," one said, his voice sounding a little tired.

"Lady Clara, Spring Knight – I am delivering the northern villagers to the palace as ordered by Sir Venostac."

The man nodded. "A pigeon has arrived; you have been expected. Thank you for your service, Knight of Spring."

"Upon my honour it was my fierce duty," she replied.

"Return to your post. If you are required, you will be sent for."

"Thank you, Sir Knight." Lady Clara turned to Kilek, glancing at everyone. "Remember your manners here, and expect to be asked about the insects after you have delivered your news, as I will be making my own report."

"We will," Paxoph said.

She strode from the chamber, heels clapping on the marble floor.

Her words echoed in Kilek's ears; the insects were not going to be forgotten but for now, he had to focus on the myths that had interested Prince Yan. And do his best to convince the king that more had to be done to rescue everyone... as well as figuring a way to speak to the queen.

One of the guards cleared his throat. "Follow me, please." He took them to the nearest corridor, a long hall also lain with marbled floors – more evidence of an almost unbelievable wealth.

Here they passed narrow windows with tapestries between them – armies clashing on dark fields, along with more of the statuary too, these also Gods or deer for the most part. They stopped before a large door set with ornate handles. "Someone will attend to you soon. Please do not stray from these chambers."

He opened the door and admitted them before leaving without any further instruction.

Inside, soft chairs of red, each wide enough for two or three people, were arranged around an indoor garden plot filled fragrant violets and roses. More paintings of Luargot heroes, like Sireac the Stalwart, hung on the walls, split by a single window. It looked out over the neat lawns, a silent fountain visible through the burgundy leaves from a shrub; small bird chirping away within.

Tyar slumped into one of the chairs. "Finally, we're here."

Paxoph joined him, Mathi too, taking a deep breath before the centrepiece with a nod.

"And now we wait," Alira said.

"What do we say when they ask us about the insects?"

Paxoph said after a moment. "Whoever it is will probably not be satisfied with half answers, the way Lady Clara was."

"I think we stick to the same story," Mathi said. "We can't convince them about the Goddess, they won't believe us. Who knows, they might even lock us up."

Kilek moved to the window. Being locked up… maybe it wasn't likely and maybe it was, but no matter what, they *had* to persuade the king to help somehow. And then, find a way to speak to the queen – both of which would be impossible from a dungeon.

Chapter 36.

"How long has it been?" Tyar demanded as he paced, the carpet here swallowing his stomping. He stopped to glare at the door. "I'm going to ask that knight again."

"He won't like that," Mathi said from where she lay across one of the long chairs, legs dangling over the arm. She'd been twirling her hair around a finger as she waited.

"Good. Maybe he'll do something about it then."

Kilek nodded, half to himself. It *had* been quite a long time – the light outside was dimming. Paxoph had lit the silver lamp upon the wall, and even he wore a frown as he examined one of the paintings once more; not, it seemed, the work of the great Nicale, since Kilek had also had time to check.

Footsteps echoed from outside.

Mathi straightened and everyone else turned to face the door. "Ready?" she asked.

The door swung inward to reveal a young fellow with slicked-back blond hair, his no-nonsense doublet white with ivory buttons. A stag's head of gold had been pinned to his clothing and seemed to proclaim some importance. Perhaps an immediate servant of the King himself?

"Forgive the interminable wait, dear citizens," he said, his voice clear and stronger somehow than his slight frame suggested.

Tyar rose. "Well, if you're taking us to see the king now then that's a start."

The man paused. "The king? Oh no, King Hadeon is quite unable to see you personally, concerned as he is with the north."

"But, Sir Venostac told us to speak to the king."

"Indeed. And your words will absolutely reach his majesty's ears but let me relieve you of that burden. I will carry your story to him, exactly as you share it."

Tyar opened his mouth, no doubt to complain but Paxoph was quicker. "That is kind of you... ah, My Lord."

"Please," he said, raising a hand. "My title is of little consequence in the palace, simply call me Peycu. I am Master of the *Decaur* in the old tongue."

"The Day-to-Day?" Kilek asked after a moment of thought; the word seemed familiar.

"Indeed, that is a fair translation, young man," Peycu said with a smile. "Now, I do believe that I recognise you all from Sir Venostac's letter, and I would like to hear your tale but let us find more comfortable quarters and perhaps a meal."

"You might not be the king but you've still got some great ideas, Peycu," Tyar said.

He chuckled. "Very well, accompany me upstairs – I'm sure the cooks will have something suitable ready for us by now."

The Master of the Decaur led them from the room and

along the hall to a stair, the tips of each step lined with gold and then along another two passages, similarly decorated. The only difference Kilek was able to note was here, the statues no longer featured stags and does, but instead, great birds.

Peycu stopped at a pair of doors inlaid with glass panels. A small dining room sat beyond the glass, table laden with meats and vegetables with wine and rich sauces, warm lamps giving the room a pleasant glow.

Kilek's first bite of the thinly sliced beef caused his mouth to water before the meat reached his tongue – and it was all delicious. The peppery sauce and the roasted carrots had him no doubt make something of a pig of himself while somehow managing to speak. Throughout the meal they still shared all they could about Prince Yan's interest in the old myths and particularly the Night Thorn, and Peycu listened attentively, drinking only a sweet lemon tea while they ate.

"This is indeed troubling. Here in the south, we are missing some details of the legend, but we *do* have an account of a young nobleman who supposedly fled to the great forests of Jasoria with one of the Thorns. It has long been regarded as fanciful but perhaps not, considering your tale." He leant back in his chair. "I fear it has been remiss of us to focus so much upon stories here in the south."

"We'd be happy to share any other northern legends, if you wish?" Alira offered. "Especially if you believe it would help get our families back."

The man tapped a finger upon his cup. "That is something we may well ask but I am also curious about something Lady Clara showed us earlier."

Kilek blinked. Of course; the insects, he'd forgotten.

Peycu could have read their report in the letter, as he doubtless did, and had someone less important conduct the actual interview. For if a king could not see them to talk about myths and legends, why would the Master of the Keep bother?

Unless he wanted different information just as much. Or more.

No-one had answered the man.

Peycu raised his hands. "Worry not, this is not some devious trap – none here believe you have done ill, we are simply concerned about what you discovered."

"You saw the two insect-things Lady Clara carried?" Mathi asked.

"We did." Peycu's eyes lost some of their welcome. "We found them... troubling."

"Do you know what they are?" Alira asked.

"Theories only, but nothing worth repeating, as we have barely had time to examine the specimens. But if they prove to be a larger threat than we anticipate, we need to understand these creatures. Lady Clara believes they are drawn to you for some reason." He turned to Kilek. "One even attempted to abduct you, it seemed."

"Yes."

"Can you guess why?"

He shook his head. "We're just villagers." And it was no lie; for beneath the changes to his friends, they were still as young and unworldly as he, truly.

"Perhaps. But based on our estimations, the first appearance of the smaller insect seemed to have been near Hasere – something may be afoot that you are not aware of."

Paxoph lowered his fork. "Such as?"

"Again, we could not possibly guess. But we cannot do *nothing*, as I'm sure you agree."

"That's why we came here," Mathi replied. "We want to convince the king to find our families."

Peycu nodded. "Of course, a noble intent. And you have passed the forces Sir Venostac rode with and so you know King Hadeon takes the western incursion very seriously."

"But is there more he can do?" Tyar asked. "Like, send the whole army west? Yan had mages and a head start – we risked everything to come here; my uncle could still be alive somewhere."

"All out war would mean the loss of many, many lives – a notion which may not be of much comfort to explain what must seem like a restrained response from your own king. But the dearth that is the Wickerlands lives large in our collective memories, and so I understand my liege's prudence. Still, you deserve assurance and I will do my best."

"How so?" Tyar asked.

"There are forces tracking Prince Yan's movements west as you and I sit here."

"What?" Mathi half-rose.

"Yes. You are, of course, aware of Luargot's own magic-users, the Silent Knives? Individually, we refer to them as *dagua*. They are generally sorcerers but we rely upon them for their more… stealthy skills also."

"Spies and assassins," Mathi said.

"A sad necessity, but yes. And they send reports, so we are aware the conscripts continue west and are, for the most part, well enough." He raised a finger. "And before you ask, the Knives are certainly too few to intervene."

Tyar's shoulders slumped a little.

"But Prince Yan is alive?" Alira asked.

"For now."

She exchanged a glance with everyone, worry clear in her eyes.

"My dear?" Peycu asked.

"It's just that, someone helped us escape. He was a magic-user too and the last we saw, he was facing Prince Yan."

"Ah. Sad news is possible then, for Yan is one of the Emperor's most powerful sons – in every sense of the word. Still, hope is not to be discarded when magic is concerned."

She nodded.

"Couldn't all this have been avoided?" Paxoph asked, a deep frown upon his face.

"How so?"

"I should have realised this before, it's silly of me, but doesn't the king have spies in the west or at the border at least?"

"Indeed. But your report along with many others, have told of Yan somehow using his mages to cloak their movements long enough to surprise us. It is awful but we must now focus on learning the truth and fighting back."

"We can be a part of that," Mathi said.

"I believe so, yes," Peycu said as he rose. "Firstly, by continuing to help with our investigation into the insects, which is something I think should continue tomorrow. You have had a long and, I suspect, truly arduous journey to reach the city. Rest now in the rooms that have been provided, and upon the morrow I will arrange for a more comprehensive exploration of what can be done to help."

Chapter 37.

Kilek woke in the deep bed, staring up at the forest-mural on the ceiling in the opulent room the servants had shown him to after the meeting with Peycu. He did not rise to open the heavy, velvet curtains, instead relishing a moment of quiet. For the first time in so long, he did not have to share a room, or even a campsite. Not even back home, did he have that luxury.

Still, how did Camilea fare?

A flush of guilt came with the thought; he'd not spared her even a moment of his worry until now. Either way, she was probably safe enough, and hopefully doing her part to help rebuild Hasere.

"And maybe that's where you should be too," he muttered. After all, chasing Prince Yan west and then abandoning that path to reach the capital was beginning to feel fruitless. No-one was going to convince the king to do more, let alone be allowed to even *speak* to the man directly. Kilek gave a bitter laugh. He'd been a fool not to realise something so obvious.

King Hadeon had never been going to speak with a

handful of villagers.

Peycu, despite his apparent kindness, would want the truth about everyone, since that was related to the Cabeku. And the moment they discussed meeting the Goddess, that'd be the end, everyone locked away. Then there was no chance of finding the Clarion Song, let alone the dragons. Just as the king was not going to see them, no queen would be visiting the dungeons for a lovely talk about an ancient song she may not even have.

How to convince everyone?

The best way was to bring the dragons back – no room for doubt then. He snorted.

Someone knocked on his door.

"Kilek, are you awake?"

Mathi.

Kilek sat up, grasping for his tunic and pants where they lay strewn across the foot of the bed. He scrambled into them, bumping into a sideboard as he did. Crockery rattled toward the edge and he lurched forward to catch it with a gasp.

"Are you having some trouble in there?"

He strode to the door and jerked it open. "No, everything's fine."

"Nice hair," she said. "Sleeping late I see."

"You didn't?"

She sighed as she entered, moving to the curtains to let light burn its way into the room – or so it seemed to Kilek's eyes. "I was too worried about today."

"Me too, I suppose."

"How can we get them to listen, Kil?"

"I don't know." He rubbed at his eyes. "It's not possible, is it? What does everyone else think?"

"Not much. All their ideas hinge upon being able to demonstrate our gifts on cue, since there's no way to prove we're all the same age."

"And you can't control when you... ah, change?"

"As it turns out, I don't think so. And Tyar's a great shot but he doesn't think he could perform on demand either."

"We need the Goddess herself, but that's not happening," Kilek said as he found his sword and belted it on, frowning down at it as he wrestled with the buckle.

Mathi made a fist. "Hold on, maybe we need the next best thing."

"You mean, one of her Servants?"

"Exactly."

"Do people in the south worship her anymore, or is it all Yaende down here?"

"I think we need to find out." She punched his shoulder. "Good work."

He grinned. "It was your idea."

"But you led me there. Come on." Mathi half-dragged him from his room and into a hall so clean that it gleamed under the skylights, then rapped upon the next few doors.

Despite some rare grumbling from a sleepy-looking Paxoph, she soon had everyone in the hall, explaining the idea. "So all we need to do is find a temple or maybe a Servant here in the palace."

"Makes sense," Tyar said with a grin.

Alira was smiling too. "If anyone is going to believe us it would be a Servant."

"Then let's find one and ask..." Paxoph trailed off.

The white-clad shape of Peycu approached at a brisk walk,

two men in tow. The first seemed to be a knight but he wore no armour, just a sword belted over a black tabard, the three poplars no different to the two Kilek wore. The man, like most knights, had a moustache but no beard, and a friendly countenance, despite a long scar running across his jaw.

The other stranger wore his long blond hair in a plait, a bone clasp at the end visible when he turned at the sound of someone hailing a 'Lord Inacien'. The fellow who gestured for the Lord's attention was dressed the same as his superior – grey tunic and pants with white hand wrappings and softer shoes that made for quiet footfalls when they met.

"Good morning all," Peycu said. "I trust you had a restful night and can forgive me now as I come to postpone any breakfast plans you may have," he gave them a short smile. "I would like to first introduce you to Sir Eciven, King's Sentinel and Captain of Knighthood here, along with Lord Inacien the Singing Blade, who leads the Alaycron Knives."

"Welcome to the royal city and the palace," Sir Eciven said. His voice was gruff but warm. It seemed odd that as a Sentinel he wore no identifying markings. "Peycu has arranged something for after, but I felt we should talk first, while everything is still fresh in your minds."

"We'll certainly do our best," Paxoph said.

"Grand. In that case, follow me to the barracks and you can see some more of the order that has shielded you with its name." He slapped Tyar on the back. "Who knows, maybe you'll be taken by a sudden rush of patriotic fervour and ask to take the vows – providing you have the backbone, of course."

"I have studied many accounts of the trials," Mathi said, her expression brightening.

"Good to hear. And now you can witness one of them in action while we talk about those insects," he said, gesturing toward the hallway. "Simply follow me."

Kilek started after his friends, but a hand fell upon his shoulder.

Lord Inacien's grey eyes stared down at him from an unshaven face – not that the man was by any means slovenly. "Not you, Kilek of Hasere."

"Ah, I had hoped to go with–"

The man's grip tightened briefly. "In time, you will join them. But the Master of *Decaur* thought you and I should speak first."

"Me?"

"Yes." Lord Inacien turned to Peycu. "Thank you. Will you send someone to escort him to the barracks when we are finished?"

"Of course, My Lord," the man replied with a bow. Then he returned the way he came, leaving Kilek with the Head of the Knives.

"You are tense, lad – do not be."

"I am?"

"In your shoulders. Your breathing – the signs are there. Come, into your room a moment," he said as he gestured to the row of doors as if unsure of exactly which one.

"Ah, yes, My Lord." Kilek led the man into his room, swallowing hard as he did so. What could the leader of spies and assassins possibly want? Despite the man's assurances the whole request seemed odd – and why wouldn't Kilek be tense?

Lord Inacien closed the door but stood before it, as though listening for sounds from beyond. Finally, he nodded to one of the simple chairs. "Sit a moment."

"What is this about, My Lord?" Kilek asked as he sat.

"You are named for your father, are you not?"

"I am," Kilek said slowly.

"As I thought. Few would bear that name and hail from a small village in the north called Hasere."

"You knew my father?" The *dagua* did not seem so old, though he was no youth either.

"And mother," Lord Inacien said. "They trained me in certain skills when I was younger, though it was your father I knew best. I owe him a debt and mean to take those first steps now with you."

Then the man obviously knew about their deaths in the war... but what exactly had Mother and Father taught the man? There was a more urgent question. "Can you help us rescue the people of Hasere?"

"My Knives are watching the conscripts but that is not what I mean. I am speaking of Alaycron here and now. You should leave the moment your business with Peycu is finished."

Chapter 38.

A chill ran across Kilek's body. "I should?" He glanced around the room – was he being watched even now? What did the man mean? No-one in the palace seemed to bear him any ill will.

Lord Inacien nodded. "Your name carries with it painful memories for one in the palace. I am not clear on what their reaction will be."

Kilek rose. "Then, I'm in danger?"

"I would not say physically."

"But *something* could happen to me – you wouldn't warn me otherwise."

"I would not."

Not much of an answer. Kilek frowned. "So are you saying my father was not a good man?"

"Quite the opposite. It was his principles that made his life difficult here back then but any more is not my tale to tell."

"Then who should?" he said, his voice rising.

Lord Inacien smiled briefly. "Not unlike your mother in that regard, young man."

Kilek searched for words but had no response – he couldn't manage to order his thoughts either. Who had Father upset? How long had he spent in the palace? What kind of danger? And Mother had a temper? That wasn't how he remembered her at all.

"Listen, I do not believe the threat is immediate but once again, do not linger here," Lord Inacien said. "Share all that you might about the Cabeku and then be on your way, Kilek. And before you ask, you can certainly trust Peycu and Eciven."

Kilek stepped closer. "Wait – you said 'cabeku' just now."

The man lowered his voice. "Avendria is not the only one concerned about them."

"Are you saying –" Kilek stopped when Lord Inacien raised a finger.

"Carefully."

Kilek glanced around the room once – nothing amiss, no sounds from outside, either window or hall. A general warning only? "Then you *can* help us, can't you?"

"I have my own tasks. Tasks which may not always align with yours, Kilek."

He frowned. "But... I thought you wanted to help."

"Those insects threaten us all. Those you have encountered are but scouts, I fear the greater horde lurks somewhere." His jaw was clenched. "But we cannot find them."

Kilek shook his head. "Shouldn't you have told the king or someone else, if you already knew about them?"

"You misunderstand – I know only what *you* have been told and what I have seen Lady Clara show the council after your arrival."

"But still, I cannot believe that whoever you work for is unwilling to join forces or at least help each other."

Lord Inacien opened the door. "If you are anything like your parents, I believe you will end up being more than capable. But again, I have my own threats to face."

Kilek took a step after the man. "Worse than those... things?"

"I fear so."

And then he was gone, striding down the hallway, almost soundlessly despite his speed. Kilek stared after the head of the Knives. Worse? What was worse than a plague of Cabeku and the other, human-like types of them?

It wasn't the only troubling question.

For which God or Goddess was Lord Inacien a surrogate? Who exactly would be at cross-purposes with Avendria, yet not be an enemy, precisely, if Kilek had read Lord Inacien correctly? Was it Yaende? Had the God of Warriors thrown his own gauntlet?

And more – there always seemed to be more questions – how had the man known his parents? Who was a threat in the palace?

"Kilek?"

He turned. A young page, barely more than a boy, approached, his red livery seemed a touch ill-fitting and his expression one of some weariness – yet not the kind brought about from lack of sleep; from the slight sneer on his face did it come from another place?

"Yes."

"Allow me to show you to the barracks."

"Thank you."

The lad set off at quite the trot. Kilek trailed him but did not match the boy's speed as they passed more sculptures and paintings – the artworks were everywhere – and descended stairs before eventually, exiting into the warm morning air.

Outside, they crossed one of the lawns to head for the barracks. The buildings spread around a grassless yard where soldiers in grey and blue trained, their shouts and grunts of effort clear. Not halfway to the buildings, the page lifted a hand to point to smaller outbuildings, perhaps used for storage. The nearest lay nestled within a row of trees that formed a shaded garden.

"If you no longer need me, simply follow the path between the trees to reach Sir Eciven."

"Thanks again."

Kilek picked up the pace a little as he slipped beneath an arch of deep green vines and started along the shaded path. More vines hung from the sheds, little orange flowers giving off a heady scent. Protected from the sun by a row of taller trees, it was a pleasant garden in an out of the way spot–

Steel flashed.

Pain erupted across his chest.

Kilek flinched back with a shout. A shadowy figure appeared, pouncing upon him before he could draw his blade. Kilek hit the ground hard and his head cracked against the stepping stones. Something hot bit into his side almost the moment he landed.

The dark shape loomed above him. "Worry not, boy. You will not feel the final blow."

Who? Kilek's vision was already dimming, the panic that ought to have been raging within him dulled, but he could see – the mouth and nose beneath the hood, the glimpse of

glittering eyes – the voice, they all seemed familiar...
  Nakir!

Chapter 39.

A gasp tore Kilek from sleep.

Or at least, from blackness. His body ached all over; he hadn't been sleeping at all. It had been something deeper; a thicker muck to swim up through, starting far from a distant pin prick near-lost to shifting shadows.

But now, he lay upon a cool bed. White walls surrounded him, half-cloaked in green plants with yellow and blue flowers in spiral form, their scents too subtle to place. They were everywhere it seemed, stacked in rows, spilling from pots and climbing lattice, covering long benches littered with clear vials and small pouches. He blinked; the white wasn't stone or marble, but light from a grid of windows, the steel between each frame of glass thin enough to almost recede into the brightness.

Or maybe his eyes weren't working too well yet?

What had happened?

"Amazing. You should be dead, you know."

He turned his head, wincing at the effort. A woman in a black robe and leather gloves approached, vial of pale pink liquid in hand. Her hair was cut to her chin and it was somehow like silk, catching the light. She smiled down at him and her lips had been painted with just enough red to make them more vibrant. The look in her eyes seemed to contain as much curiosity as relief as she set the vial in a stand upon the nearest bench.

"I was attacked," Kilek said with a frown, his throat dry. Then he rose to a half-sitting position. "Wait, Nakir! I have to warn–"

She pushed him back to the pillow, hands on his shoulders firm but not rough. "Rest, Kilek. You've lost a lot of blood and your wounds are still healing, despite what seems to be a true miracle."

Odd, he didn't feel much pain. "Is everyone safe?"

"Yes. They fought off this Nakir person – your friend, one of the lovely young ladies, I believe it was Mathila? She helped Sir Eciven and Lord Inacien drive him away. She is now quite the darling of the palace. In fact, you all are; the halls are afire with gossip."

Kilek took a moment to respond. "Gossip?"

"They want to know about the Northern Heroes. Supposedly, you single-handedly drove Prince Yan back to the Wickerlands and Sir Venostac sent you south to be rewarded."

He groaned. "That's not true."

The woman shrugged. "But it's interesting, and that's why people will repeat it, even if they don't truly believe what they've just said."

Kilek closed his eyes. Gossip and rumours? Heroes? It was... impossible to deal with. Even if he wasn't abed with no idea about where he was or who cared for him. He looked to the woman again. "Did you save me?"

"No. A pair of Knights did that; said they found you bleeding behind the barracks not long after the attack. They carried you here."

"But you healed me?"

"There's some debate as to how much I actually did, but I suppose so," she said with a smile. "My name is Amil."

"Thank you, Amil. I'm Kilek. Do you know why I healed so..." He lifted the blanket to check on his wounds – then pulled it around his chest once more, face heating. "I'm naked!"

"Yes." Amil lifted the vial once more, seeming to ignore him. "I want you to drink this today and tomorrow, to make entirely sure you suffer no infection."

"But–"

"The wound in your side was particularly deep. It may still give you pain despite the clean heal – the blade missed your ribs *and* your heart, so you were lucky. But despite that, you had lost too much blood when they brought you here." She shook her head in disbelief. "Yet you clung to life somehow, it really was impressive. And so I cleaned and sewed you back up. It has now been two weeks since the attack."

His shame receded. "Two weeks? I survived for two weeks? You must have saved me." Either that, or Mathi's theory about him being lucky was looking more and more likely.

"As I said, no doubt I helped but I believe that pendant of yours was far more instrumental in allowing you to live."

He lifted it from his neck. "My pendant—"

A door opened, bringing new light. Kilek shielded his eyes, pendant falling back beneath the blanket.

Three women entered, followed by a familiar man – Peycu, but the women drew his gaze, two servants wearing pale dresses with bell-shaped bottoms, hair arranged atop their heads. Leading them, an older woman, beautiful and refined, her own hair almost sculpted where it curled down toward bare shoulders. Her gown was a bright yellow, trimmed with silver. A matching coronet set with a ruby glittered as she neared, extending her hands, encased in white gloves that reached her elbows, to Amil.

"My dear, you are truly gifted."

Amil bowed. "You flatter me, My Lady."

The noble drew close to Kilek and smiled down at him, a warm expression. "I am relieved to see you recovered, young man."

He kept the blanket clasped around him. "Ah, thank you, My Lady."

Peycu cleared his throat. "Kilek, you are now in the presence of Her Majesty Queen Mae."

He shrank back into the pillow, eyes widening. "I'm sorry, I didn't know, Your Majesty." His words came out in a rush. He was practically naked before the Queen of Luargot! Before *many* women, for that matter – with only what now seemed like an entirely too-thin blanket protecting him from mortal shame.

"You did not know," she said, and it seemed not exactly an acceptance of his apology so much as an acknowledgement. "As I trust Amil has informed you, your companions are alive and well. They have been asking after you but we thought it best not to tax you with too many visitors at first."

"You knew I was to wake?" Kilek asked. Then added, "Your Majesty."

She smiled. "I had hoped – Amil must not have told you but you have been speaking in your sleep the last two days."

"Oh."

"Not to worry," she said, reaching out to stroke his cheek. He flushed. "You said nothing untoward, according to Amil." Kilek glanced at the healer and Amil was nodding, though she bore a faint smile. Gods, what had he said?

"I'm... ah.... very honoured that you would come and visit me," Kilek said. Was that the right thing to say?

"Of course – you and your friends are heroes and you will be acknowledged as such once you are fully recovered."

"I wouldn't want everyone to go to such trouble, not for me. I didn't do anything."

"Your warning about the insects is valued, young man." She paused, some emotion fleeting across her gaze but nothing clear enough for him to understand. "You do have a look about you that reminds me of him, truly."

"Your Majesty?"

"Your father, Kilek," she said with a sad smile. "He is missed here, even now, and I mourn with you."

Kilek had no response, only the warning from Lord Inacien ringing in his ears. Surely the leader of the Knives hadn't meant for him to be wary of the Queen?

One of the maids stepped forward, but not close enough to interrupt precisely. "My Lady, you do have a prior engagement."

"Yes, of course, Clarece." The Queen turned to go.

"Your Majesty, I would like to ask you something before you leave," Kilek said, sitting up a little.

"Quickly, you may."

"Ah, I wondered if you had ever heard of the Clarion

Song?"

"Not that I can recall... I must say, it is fascinating to learn that you are interested in music, young man." She nodded in approval. "Well, let me send you my bard when you are recovered."

"Thank you, Your Majesty."

Queen Mae left, her ladies-in-waiting close behind. Peycu and his white doublet remained. "If I had known you were interested in music, I might have sent Amil someone to sing, maybe you'd have woken sooner," he mused.

"I don't think so," Amil answered. "I'm still shocked he survived at all."

"Well, let's give him some more time before reuniting him with his friends, just to be certain."

"What happened?" Kilek directed his question to Peycu. "Nakir just appeared from nowhere."

"That is how many of us feel – Lord Inacien is furious; he is still searching for this Nakir. I believe you have encountered him before?"

"Yes. Mathi fought him off, outside Jecomar."

"So she told me. Do you, Kilek, know why such a powerful assassin might have targeted you before going on to attack your friends?"

"You don't think Sir Eciven or someone else was the target?"

"I think many things and have decided nothing; but one thing is clear, you and your fellow villagers appear to be quite remarkable."

Kilek tried to laugh – and maybe the false cheer didn't come through, but a hint of bitterness did. "I don't feel very remarkable. Look at me – I didn't even see Nakir coming.

This is the second time I've had to be saved in just a few days. It feels like I'm always waking up after something terrible."

"Don't forget what I told you," Amil said with a grin. "You're all important now – and once word gets out that you recovered, I'm sure everyone will want to meet you, the Boy who Cheated Death."

"Cheated Death?"

She shrugged. "They'll probably come up with something better to call you."

"Oh." Kilek fidgeted with the edge of his blanket. "That sounds unpleasant."

Peycu chuckled. "I can barely imagine what a cruel fate it would be to leave a quiet place and come to the royal city and have people seeking you often – I fear you will indeed find it unpleasant, Kilek. But I will fend some of them off, though I believe you and your friends will become an important part of the palace, at least for a time."

"But it can all start tomorrow?"

"I am sure we can keep news of your recovery quiet a little longer," Peycu said. "But I will need you to speak with several people first."

"Who?"

"Lord Inacien whenever he returns for one, but the king himself expects to see you this evening – and your friends. A few other advisors are most keen too, along with Sir Eciven once more."

"King Hadeon?"

"Yes. Though you will find him as gracious as his wife."

Amil held up the pink vial from before. "Let's leave it at that, shall we? I think my patient should rest a little longer before that meeting."

"Sound thinking, Amil," Peycu said, then excused himself after a promise to return and reunite Kilek with his friends.

"Drink," Amil said.

He took the vial and swallowed the cool liquid. It splashed down his throat, refreshing and sweet.

"Surprised?"

"Yes. Most medicine tastes terrible. Jeona back home used to offer mint leaves to chew on afterwards, when we were younger."

"Not a bad idea when dealing with children," Amil said. "Now, let's get back to the important things – that Herisman pendant."

Chapter 40.

Kilek drew the pendant free. "You recognise it?"

Amil leant closer, the scent of dry flowers following her. It was not unpleasant but still unusual. She pointed to the engraving. "The Raven is a symbol of the Herisman Healers, they who passed between life and death so often when working on their patients. It is said they flew back on raven's wings."

"From death?"

"Yes." She spread her hands. "And who knows, for they are gone now in any event, along with their records, their knowledge."

"But you know what this is," Kilek said. "Do you have Herisman blood?"

"No. Just Luargot and supposedly a bit of Minjao, if you believe the rumours about my great grandmother."

"Oh."

Amil snickered. "Scared now?"

"No, I just, you don't seem like the Westerners I've met."

"That I can believe. Now, let's return to your pendant – I

think I have found it in one of my teacher's tomes," she said, running a hand across the worn cover of a large book, its pages lined with folded paper and markers of what looked like leather and velvet. "It is a War Heart."

"It's a weapon?"

"No Herisman Healer would forge a weapon, no. But it is an incredibly valuable piece – used as a ward against death. In fact, I believe it stores the wearer's life."

"Huh?"

"How long did you carry it before the attack?"

"Weeks, but what does that have to do with–"

"Good, then listen to this." She lifted the book carefully, pages creaking as she opened the old tome. The musky scent of age rose with her action and triggered a memory of his mother, reading to him – the sound of her voice but not the title. "This speaks of such an amulet, claiming that 'the *sum-an* falls cold between bearers, but when a new owner is given the responsibility over this immense gift, the *sum-an* must be worn around the neck for a minimum of five days before a bond is forged. Once the bond is made then the true nature of its power begins to reveal itself'."

"It *was* cold when I found it. Almost too cold to wear."

"But it warmed over time, didn't it? And once it did, it stayed basically warm, no matter the weather."

"Yes," Kilek said softly. "I think it did. Are you saying I've bonded to it, and that's why I survived?"

"Exactly." She gestured down to the open page. "It earns its name from *how* it gathers and stores life. Do you know how many times the average heart beats each day, Kilek?"

"No."

"Perhaps one hundred thousand times. Imagine that

number across weeks, months or years."

"So... this is like... being able to cheat death," he said. "And my heartbeat is what builds its power?"

"Yes. But there are limits, as you are no doubt aware."

"The last wearer."

"Exactly, Kilek. So perhaps those limits were tested recently but my theory is that you could certainly not withstand any such attack again now, so soon after Nakir."

"But still, if I can give the War Heart time, I should be protected."

"From death, but not pain or despair... but yes, for the most part." She raised a hand when he opened his mouth to answer. "Again, remembering that the War Heart *does* have a limit, else they would never need to be passed between owners."

"Even so, this is even more valuable than... than *anything*, surely!"

Amil sighed. "Youth."

"What do you mean?"

"Simply that many things have great value," she said, closing the book. "But that's not important now – I need to ask something of you."

"You saved me; I will try my best, Amil."

"Wonderful. What I need is for you to keep the pendant a secret from all but your friends and I."

"I don't think even they know I carry this," he said.

She raised a thin eyebrow. "So be it. What I want from you, in exchange for keeping your secret, is two things. First, I want you to tell me everything you can about the pendant; how it reacts, how it feels, how *you* react to injury, especially in regard to healing. How quickly, how fully."

"I will. What's the second thing?"

"I need to know *where* you found it."

"The Wickerlands, beneath the earth... I don't think there are any more."

"No?"

"Well, a giant lizard creature had eaten the torso of whoever wore it last; it was no treasure trove."

Amil hung her head a moment, silky hair sliding across her face. "That is disappointing – I had hoped to study one in more detail. Possibly even attempt to forge them."

"Is that even possible?"

"I have no idea... perhaps it is just a silly girl's fancy, but while you recovered, I had begun to let myself become caught up in imagining how many people I could nurse back to health with just one." Tears built in her eyes and she shook her head, as if at her own foolishness.

Kilek met her gaze. "I could give you this one when all the madness that's going on is finished."

She smiled then. "Aren't you sweet?" She took him by the shoulders and kissed his forehead, then pulled back. "But listen. Horrible things tend to return, no matter how many times we put a stop to them, so why don't you keep it, Kilek." She smiled at him again. "And keep it secret because not everyone bears my wonderfully noble heart."

"I will, Amil," he said, clearing his throat. Her lips had been cool and soft against his skin. "And I know what you mean... someone already tried to take it."

"Then you already understand, good. Now, get some rest."

Chapter 41.

King Hadeon was not dressed as a royal, with only his longsword over a simple red tabard where he paced before the wall of glass, windows tall enough to reveal sparkling stars overhead. Most of the stars seemed to merge with reflections from bright chandeliers, which by some marvel, rotated slowly from where they had been affixed to the high roof.

"And that is still all we know of these insects?" the king asked. His heavy brows were drawn together, not in displeasure but worry. His dark beard was neatly trimmed, giving him a look perhaps closer to the knighthood than the other nobles present, who were clean-shaven and dressed more lavishly; in doublets or frilled shirts beneath coats. Their colours were more varied, giving a festive air that did not suit the conversation.

"Forgive me, Sire," one of the nobles said, bowing deeply. He was a rotund fellow who appeared too young to be fully bald.

"You are not to blame, Raqfoir. I am simply feeling the

sands sifting through the glass – this is yet another sign that something vast and dark is afoot and we are still playing catch up. Any word on Inacien?" He glanced to Peycu, who stood amongst the other nobles in his clean white clothing, one of several who'd been gathered to hear from Kilek and his friends, though no-one had asked much in the way of follow-up questions since they'd given their story.

Yet nor had they been dismissed.

Kilek tugged at the tight collar on his own rich blue coat as Peycu answered. "Last we heard he was in close pursuit of the assassin known as Nakir."

To a man with a long beard, the king asked: "I want the locations of the first sightings searched again."

"Yes, Your Majesty," the bearded man said, then bowed before excusing himself.

"What of the Minjao, Your Majesty?" Sir Eciven asked. A bandage wrapped his forearm and a fading bruise covered his cheek but he stood tall, unbothered. "We continue to receive reports from smaller villages each day, many of them old messages now."

King Hadeon sighed. "I know, Eciven. And I know what you are asking but still I will wait for the final word from the *dagua*. I cannot risk another atrocity like the Herisman War or those that followed."

"Yet the incursion cannot go unanswered."

"On that we still agree, old friend," the man said. Then he glanced to the other nobles and spoke before dismissing them. "Take you now to your tasks and know your kingdom is counting upon you to excel at them."

The men filed out with low bows to their king, leaving only Peycu and Sir Eciven alone with Kilek and his friends.

Kilek couldn't hold back a slight frown – though it was not directed at the king. The man *did* seem to care... more than Kilek had assumed before.

The king finally turned his full attention to them now, striding to stand before them with a smile. "Welcome again heroes – especially Mathila of Hasere. Sir Eciven tells me you saved the lives of many, and that truly, you all helped. I also appreciate the vital information about the dark creatures you bring."

Kilek and his friends expressed their thanks but Mathi went to one knee. "Your Majesty, as I fought before I would do again, gladly." She paused, and it seemed she swallowed before she spoke. "But I want to fight for a man I believe in."

Alira gasped and even Peycu raised an eyebrow.

King Hadeon glanced down at her, welcoming expression unchanged. "I once spoke similar words to my own father, so I understand and can certainly forgive your impertinence, daughter of Hasere."

"Our people have been taken."

"And so with words I hope to return them," the man said. "Though our swords are both in pursuit of and waiting ahead of Prince Halic's ship, as I am sure Peycu has informed you."

"Your Majesty, is diplomacy truly an option now?" Paxoph asked.

"We have leverage should we choose to use it," the king replied. "But the truth behind Prince Yan's attack must be uncovered."

"It does not feel like they are being used as bait, My Lord," Paxoph said. "Is that what you fear?"

"If we had learnt of Yan sooner, we would know the answer to that question and more, we would have stopped him going as far as he did, on that you have my word as King."

"But you aren't rushing after him," Tyar said. Then added, "Your Majesty."

Once more, King Hadeon bore the criticism with only a patient expression. "And why would that be, do you think, Tyar?"

"That's what we came to ask."

"Well, you are an archer, yes?"

Tyar nodded.

King Hadeon turned to Peycu. "Pey, will you join me a moment?"

"Of course, Sire." Peycu strode to the king's side, but the monarch moved around to stand behind his servant, placing one arm around Peycu's shoulder. A blade glittered in his hand, which he held to Peycu's neck.

Only part of the King's head was visible now.

Peycu did not even blink.

"Imagine only *you* can save Peycu, Tyar. You draw but do you let loose an arrow?"

Tyar folded his arms. "No."

"Half a step forward, Peycu," King Hadeon instructed, moving his arm.

Peycu complied.

The king was still within striking range, but presented a clearer target for Tyar. "Do you loose your arrow now?"

"I might. If I was sure I was faster."

"Are you?"

Tyar frowned. "I don't know, Your Majesty. You're as old as my father would be if he lived, but that doesn't mean you're slow."

King Hadeon smiled, and took a full, large step back. "What about now?"

"Yes."

"Then do you see?"

Tyar nodded, though his expression did not suggest he took much comfort from the realisation, one that Kilek experienced at the same time – the king did not want to risk innocents dying in the clash of soldiers.

"Let me assure you all, that when the time is right my strike will be swift and precise but that I cannot risk the lives of my people on rash action."

"What of those who have already died?" Alira asked, her eyes suddenly brimming.

King Hadeon approached her, reaching out to take one of her hands, his own face full of sorrow. "Alira, I know you fear for your family but you and I must take up that question with Prince Yan, who chose to come to our land and do such unforgivable things."

She drew in a shuddering breath, managing a nod.

"Now, please people of Hasere, I seek your help. We know Prince Yan had two purposes in heading to the north. One was to search for legends about the Night Thorn, and the other to conscript your families and friends. As yet, we do not know for what purpose but our fear is that one action is a cloak for the other."

Peycu nodded. "After all, if the man needs soldiers, why travel across the Wickerlands to conscript Luargot villagers?"

"He told me he did it to protect his people," Kilek replied.

"From *what*, is the next question, isn't it?" Peycu said with a nod.

"But we've told you everything we know about the myths,"

Kilek said.

"Yes, and you will compare that knowledge with what lies in our archives and see what more can be discovered," the king said. "But more importantly, I would seek your help with another problem – that of the foul insects. I know your concerns are chiefly with your village and your families and friends, but the insects are a threat to us all, a threat to your rebuilding, to your lives after."

Kilek nodded. His friends did not argue with the king either, though Kilek had no doubt that it was painful for each to continually set aside their desire to give chase to Prince Yan.

King Hadeon continued. "There have been unverified sightings of strange, winged creatures in the south. Yet never in highly populated areas, and never in the same place twice. And until your arrival, we had no proof either."

"Then they were here too?" Mathi asked.

"As best we can tell, but only *after* the one you found in Hasere. And so it may be that some of you help my men search the north, since a possible first sighting must be investigated and your knowledge would be a boon to them. Once there too, my men will be instructed to help rebuild Hasere."

"And the rest of us?" Tyar asked. "Could we travel on to the Wickerlands and help there?"

"Perhaps," King Hadeon said, glancing at Kilek. "Yet some I will ask to stay here and work on the legends of old."

"You want to split us up?" Mathi asked.

Paxoph's expression was equally troubled.

"I have decided nothing at this point, Mathila. And such a search would not occur tomorrow, by any means," the king replied. He gestured to Peycu. "Please now follow Peycu to the next room, where a meal has been arranged. Enjoy the relative calm of this night too, for tomorrow there are more who would meet you."

Kilek stepped forward. "Ah, Your Majesty? I would like to meet someone myself, if possible," Kilek said.

"Oh?"

"The knights who carried me from the barracks – I want to thank them."

King Hadeon offered an approving nod. "Sir Eciven will arrange that." He paused to look to the knight, who offered a short nod of pleasure. "In fact, Kilek I would have you stay a moment for there is something I would ask you myself."

Chapter 42.

The large room seemed far emptier, far quieter now that only he and the king stood within it, the large man regarding him as he waited for Peycu to escort everyone else out. Somehow, shadows in the corners now seemed darker, fuller. Too easy was it to imagine Nakir lurked within.

Kilek did his best not to squirm, yet composure evaded him. The coat was twice as uncomfortable now, his shirt collar too tight. Even the polished boots were suddenly two sizes too small.

Was *this* moment the one Lord Inacien's warning had been meant for?

"Worry not, Kilek," the king said.

"I'm sorry, Your Majesty. It's difficult... all the attention, I mean. People here seem to think I'm special."

"You did survive quite the brush with death. And I am pleased to learn you appear to have a fine sense of honour."

"You wanted to tell me that?"

He placed a hand upon Kilek's shoulder. "I have but a final question. Peycu has asked your friends about Mathi's abilities when facing Nakir. All are at a loss in terms of describing the source of such a remarkable change. It does not seem to be magic, yet it is certainly beyond the scope of regular people. Tell me, Kilek, since I deem you a young man of integrity. What do you believe?"

Kilek blinked. Mention of Nakir caused a new shiver and he nearly raised a hand to touch his chest. More, how could he answer such a question in a way that would satisfy the king? Would the same half-truth be enough? "Maybe she's somehow blessed by the gods?"

"Hmmm. I believe Tyar offered a similar throwaway comment to Peycu when you first arrived."

"Did he?"

"Yes." King Hadeon waited.

But Kilek could offer nothing other than the truth. "That's what I believe, Your Majesty, because nothing else makes sense. We're just ordinary people from a small village, where else could it come from? Mathi's father was once a soldier and her mother cooked in Tyar's inn."

"I see." Again, the man waited, straightening as he regarded Kilek, his gaze stern but not yet, it seemed, one of anger. "You yourself recovered from mortal wounds, did you not? Are you also, blessed, Kilek?"

"I don't feel that I am." And that was not a lie, either. At least, he couldn't be sure either way anymore.

"No?"

He looked down. "I don't think so. I couldn't save the village. I couldn't stop Yan. I have no skills, no magic, nothing. I'm just... I'm just alive. It's not very impressive, Your Majesty."

King Hadeon shook his head. "Do not be so hard on

yourself. I, for one, am impressed, Kilek. You honour your father and mother."

Kilek raised his head. More and more, it was growing clear that Camilea had shared far too little about his parents. "You knew them too?"

"Yes. And one day, I will try to make the time to share some stories but I will not keep you from your meal any longer."

"I would like that, Your Majesty."

King Hadeon nodded as he walked Kilek to the door, where he paused and placed a hand upon his shoulder. "Let me leave you with one more thing, young man. Whether you see it or not, I sense something remarkable within you – be it a blessing of Gods or your own determination, I trust you will achieve fine things for your kingdom and yourselves."

The king ushered him through the door before he could answer, and into a bright dining room where his friends and Peycu were seated at a candle-lit table.

Kilek glanced over his shoulder but the king had already closed the door. Did the man mean what he said? The words had somehow warmed Kilek... did King Hadeon believe the story or simply believe *in* Kilek for some reason?

"Hurry up, it's getting cold," Tyar called, his mouth full by the sound of it.

Kilek took a seat beside Paxoph.

"What did the King want?" his friend asked.

Kilek looked to Peycu, who was explaining the other Cabeku sightings to Alira, Tyar and Mathi. "He mentioned knowing my parents." He lowered his voice. "We should all talk tonight."

"Good idea."

The rest of the meal became a blur, glimpses and impressions of forks, spoons and rich sauces, tender meats, as was the walk back to their rooms through lamp-lit halls and marble floors. The servant who led them was barely more than a splash of red – Kilek couldn't keep his concerns together.

Did the king know about *Anesca*? It seemed possible. Why wouldn't a royal know about such things? Almost as troubling, would the king split everyone apart? Already, the man was planning to keep Kilek behind… was it really to help in the archives? Or was Lord Inacien correct? And above it all, Kilek *wanted* to return home and help – even leaving the Goddess' important plan aside, his friends had suffered more; he had to help them.

And the dragons still needed to be found.

Finally, he reached his door.

In the darkened room, tension filled his muscles as he strode immediately to light the lamp. Better. Once its glow filled the chamber, he searched the wardrobe and then beneath the large bed. Nothing.

A vial of Amil's pink medicine waited on his bedside table, the scent of mint strong. He reached for the glass and drank quickly. The aftertaste was still quite pleasant. He exhaled then and slumped down to the mattress where he began tapping his foot. The faint hiss of the lamp kept him company while he waited.

When to seek the others?

He stood and began to pace.

Yet the moment he decided to get Paxoph, a knock came upon his door, followed by Alira's voice. "Kilek?"

"Coming." He joined her in the dim hall. Tyar, Pax and

Mathi already stood nearby, whispering.

"Tyar thinks he has a good place to talk," Alira explained.

"Not one of our rooms?"

"He's worried that someone might be listening," she said. "I suppose it's better to avoid the risk."

"Right."

Tyar waved them over. "I know a place – it's not too far. A rooftop garden. It's quiet."

"Let's go then," Paxoph said.

Tyar led them down the passages, guided by moonlight from the skylights overhead and windows beside them. Kilek kept close to his friends as they walked, soon climbing up several flights of stairs until stopping before a door marked with the words 'Gian Garden'.

"How did you find this?" Kilek asked.

"Just wandering one day," he said. "There wasn't much to do while you healed, you know. They had us meet a few nobles here and there but other than that, and training with Sir Eciven, we haven't done much else except explore." He opened the door. "Here we go, welcome to my private garden – be thankful I let you see it, you pitiful, grubby little villagers."

Mathi shoved him inside.

The garden was mostly pale stone and trimmed shrubs in stone pots, many of these ringing small benches. Taller shrubs spread broad leaves with white flowers and vines spanned lattice work. In the day, it would have been a cool, shaded place.

Kilek took part of a bench and everyone else followed suit, half sitting across from him.

"Where do we even start?" Kilek asked.

Paxoph nodded. "I know what you mean, but I think our first responsibility is still to locate the dragons – we have to recover Daciael's song somehow."

"And what did the king ask you about, Kil?" Tyar asked.

"Mostly about Mathi – he's looking for an explanation as to why she can fight like that."

"What did you say?"

"I used your answer," Kilek said. "And told him that I didn't know and that maybe she *was* blessed."

"Did he believe that?"

"I don't know... maybe? I was thinking about it, why *wouldn't* a royal know about the possibility of Surrogates? Avendria didn't tell us how long it had been since she sent people out to do her bidding – maybe it's not so far-fetched for him?" He stiffened. "Wait – there's something I forgot."

"What is it?" Mathi asked.

"Lord Inacien is a surrogate for another god."

"What?" She half-rose. Everyone else wore expressions of shock. "Are you sure?"

"He told me. He knows about the Cabeku. He said he's had his Knives searching for the horde but he can't find them."

"Well, that's something," Tyar said.

"There's more," Kilek added. "He also said that his goals and ours might not always align."

"But he's chasing Nakir, isn't he?" Alira asked.

"Who is likely another of the *Anesca*, right?" Paxoph said.

Kilek felt his arms twitch, a somehow involuntary response, but no-one seemed to notice.

"Whether Lord Inacien will be our ally for always or not, he *is* right now, while he's keeping Nakir busy," Mathi said.

"So I guess we're back to the original question – what do we do? We were going to find a Servant, remember?"

"Will that be enough?" Paxoph asked. "While I think it's clear King Hadeon is a good man, he seems to have made some decisions for us."

Mathi sighed as she leant back against one of the trunks. "You're right. We might be trapped whether it's in a cell or not."

Tyar frowned. "Do we have to do as he says?"

"Everyone will expect it," Mathi said, "I know that much. Now that they've seen what I can do, I doubt they'll want to let me just wander around the countryside. I'm like a weapon in the king's eyes."

"He didn't look at you that way," Kilek said.

She shrugged. "I know, but he's probably thinking it. I don't blame him in a way... I'd want to use every tool I had to rescue my people. And I always wanted to be a knight anyway."

"You're not a tool, Mathi," Tyar said, a hint of anger in his voice.

"I know that too."

"Then you'd stay here instead of going home, if we got the chance?" Tyar asked.

"I don't know," she replied. "Even if we take them north and explore the possibility that the first Cabeku appeared there for a reason – will they let us chase down Prince Yan after we find nothing?"

"Don't we need the dragons for that?" Alira asked, lowering her voice.

Pax nodded. "And I think you might be making an assumption there too, Mathi. How do we know that the

Cabeku *aren't* close to Hasere somehow? It's a troubling thought that I completely overlooked this whole time."

"Hmmm."

"Wouldn't the village have been overrun by now?" Kilek asked.

"How do we know that hasn't happened since we left?" Paxoph replied, head in his hands a moment. He looked up. "We don't know anything anymore."

"Maybe not, but it feels that way."

"Should we confront the possibility that it would be better to simply ask for help?" Pax said.

"Should that be a last resort?" Alira replied.

"I don't know." Pax sighed. "What about you, Alira? Do you have one of your feelings, can you guide us?"

She shook her head, slowly, sadness clear in her movements. "I have tried... but I sense nothing about what is the right choice... I wish I did have an answer, I'm sorry, Pax."

Before anyone else could respond, Kilek spoke. "I have something else. Queen Mae visited me when I was still at the healers."

Soft exclamations echoed around the garden. "They've taken quite the interest in you, Kilek," Alira said.

"I know. Apparently, I... ah, reminded her of Father," Kilek said.

"Your father knew the king and queen too?"

"So they say."

"As curious as I am, I think it's a mystery for another moment," Mathi said as she leant forward. "Did you ask her?"

"Yes, in a way. I asked about the song itself. I didn't want to seem like I was out of my mind."

"So what did she say?" Tyar asked.

"She offered to send me her bard. Maybe he'll know it?"

Mathi frowned. "Didn't Daciael mention a Queen Liana?"

"I know, but it's a starting point, isn't it?"

"It is."

"I could try to speak with him tomorrow," Kilek asked, though he could not force much cheer into his voice. "Before we get sent to different places, that is – because I think it's clear the king wants me to stay here and work on the Night Thorn."

"That won't be for several days, hopefully," Mathi replied.

"Why?" Tyar asked.

"King Hadeon has to gather whatever troops he wants to send as the search party at least. But there's more, I think he's going to wait for Lord Inacien to return before he sends anyone he considers too important from the palace. He needs me here in case of another attack."

Paxoph was nodding along. "That makes sense. We'd be more vulnerable on the road too."

Kilek frowned at the stones beneath his boots. Maybe Pax was right, maybe not. Nakir didn't seem to have faced much trouble getting into the palace. He reached up to touch his chest with a shiver – but there was no pain, only the reassuring shape of the War Heart.

The War Heart. He needed to remember it protected him.

And Lord Inacien was going to deal with Nakir; he *had* to.

"So have we decided? For now, we try to stay together and locate the song, and keep our secret a little longer?" Paxoph asked.

"I guess so," Tyar said.

"Everyone else?"

Mathi and Alira both nodded, then all eyes turned to Kilek. "I think we should still try to meet with a Servant soon, just to be safe. Maybe they could even help us contact Avendria for advice."

"Good idea," Alira said. "I'd call the hawks if I knew how but I don't have any idea and the feathers themselves don't allow me to call *her*. Maybe Florique would know more, if he were here."

"Then it's settled," Paxoph said. "Let's get whatever rest we can and tomorrow, finally find the Clarion Song."

Chapter 43.

Kilek swung his wooden practice sword.

A week had passed already and their plans had come to naught – the bard was still returning from farther south and the palace contained no temple or shrine to Avendria; it was all Fiana and Yaende. And escaping the palace to find one in the city had proved impossible so far, since they were refused leaving at the gates and had found no hidden alternative either.

After several failed attempts it had seemed best to simply wait for the bard to return.

Which meant enduring Sir Eciven's training each day.

And though Kilek knew he was improving, it didn't seem like much as his next swing was met by Paxoph's sword with a crack that echoed among the others in the dusty barracks, sun beating down upon them. Sweat flew from his limbs as he moved, skipping back to catch his breath. But Paxoph kept on, his plain grey training tunic swirling as he thrust.

Kilek deflected the blade but found himself jammed up as Pax moved inside his guard. The bigger man dropped his shoulder and thudded into Kilek, not a true ram but hard enough. Kilek crashed to the ground, puffs of dust rising around him.

He rolled. A smack behind him suggested Paxoph had swung down. Kilek found one knee – and Pax was already attacking again. Kilek met the blade with his own, using two hands to block. His friend leant down, bearing his superior weight to the task. Kilek ground his teeth, pushing back but Paxoph was stronger.

Pax gave a shove and once more, Kilek sprawled in the dirt.

This time Paxoph had his wooden blade at Kilek's throat before he could rise. He sighed, spitting dust. "I yield."

Paxoph extended a hand. "You're being too hard on yourself, you know."

Kilek took the offered hand and Paxoph helped him up. "I guess so."

"Truly, Kilek. The difference in our strength can hardly be considered *your* failing."

"Well, I'd hoped that after a week of this I'd be improving faster at least."

Sir Eciven chuckled from where he stood watching. "You are – each of you. At least, most of your technique and upper body strength. But what you forget, Kilek, is to use your head."

"Sir?"

"Battles are not won and lost on pure strength alone. Tactics and strategy play a vital part – and even luck," he said, stroking his moustache. "While none can control luck, we have our minds for the rest. You can strategise here – it is just on a smaller scale than that which a general might do."

Kilek wiped sweat from his brow, his breath only now starting to calm. "How so?"

"If you know your sparring opponent is stronger, then consider developing your speed or prepare different techniques, such as using their strength and weight of stroke against them. I understand we have yet to show you many such options but you need to realise such things and ask."

"Oh."

"That is why, though her stamina seems to lag quicker than yours, your bouts with Alira tend to be more even. She's still quicker than you so it's difficult to best her swiftly but she uses her speed well. However, you tend to outlast her when the bout is closer."

Kilek nodded slowly, then grinned. "So, what can I do about Mathi?"

Sir Eciven laughed. "A question upon the lips of many recruits and a few of the knights as well."

So far, Mathi's bouts tended to result in an entirely predictable outcome, no matter who she faced, unless it was Sir Eciven himself. Though her eyes had not bled blue her skills grew every day, and swiftly. Kilek himself barely lasted a handful of strokes before earning a bruise or two and conceding defeat.

But there was one other knight-in-training who held her own and often bested Mathi; even now she stood watching his friend from across the yard, her expression one of fierce excitement. When Mathi managed to trip then pin her opponent – a grumbling Tyar – the girl cheered.

Mathi gave her a wave, smiling as she did.

The girl, who seemed close to Kilek – and everyone else's – age, had introduced herself as Zenia when they first arrived at the training ground. She'd smiled and shown them where to store their belongings when they sparred, where the practice swords were kept and half a dozen other useful things. Kilek had found it hard not to stare at her the whole time – she was beautiful in a refined way yet the smudges of dust upon her grey tunic and face, the way she tied her dark, sweaty hair up on the back of her head gave her a look quite distant from a wilting noble's daughter, despite the fine manner of her speech.

The few times he'd trained opposite Zenia he'd not managed to last very long but she only ever smiled or took the time to show him what he could do better.

"Has the palace received word from Lord Inacien?" Paxoph asked Sir Eciven.

"Not yet, but don't worry about him. He'll sort that bastard Nakir out and return in one piece."

Kilek gripped his blade harder at the mention of Nakir, but asked, "What about the Knives in the west?"

"Nothing new. Last we heard, Yan's forces were nearing the border."

"Aren't we running out of time?"

"Not precisely – Yan still has to navigate the most deadly part of the Wickerlands – I imagine you've heard of the *Stemyonak*?"

"The Vanishing River?" Paxoph asked.

"Yes."

Kilek nodded slowly; he'd read about it several times. "It's called that because it dives down to the roots of the Persina Mountain Range. I think a furious Herisman mage left it behind in an attempt to stop the Minjao and Luargot from meeting there ever again."

"Precisely," the knight said, giving Kilek a quick smile. "That is more than most know, to be honest. But you perhaps have not heard that crossing the river is difficult since no bridge survives more than a day, such is the fury instilled in the river."

"You mean... the water attacks the bridge?"

He glanced over at some of the other bouts as he spoke. "I have seen it, lad. And will never be able to forget it. But it serves our purpose now, since circling the mountains will slow him too much. They will have to proceed over the river."

"Then isn't this our chance?"

"It may well be if Yan stops long enough to lower his guard while building a bridge, which we all hope he might."

"Aren't we too far to strike?" Paxoph asked.

"Perhaps you and I, yes," Sir Eciven said. "But General Sanulcon is far closer than we, and Prince Halic sails west even now, his risk greater than ours. Do not forget also, the Knives are watching."

Paxoph hooked his wooden blade into his belt. "Would not Prince Yan have predicted at least some of our responses? His actions seem increasingly foolhardy."

"Not quite so foolhardy if we accept the idea that he may not wish to escape with his own life."

"So... what does that mean?" Kilek asked.

"Yan probably knew at least some of the ways we'd respond and he knew the *Stemyonak* would slow him and give us time to catch up. And this is perhaps more my musings rather than anything we can prove. But whatever he sought in the north, he believes he has. He gambles that it will cross the river even if he himself does not." The knight shrugged. "Or so I believe."

"You mean, he'd fight a losing battle to get... information or the conscripts into the west?"

"I believe it possible."

A flash of disappointment twisted within Kilek, despite the Knight's somewhat hopeful theory. There really was no way to help – it would come down to finding the Clarion Song, as he already knew. "And is General Sanulcon strong enough to take on Prince Yan?"

"We sent him north for a reason, lad. He'll get the job done, whatever he faces." He put both hands upon his hips. "Now, back to work – I'm pairing you with Zenia now; she's the better fighter but your weight will be closer to even. And don't forget what I said about using your head, I want you ready for the formal entry assessment when it comes around."

"Right."

Entry into the knighthood was still a dream... just not the way it was for Mathila, and so while Sir Eciven's words did offer something of a thrill, the search for the song filled his mind more.

Kilek crossed the dirt, giving space to Alira and another recruit as they worked, the sound of their blades beating a fast pattern. And she really was fast – it was impressive; but he couldn't squash a feeling of what had now become an old, familiar bitterness: where was his gift? Mathi's idea of luck seemed... possible but surviving Nakir had been due to the War Heart and nothing the Goddess supposedly gave.

"You look like a dark cloud." Zenia stood before him with a smile, her green eyes twinkling. She lifted her practice blade. "I assume Sir Eciven sent you to me?"

"Ah, yeah."

"Right. Why don't we start with the Dancing Spark? Last

time you were a little slow to switch into that pattern."

"I can never remember what the names mean," he said with a grin.

Zenia hung her head in mock defeat. "They're supposed to make things *easier* to remember."

"Sorry to make extra work for everyone."

She looked up with a smile. "It's fine, just remember – it's Spark so we're talking speed. And Dancing just means move left to right and right to left."

Kilek nodded. "Right, I remember now. Thanks, Zenia." He lifted his wooden blade. "Maybe if you tell me what we're going to switch to, so I can begin thinking about it?"

"Bad idea," she said. "Training is only training, of course, but we have to let you practise reacting and predicting what might come. In a real fight, you won't know, even if some patterns lead in to one another more naturally."

He raised a hand. "I remember now – you sound like Sir Eciven," he said, then added, "Which I mean as a good thing."

"Well, just for that wonderful compliment I'll let you choose the change." Zenia winked at him. "Which do you remember?"

"There's Avalanche and Howling Valley. And, um... Moving Web?"

"Close – it's Lunging Web," she said. "Anyway, from Dancing Spark to one of those two."

"Three?"

"No, just two. Howling Valley isn't suitable here as I'm not on horseback."

"Oh. Right."

She lifted the wooden blade. "Ready?"

"Ready as I'll ever be to earn a few new bruises."

Before they could start, a servant appeared from where he'd seemingly run across the yard, waving an arm. "Kilek, I bear a message from the Royal Bard."

Zenia lowered her training sword. "Why don't we put a hold on this one?"

"You don't mind?" he asked.

"No trouble at all; I'll try and come up with something more difficult for you."

Kilek sheathed his weapon. "Ah, thanks, I think."

Zenia laughed.

Chapter 44.

The bard's quarters were just as opulent other palace rooms but it was unable to sparkle. Every available surface – save one – had been covered by instruments or books or sheets of music, the dark script flowing across the pages in graceful yet almost illegible forms.

Only the bed remained free from strings or sheets of music; soft blankets and pillows arranged quite neatly.

The bard himself was younger than Kilek had expected but he was still a little older than Kilek's friends; he looked quite refreshed considering his recent return from wherever he had been, suggesting perhaps a short trip only. He stood at the window in red and black robes, embroidered across the chest and at the sleeves with a blood-coloured thread that depicted roses and thorns. In one hand he held a silver lyre and the other an open book, which he looked up from when Kilek knocked.

"Ah, Kilek of Hasere," the man said with a broad smile. His voice was smooth and quite pleasant to the ear – which should have been no surprise. "Please, join me. I believe I have found something that may interest you greatly."

"You know what I'm looking for, My Lord?"

The bard nodded as he gestured down to the tome he held. "I do. And please call me Dionarc."

"Thank you," Kilek said as he looked upon the yellowed page and there, in a square-looking script, the words 'Song of Clarion'. "Is it the same as the Clarion Song?" he asked.

"Doubtless – it is an old, old song used to rally men upon the battlefield. Though this is only the first verse, I believe."

"Oh." Would that be enough? Doubtful.

Dionarc snapped the book closed. "But do not despair. This is the last of my master's tomes that she left behind – a biography of the writer who collected such songs. There are others on her estate and I am sure that I recall seeing the name Orille upon a spine or two. Perhaps the *Songs of Glory*."

Kilek straightened. "And that might have the full song?"

"I believe so," he said. "Or at least, one of his works. However, the mansion is some distance from Alaycron, near the old capital."

"The Ocean Palace on the coast?"

He nodded. "So a few days east, I am afraid."

"Would it be possible to go there?"

"I am sure Queen Mae will approve; there is a particular song that she has been asking me to perform for her but I have not been able to recall it; and to be honest, the flute was never my best instrument, so I could use a brush up."

"Do you think my friends and I would be allowed to travel with you?"

"Possibly." The Bard rubbed at his clean-shaven chin. "You are quite interested, just as the queen said."

"Well, I read as much history as I could find, back in the village," Kilek said. "I think I remember the Ocean Palace being the capital back when Queen Liana ruled?"

"Ha, yes! Precisely. I am impressed, young man. In fact, my master was a direct descendant of Liana herself."

Kilek straightened. "Ah, is your master still in the east?"

"Yes, Lady Wen will be happy to see me, I'm certain."

"So, should I try to speak to the king?"

"I understand your concern, since all know he has taken an interest in you and your friends, but we will instead rely upon the queen to ensure such a trip is supported." He strummed the lyre, a tinkling sound. "And of course, if required, I will simply retrieve it myself and you can hear the song upon my return."

"That would be wonderful," Kilek said.

"Wait until you hear me sing it!" Dionarc said. "But for now, I've a performance to prepare for so I won't keep you from the rest of your day but I'm sure you'll have a chance to hear me upon our journey."

Kilek thanked the bard again as he left. He started back toward the staircase and the lower floor so he could reach the barracks once more but slid to a halt when he saw Zenia approaching, her expression dark.

"Is everything well?" Kilek asked.

"Nothing that can't be sorted out soon enough," she said with a quick smile. "Why don't you get back to the yard and work on sliding between stances, it'll help you with Dancing Sparks – give me a challenge next time."

Kilek returned her smile despite his confusion. "I will."

But he did not head for the training grounds at first, instead, he sought out a servant and was escorted to Peycu's chambers – the man met him from a giant desk half-buried in stacks of papers. From around one pile, he waved Kilek closer.

"Taking a break from training?" the man asked.

"Yes, but I wanted to ask something before I returned."

"I will do my best to accommodate you if I can."

"Do you think you could send a message to Amil?"

He readied a slip of paper and quill. "Of course."

"I just wanted to let her know that I feel fully recovered now, that's all."

Peycu wrote the message. "Done, and no trouble at all, Kilek."

"Thank you," Kilek said as he excused himself then started for the barracks.

Yet when he neared the training yard, he caught sight of the garden and the storage sheds. He faltered, and a memory of the pain blossomed in his chest. How could he be sure Nakir didn't still lurk somewhere within the palace grounds?

His breath became laboured and his limbs trembled.

"No." He had to fight.

Kilek stamped a foot upon the ground and forced himself to take a step, pushing through the fear that gripped him. One step. Then another. Another. He passed the sheds and managed to regain control of his limbs.

Before he reached the yard, a young pair of recruits hailed him. Kilek tried to hide his flinch as he studied the two; the poplars on their clothing marking them as close to completing their training. They both smiled, and Kilek relaxed a touch as the taller, dark-haired fellow spoke first. "It's good to see you up and walking," he said.

"We weren't sure you'd survive, considering the shape you

were in last," the second added, his slower speaking pattern making him seem quite relaxed.

"Ah, thank you," Kilek said, struggling with a moment of confusion before blinking. "Oh, you were the ones who saved me?"

"Sure were."

"Thank you both. Amil said I wouldn't have survived without you."

The dark-haired man shrugged. "Well, we carried you – same as anyone else here would have done." He extended his hand. "I'm Renau and this is Paidom."

"I'm Kilek," he replied, shaking both their hands.

"We would have tried to find you sooner but we've not long returned from the First Trial," Paidom explained. "Hard work, right?"

Renau nodded. "Something for you to look forward to one day, Kilek. You should come and have a drink with us one night."

"Yes!" Paidom said, a little excitement entering into his voice. "We're usually at the Five Stones Tavern."

"Ah, I will," Kilek said as they set off once more.

He returned to the yard at a jog, even more pleased now, but despite the good news he wanted to share with his friends, he could not maintain any real energy for the rest of the training. Defeated quickly by every opponent, he found himself simply waiting for the training to end so he could share Dionarc's promise.

Once they had finished working and each bathed in wonderful, giant brass baths, he gathered his friends and explained what Royal Bard Dionarc had found, along with the less encouraging news.

"So we wait, right?" Tyar asked, leaning back upon one of the chairs.

"Right."

And when finally one of the queen's servants did appear at his door, it was to inform him that the king did not believe it prudent to leave the palace until Lord Inacien returned. "He trusts you understand that this is for your own safety."

"Of course," Kilek said with a sigh, then closed the door and turned to his friends. "You heard?"

Nods.

"So, do we simply let the bard return with the song?" Tyar asked.

Alira slumped into one of the smaller chairs. "Shouldn't we warn him, and maybe the king or Peycu, about what will happen? What if he sings it without us?"

"Assuming it works," Tyar said with a frown.

Mathi exhaled. "I suppose we can wait for him to bring it back and then explain *after* the dragons appear, whether with us present or not."

"Perhaps we don't need to," Paxoph said. "Isn't now the perfect time to be truthful, now when there is the highest likelihood of being believed?"

"Will anyone believe us, even with what they've seen?" Kilek asked.

"We've been over this," Tyar said.

"True, but things are changing," Paxoph replied. "And really, all we need is enough for the king to want to *investigate* the possibility."

"We could go back to Kilek's idea from before – we leave the place and see if we're believed by a Servant in the city?"

"I fear asking will only win us the same answer – it's too

dangerous to leave."

Mathi nodded. "And we've failed at sneaking out so far."

"So, assuming we can't find a way to join the bard, I wonder – will he fail somehow, because it's not us?" Alira asked.

Kilek leant against the door. "What do you mean?"

"If the Goddess sent us into the world, is it because she wants us or needs *us* to bring the dragons back?"

Tyar sat with his head in his hands a moment. "We won't solve this tonight, will we?"

"Maybe not," Mathi said.

"Then how about we make one final effort to get out of here and then if we're caught again, we tell the whole truth. If we find a Servant, we decide what to do based on the reaction we get?"

"Good idea. Any objections?"

No-one spoke, instead rising to leave, their expressions weary, movements slow after a long day at the barracks. Kilek closed the door after, then dragged himself to his own bed. He lay atop it first, not yet kicking off his boots.

Sleep was impossible for now.

Maybe Avendria wanted the dragons back but did it matter *who* was responsible? There was just no way to know for sure. Was the best thing to just act like the adults they were supposed to be, and lay everything before the king, and convince the man and let *him* decide who to send? That way, he'd send the best, most capable people east and there'd be no chance of failure.

That was the most important thing – to save the nation by bringing the dragons back.

Only, the thought of not being part of the eventual

triumph stung.

Kilek rolled onto his side. "Avendria, what should we do?"

Chapter 45.

Kilek hurled the blankets aside and fumbled around for his clothes and then his boots in the dark.

Sleep eluded him.

Still.

And it was due to lingering doubts. Finding a Servant and winning over the king meant giving up any meaningful role in the most important moment in their entire lives. And maybe, he wasn't strong enough to do that.

Whoever did go would be regarded as true heroes.

He reached for the curtain, drawing it open to let in the moonlight.

Another thought lingered. What urgency was there truly? The hordes of insects had not appeared, they were not a real threat yet, were they? Without a way to know whether the blasted things were even close, or where they came from, was there a need to rush at all? Once Dionarc brought the song back, then it could be solved.

And if he played the song in the east and it worked then the dragons would return anyway.

He paused, one boot in hand now. And yet, the Goddess had rushed the growth of his friends, suggesting that she knew the threat was near enough.

"You did not give us nearly enough answers," he said aloud.

It all came back to them being chosen – why bother with any of it, if *she* could just whisper in the king's ear and have him go and pick up the song?

"*We* have to be important to it all… somehow."

He skipped around the foot of his bed and made for the door. He had to tell someone: whatever they decided, they *had* to be a part of the effort to return the dragons. Even if that meant at least giving Dionarc a proper warning about his short quest.

Outside, Kilek hesitated before Pax's door – movement at the end of the hall.

Kilek stiffened.

Was it another attack from Nakir? Or something to do with Lord Inacien's warning?

But it was only Tyar, walking quickly. Kilek hesitated. Speaking to Ty would be better than waking someone else up, but the tension between them still lingered. Had they even spoken alone together since the Highway Post? Somehow, they hadn't even sparred in the barracks yet – perhaps not unusual, considering Tyar spent about half his time with the archers.

And yet, of all his friends – aside from Mathi – it'd be Tyar who'd want to avoid missing out most.

Kilek followed.

Yet he'd barely turned the first corner when he lost his friend. He paused… there, the faint sound of footfalls. Kilek changed direction, doing his best with the lamps few and far between. Even the statues weren't helping; not all were familiar and Tyar's footsteps had faded again.

Ahead waited a set of stairs flanked by twin statues of Yaende, God of War, and he quickened his step now. "Ah." *That* stairway was familiar. He climbed and soon enough found the rooftop garden where they'd spoken before and started in, about to call softly for his friend when something stopped him.

An odd sound from beyond the greenery – heavy breathing.

Kilek frowned. Was someone hurt or... a moan slipped through the leaves. A woman's voice... and it did not sound like pain. At all. It had been a sound of pleasure. A heavy dread spread through his body and he took a single step forward, almost unbidden.

For he didn't want to see what he feared he would find.

Yet couldn't stop himself.

He moved as quietly as he could but from the new urgency in the voices, he could have tripped and not been noticed.

Pausing at a bush that blocked most of the bench seats, he peered between branches.

Only half-visible, a woman straddled a man's lap, her bare back smooth in the beams of moonlight, the rest of her nakedness cloaked by darkness; the man's chest concealed too, his head flung back.

And though Kilek stood frozen in place, something in his mind screamed for him to leave.

But even without their voices, Kilek knew.

Curls of her golden hair fell down her back – Mathi and

Tyar.

Kilek swallowed back a hot burst of bitter disappointment, jealousy and hurt. Mathi had made her choice, had promised him nothing. Not in any way.

It hurt nonetheless.

He backed away until he was sure they wouldn't notice, then crept back to the stairs, forcing himself to be quiet yet wanting, *needing* to escape the sounds of their pleasure. At the bottom of the stairs, he broke into a stride, then a jog, and finally a sprint down the darkened halls, the patches of moonlight flashing by.

Tears grew chill on his cheeks from his flight and he wiped at them as he ran.

Somehow, he'd managed to find both the correct floor and wing, where he stumbled to his door and burst into warm light.

A tall man stood in the middle of the room, dressed in black and wearing gloves of white, his blonde hair in some disarray. "You left your room unlocked, Kilek."

Florique.

Chapter 46.

Kilek fell against the door, bumping his head.

Florique grinned, then swept an extravagant bow. "You all missed me, didn't you?"

"Florique?"

"Yes, lad. I am he – come now, have your eyes ceased to function?"

"But..."

The mage crossed the room and gave Kilek a light slap on the cheek, more of a tap, in truth. "There, you're awake now so believe what you see, this is no dream. But we've no time for sleeping, either."

"What... I can't believe it. We thought maybe you were dead!"

Florique snorted. "Hardly. You think Prince Yan could best me? Highly unlikely."

"But you didn't kill him?"

He gave a small shrug, glancing away a moment. "It turns out he was rather competent after all. Still, I bought you time to escape, didn't I?"

"Yes."

"Well, I'm doing it again – only, this time I'm coming with you."

"Escape? Where? And why?" Kilek asked, and still his mind was reeling. One shock upon another was just too much. He could barely keep up with the mage, let alone deal with what he'd witnessed in the darkened garden. "What happened?"

"A tale for the road, I think," Florique said. "Now go, gather everyone and let's get moving."

"Wait, why?"

"Because something is coming and we must draw it away from the palace for the safety of all."

"What?"

Florique met his gaze and there were no more traces of humour or joy now – only a forcefulness that seemed part the man's fear and part an almost magical compulsion. "Kilek, you must go."

He stumbled into the hall and burst into the next room. "Pax, you have to wake up!"

A groan from the bed. Kilek fumbled for one of the lamps, lighting it to reveal a blinking Paxoph. "Kilek?"

"Florique is back, come on – he says we have to leave."

Pax rose, blanket falling away. His muscled torso gleamed in the lamplight – another of many constant reminders of the way the Goddess had given Kilek nothing. Yet the thought was fleeting; he had to hurry. "Florique?"

"Yes, I can't believe it either but we have to leave."

Paxoph nodded, even though he was frowning deeply. "All right. I'll wake Alira, you help Tyar since he's probably lost his bow by now."

Kilek hesitated. "Ah...."

Paxoph stopped, a piece of clothing in hand. "What's wrong?"

"I don't know... where he is, exactly." His cheeks were heated but hopefully Pax didn't notice...

"Again?" Paxoph sighed. "Fools, they're always sneaking out of a night..." he trailed off after noting Kilek's expression. "Oh."

"I'll get Alira," Kilek said, leaping from the room, his voice unsteady.

He was a fool. *Of course* it had happened before.

But Florique's voice echoed in his mind, the tone was clear – the mage was deeply concerned. *Focus, focus, focus.* He knocked upon Alira's door. "Are you awake?"

He'd barely finished speaking when the door opened, Alira with a look of worry upon her face, dressed and ready. Her cheek bore a crease and over her shoulder, lamplight glowed at a writing desk. It was covered in open books – she'd fallen asleep while reading. "Kilek, I could hear you shouting next door. What's happening?"

"Florique is here and we're in danger. We have to leave."

She blinked but moved immediately back into the room and started collecting her things; belt, pouches and a pack for the books she gathered up from the desk. "Get your things too, Kilek."

"Right." He ran back to his room, passing Paxoph's empty one, and found Florique pacing by the window, glancing to the sky.

"We're heading for the stables now," Florique said as he turned. He lifted Kilek's pack and tossed it across the room. Kilek caught it then joined the mage as he strode into the hallway where Alira was already waiting, and beyond her, Paxoph leading Tyar and Mathi through the shadows.

Pax held all their belongings but Kilek glanced away before he could see anyone's expression.

"Master Florique," Alira said, taking Florique's hand, her smile wide. "You're alive."

He grinned. "It certainly looks that way, doesn't it?"

"Kilek said we're in danger?"

"Yes. We have to leave immediately." He raised his voice. "Everyone, follow me now."

Florique started them along the hall at speed, taking each stair two steps at a time, turning down quieter halls and dashing across the brighter intersections. Finally, he came to a locked gate at the foot of what appeared to be a narrow tower, where he stopped to tap upon the lock, first once, then twice and once again.

It fell open and he started up.

Kilek climbed after, knees beginning to protest before the top – a stretching walkway that approached the palace wall, allowing a view of the entire palace. "Quickly now," Florique said, and led them along the sturdy walkway, the warm night air welcome.

The mage exited the walkway, spilling onto a rooftop that overlooked the stables – four storeys below.

"How do we get down?" Paxoph asked softly. The swinging lantern of a guard passed along the somewhat distant palace wall.

"Jump," Florique said.

"What?"

"With me – I'll handle the landing, all right everyone?"

Kilek hesitated. "What do you mean, Florique?"

"Watch me."

The mage took a running leap – and instead of plummeting to the ground, he began to float down gently. When he landed, he waved at them.

Kilek stepped to the edge. What if the mage couldn't handle them all at once? The others hesitated too – except Mathila.

Mathi was now grinning as she tugged at Tyar's arm. "Let's go. It'll be fun."

Tyar's eyes were wide, and he licked his lips, breath coming fast.

Kilek ground his teeth; *he* wouldn't be afraid. Not like Tyar was. He took a step back, then leapt forth.

Cool air rushed across him – then eased as he began to float down, a smooth and gentle landing at the bottom. The others soon landed too, Tyar's face quite pale and Kilek couldn't stop a little flash of satisfaction.

Here, sleeping bodies lay about the place, some quite comfortably arranged. One stablehand slept with his head upon his arm, another reclined in some hay. A guard even lay in the dirt, cradling his helm.

"I may have wasted a little too much time early on in my infiltration," Florique said when he noticed Kilek staring at the guard. "At least your horses are awake, right? Go on, mount up, everyone." He skipped to the entry and peered up at the sky.

"Are you sure about this?" Tyar asked as he swung into the saddle.

"I am. All too soon, so will you be, I fear." The mage strode to his own mount. "We need to clear the city before the moon falls."

Chapter 47.

The streets were near empty as they thundered along the cobblestones.

Torchlight streaked by from the inns and street corners, along with the occasional shout from a citizen forced to give way. But Florique did not slow, yet glanced to the sky often. Kilek found himself copying the mage. Just what was coming? Was it the horde, already?

If so, wasn't staying in the city actually safer?

He shivered as the pleasant summer night turned cold.

Ahead, the eastern gates loomed, blocking out half the night sky. Guards were assembling at the sound of their hooves, half a dozen of them, their armour glinting beneath the torchlight. Shouts echoed, their arms waving, and when it became clear Florique was not listening, they drew weapons.

His response was merely to raise a hand. Tiny sparks of blue, shaped almost as butterflies, appeared on his fingertips. When he gave his own shout, they streaked forth to strike the faces of each guard. The men slumped to the stones as

Florique reined in, pointing to the guard house. "Quickly, the gates."

Pax and Mathi leapt down to charge inside. A grinding followed and the gates began to open. The moment they were wide enough for a horse, Florique called them back. "Straight through the trees now, no detours."

Again, he kicked his mount into action, leading them out into the night.

The road between the massive trunks stood dark and long, a line of moonlight running up the centre. The emptiness of the lawns and shadowy statues seemed menacing now. Kilek glanced behind him to the hulking walls of the city and the sky above, yet still nothing approached.

Was Florique keeping an eye on the night's passage or was he watching for some*thing*?

The mage did not slow when the mighty trees fell behind.

"How far do we need to go?" Mathi shouted.

"Farther," came the reply.

The farmhouses and fields to the east were dark, animals silent beyond the fences; it all rolled by steadily as Florique held a direct course east along the stone highway. It wasn't until a clearing with a roadside well appeared that he brought their relentless flight to a stop.

"We rest here."

Kilek dismounted with a groan. Fleet was breathing hard and steam rose from her flanks, muscles trembling. He soothed her as best he could, then went to the well to begin working the rope and bucket. His friends were catching their own breath or drinking from flasks.

Florique however, paced, as though his energy were boundless.

"Can you tell us now?" Mathi asked between gulps of water.

"Some of it, yes." He sat upon the well's stone edge, replacing Kilek who began to water the horses. "Where would you like to start? My dazzling escape from the formidable Yan or the trouble brewing beyond the city?"

"The trouble," Paxoph replied.

"Wise." Florique put his hands together. "Something large and powerful is seeking you and I believe that if it were to find you in a largely populated area, many lives would be lost."

"What kind of 'something'?" Tyar asked.

"And why?" Alira added.

"Because you are all special, of course. Whoever is directing the terror that approaches knows that fact and they wish to prevent you from fulfilling your potential."

"Ah... why are we special?" Mathi asked.

Florique chuckled. "My dear, I think we all know that you are Avendria's chosen *Anesca*."

A hush followed his proclamation.

"You knew?" Alira finally asked.

"That she sent you off into the world a little underprepared? I did. But I felt it wouldn't hurt to help you out along the way."

"So, she sent you to help us?" Tyar asked.

He shook his head.

Mathi spoke next, her voice soft. "Then who are you?"

"Florique, as previously promised. Great mage, unsung hero of the lands and altogether charming fellow."

"You must be more than that if you know about Avendria," Paxoph said.

"A fair assertion. Then instead, consider me also an old master of magic who still has tasks that need completing before the lands turn to chaos."

"You don't seem so much older than us," Alira said, her expression caught between interest and perhaps disappointment, Kilek couldn't be sure either way.

"Then you would be disappointed to learn my true age, for it is far removed from both *your* true age and your assumed age," he said with another chuckle. "But I am no winter-beard either."

"So, what do you seek?" Kilek asked. "And does helping us truly bring you closer to your goal?"

"As I said, protecting the lands from the Cabeku protects both me and the things I desire, so yes. As to the specifics, I believe I will hold them in reserve but if you succeed in bringing the dragons back to Luargot then I will be one step closer."

Kilek shared a look with his friends. Florique left many unanswered questions... and yet he had saved them on more than one occasion. He was still trustworthy, surely. More, the mage had even known the truth about Avendria and had not attempted to use it against them.

"We don't have much choice but to continue to trust you," Mathi said.

He stood and bowed low. "You are very gracious."

"Mathila, he's saved us before. Of course we can trust him," Alira said.

Mathi spread her hands. "You're probably right."

"So what is seeking us?" Tyar asked again. "Can we stop it?"

"I believe so, yes. My concern is that it will reach us

before you have a chance to locate the Clarion Song, but even if that comes to pass, we will have drawn it away from innocents. As to its exact nature, I do not know. I feel it flying towards us even now, from a great distance."

"Flying?" Tyar asked. "As in, flying like a dragon?"

"No; it is of the Cabeku, yet it is not the horde you have been warned about."

Tyar frowned. "How can you be sure?"

"Because it is far too soon – trust my word on that, Tyar. But what comes for us will be bad enough, even if it is but one thing."

"So how do we face it?" Mathi asked.

"With all your might," he replied with a smile that now seemed touched by sadness.

Chapter 48.

Dawn approached and still the thing had not reached them, though Florique did not appear particularly relieved by the fact. He still watched the sky as it lightened, turning often in his saddle. Even unremarkable sounds from the surrounding apple orchards caused him to turn his head a little sharply – almost as if glaring a reprimand at them for the distraction.

Yet Kilek found the man's concern washing over him with barely any effect now.

He caught himself swaying in his saddle, blinking often. Once, he dropped his reins and jerked awake at a snort from Fleet. The others didn't seem to be faring too much better, though Mathi seemed to have thrown her shoulders back in defiance, even as she too, blinked.

"I hear something," Paxoph said from the rear.

Florique called for a halt.

Hooves approached from the back trail – not at a charge, but at speed certainly. Kilek glanced back to the mage.

"Do we draw?"

"I sense no danger."

Alira was nodding at his words, as though her own senses were telling her not to worry.

Three figures appeared, cresting a hill some distance back, darkened by the rising sun. Kilek squinted. It did seem that at least two were armed. Soldiers sent after them from the palace?

His weariness had vanished.

"If they are the king's men then they won't be happy," Mathi said.

Florique nodded. "Let us see who has come to join us."

Kilek frowned at the mage's response – Florique didn't seem so worried now. Hopefully it *wasn't* because he was planning a surprise. His powerful clap might be good for levelling invading soldiers but the king's men might take exception to being hurled from their saddles.

But when the three figures drew near, Kilek found himself caught between surprise and concern.

Sir Eciven in only breastplate and tabard, a greatsword hanging from his saddle, led Dionarc the Royal Bard who rode a little stiffly in a heavy cloak, and finally, Zenia. In contrast, her eyes were alight with excitement and she appeared exactly as she did on the training ground, only now she also wore a breastplate.

"We feared we would not catch you," Sir Eciven said when they reined in. His expression was as usual; open and friendly enough, though he did appear a little weary. To Florique, he said: "Phantom, I had not expected you here and yet I am not unsurprised, either."

"Sir Eciven, you honour me," Florique replied. "Greetings to the Master Bard and of course you, Princess Zenia."

She smiled. "Uncle Florique."

Kilek found himself gaping. Zenia was a princess? How? She'd never mentioned it and no-one in the barracks referred to her that way, not once!

Dionarc seemed to have hidden a grin behind his hand.

"We are honoured by your presence," Florique said. "Is the king concerned?"

"He thought it prudent you be accompanied on your trip, seeing as you seem so very determined to recover the Clarion Song," the knight replied. His warm tone faded a little. "Despite his wishes that you stay within the safety of his walls."

Zenia sniffed. "He said 'orders' Eciven. And either way, he's worried over nothing."

"Ah, well he may not be so wrong, little Zen," Florique said. "But when we return, I will be sure to let him know that I essentially kidnapped his honoured guests for very good reasons."

"Why?"

"The Cabeku are up to something and it's big. Better to have it happen out here."

"Are they chasing the people of Hasere for some reason?" Sir Eciven asked.

Florique nodded. "Yes. Perhaps it makes some sense, considering where the first insect was discovered but I am still too much in the dark."

The knight patted his blade. "Then we protect you each then take a trophy back to the city."

"Spirited as ever, Sir Eciven. Shall we continue on?"

"Perhaps after a short rest?" the knight replied. "Our mounts are quite exhausted."

Florique nodded. "Of course, foolish of me. Let us take a few hours – I will watch the sky."

Kilek dismounted and helped picket the horses with Paxoph, in turn joined by Sir Eciven. Kilek glanced to where Zenia was embracing Mathi and laughing, the bard greeted Florique as Tyar and Alira rummaged in their packs for food.

"Feeling left out, lad?" Sir Eciven said.

He looked back to the horse's saddle straps. "Ah, just surprised still," he said, his cheeks flushed but hopefully the poor light hid it. "I can't believe she never mentioned being the princess."

"Truly? Consider it a moment. She wants to set all that aside when she trains, and be treated as every other student."

"Oh." That did make sense.

"And as part of her wishes, we don't use formal titles in the yard for her."

"King Hadeon didn't object?"

The knight shook his head. "He has three sons for succession, so the Princess tends to face fewer restrictions in some ways."

"Yet you accompany her now, Sir Eciven," Paxoph observed.

"That I do. Fourth in line or not, she's still his daughter."

Light bloomed; Florique had started a blaze already. "Why don't we eat and then everyone can rest."

"A fine idea," Sir Eciven said as he approached the blaze.

Kilek finished with the horses before joining them, moving a little slowly now that the initial excitement had worn off. The party had grown, and for the better when it came to finding the Clarion Song, but even Sir Eciven's greatsword was not as comforting as he'd wished, considering

Florique's expression of worry had returned.

Chapter 49.

The sun had not risen far when Florique woke and started everyone on the road again, having broken the camp and readied the horses by himself. "It has taken flight," was all he said until they were some distance down the highway, still heading east through the green orchards and toward distant plains and bright blue sky.

"How long before it reaches us?" Kilek asked.

"I cannot say yet for certain, that is why I wanted a head start; the moment I felt its birth I knew it was time for you all to leave."

"You... felt it being born?" Alira's expression was one of distaste.

"In its way, yes." He shrugged. "Unpleasant and swift as it was, its presence rang out across the Planes like a murky bell."

"Planes?" she asked.

"Yes – the Aether Planes, something I will teach you about when we have time, my dear."

"And it already seeks us, directly after the moment of its

birth?" Paxoph asked softly.

"I suspect a cocoon-like gestation, but it rose fully-formed as the other insects."

Sir Eciven shook his head. "We could have used you in the palace to examine them, Phantom."

"There's still time for me to share what I have learned but for now, I think we should pick up the pace."

They rode on as the sun rose, heading always east along the clear road, passing few people, mostly farmers moving from one field to another. They stopped only to eat swiftly and then continue their ride. Kilek's weariness returned before the afternoon sun started to dip and when the mage slowed to a walk for a time, he caught himself blinking in the saddle once more.

"Damn it," he muttered.

"Kilek?" Zenia rode beside him, her expression showing concern. When had she fallen back? Had he been dozing, only *thinking* he was awake?

"I'm fine," he said. "Just feels like we've been riding forever, somehow."

She slapped his shoulder. "I'll make sure you stay awake."

"That helped a little," he said with a grin, but it faded. For a moment, he'd forgotten who she was! "Oh, and ah, thank you, Your Highness."

Zenia whacked him again. "Spare me that while we're out here, can you?"

"Ah, I think I can."

"Good."

He scrambled for a new topic. "So, why does Sir Eciven call Florique 'Phantom'? And you called him 'uncle'?"

"Right. He's *like* an uncle, but Florique isn't a member

of the royal family. He's more like a phantom, just like the name suggests – he simply appears and disappears whenever it suits him. No-one is really sure when or if he'll turn up."

"That sounds like Florique... even knowing him for a short time."

"He's been like this since my father's day," Zenia said.

"When he was younger?" Kilek asked.

"I don't know if he ages that much," she replied, squinting over at where the mage rode at the head of their group. He was speaking earnestly to Alira, the tilt of her head suggesting complete concentration. "He doesn't look much older than I remember from my childhood."

"What sort of mage ages so slowly?"

"I have no idea but he is by far the cleverest person I have ever met, Kilek. And I have met many dignitaries from many lands as a member of the court."

"You seem to enjoy the barracks more," Kilek said. "The princesses I read about were always clothed in long dresses and crowns, expensive jewels."

She nodded. "I can do all that when needed but this is who I am too."

"Well, I like it," Kilek said, then floundered for an apology.

But again, Zenia simply laughed off his awkwardness. "Don't worry so much about upsetting me – I'll let you know if it happens."

Florique turned in his saddle, frowning. Then he pointed to the sky. "There. A dot on the horizon, no more."

Kilek followed his pointing but saw nothing and it seemed no-one else had too, until Tyar spoke. "I see something tiny."

"Impressive," Florique said. "You've been practicing it seems."

"Practicing... my looking?"

He grinned. "Evidently."

"Will we find shelter in time?" Sir Eciven asked, his expression stern now.

"Possibly – for it is no falcon judging from its speed."

"So, we'll reach the Ocean Palace?" Dionarc asked, his breath coming a little short. "For my master's mansion is no doubt closer."

"I do not know if we will reach the old palace... if we pressed on all through the night, I believe we would find ourselves knocking on the Shattered Gates but are we really all up to that? And if we were to avail upon Lady Wen's hospitality, she may be in danger."

"Ah, well said. And thank you for attempting to conceal my exhaustion amongst the group too."

"A pleasure," Florique replied. "Wherever we land, I fear possible wreckage. It is my hope there is still an abandoned home or two out this way at least."

"Just how big *is* this thing?" Mathi asked.

"Once more, I cannot be certain but I wish to take no chances."

"Then let us at least travel as far as we might now," Sir Eciven said. "And should the creature draw near enough we will make our plans then."

Chapter 50.

Before the last pink of dusk faded even Kilek could see a small shape on the horizon. But despite its appearance, gauging its speed was impossible as it did not seem to grow larger at first. Florique had everyone galloping along the road once more, eventually slowing but continuing long after nightfall, when the pursuing creature had been lost to the darkness.

"Can you still sense it?" Sir Eciven asked the mage when they stopped to rest within the shadows of a small grove.

"Yes. I believe we have until dawn," Florique replied. "Which means we must decide whether to make a stand somewhere here in the open or seek shelter nearby. The problem I see with that choice is that we may be pinned down in such a location."

"I suspect this will not be a running battle, however," the knight said.

"True. But when I mean pinned down, I was thinking by falling beams should the structure we choose prove inadequate to the task of shielding us."

Kilek shared a look with Zenia. Again, just how large was this thing?

"Then are we safer out here?" Mathi asked.

"Possibly," Florique said. "If needed, we might send Her Highness east to bring the garrison from the Ocean Palace."

"You'd be sending me there for protection too, right?" she asked.

"Very much so. Not a comment on your abilities, my dear, more a reflection of my desire to retain my hide. I would not risk your father's wrath."

"What about *my* wrath if you do send me away?"

"That I will risk."

She folded her arms. "Well, we won't need to do that. We're going to deal with this thing together, right? The Phantom and Sir Eciven the Autumn Lord, joined by me and the Northern Heroes – no problem."

Sir Eciven laughed with fondness. "Kind of you to let us all tag along, Zen."

Yet Kilek couldn't find much mirth himself; he was no hero. Cheating death was not a weapon either; if they were to defeat whatever approached it would be because of Florique and the others.

But he had to do his part still. *Had* to make sure he didn't become a slave to fear or gloom.

"Then let us find an open space and rest once more," Florique said. "For by dawn tomorrow whatever creature has been sent will be upon us."

A cold meal this time, and everyone instead spent time on their weapons or armour while the fire glowed. Kilek let his sword rest across his knees, gripping and releasing the handle in an endless pattern.

Nakir's flashing blade seemed to lurk behind his damn eyes. The assassin haunting with each blink.

Worry not, boy. You will not feel the final blow.

"Kilek?"

Alira sat beside him now, worry clear in her voice. He almost smiled; she was good at recognising his dark moods. "We'll work together, Kilek, just like the princess said."

"Thank you – and I will live up to my end of that deal."

"I know."

"How do you know? Did you sense something?" he asked, the hope in his voice sounding a little sad, even to his own ear.

"Not about the creature," she said. "But ever since we started on the road, I have sensed something I believe to be important, though it makes little sense. Even Florique cannot fathom it."

"Is it about the Clarion Song?"

"I don't know. It's a... cradle, that's all. I get the sense of a cradle beneath a sun-lit window."

"What could that possibly mean?"

Alira shook her head. "I don't think we'll know until it's right before us." She leant closer, lowering her voice. "I wanted to make sure you weren't too upset by... what you saw when we left the palace."

"Oh."

"Pax and I, well, we thought you knew."

Now Paxoph's voice echoed in his mind. *Fools, they're always sneaking out of a night...*

"I guess I should have." And it was the word 'always' that really stuck. Just how long had he been so clueless? They'd always been close... but then, *everyone* had been close. Fool.

She offered another smile. "Listen, make sure you don't take any stupid risks tomorrow."

"You either."

"Deal." Alira left to seek her bedroll then, and so Kilek sheathed his sword before unrolling his own bedding. He lay down, tried to block off the sounds of the camp as others began to settle and the fire cracked and popped. He closed his eyes.

Nakir, blood, a cradle, Mathi's bare skin...

He rolled onto his side and clenched his hand to a fist. *Focus.* By dawn, there would be no room for such thoughts. As the weakest, he had to focus on survival. His, and the survival of his friends.

And more, he had to prove himself to everyone.

To himself too.

Somehow, he slept, since Florique's calm voice was suddenly waking everyone to the dawn. "Looks like we have no time for a morning meal, fortifications or boasting amongst ourselves about who will take the trophy of the Cabeku's head – ready your weapons."

Kilek rolled to his feet, scrambling for his sword as around him, his friends made similar movements. In the still-lightening sky there was a silhouette, something large speeding toward them. Even from a distance the creature appeared unnatural – the way it undulated through the sky.

Sir Eciven paced, kicking out kinks in his limbs and swinging his greatsword. It looked heavy enough to cut a bull in half.

"How will we face this thing?" Kilek asked in the hush.

"I believe the best course of action is for Alira and I to immobilise it so that everyone else can hack it to pieces,"

Florique said.

"That simple?"

"Let's hope so."

The Cabeku drew closer, though many details were still unclear. It was long, almost like a serpent but it did not move with smoothness, instead, it seemed to have a segmented body and a barbed tail. Not quite like a flying scorpion, since it was longer, but the tail was an ever-present danger.

Kilek gripped his blade, in part to fight the trembling.

"Spread out – we don't want to give it a clear target," Sir Eciven said. "Dion, I want you to take cover in that stand of trees. Take the horses and be ready if the worst should befall us."

The bard nodded, almost stumbling as he moved, and everyone else settled into a half circle, Pax staying near Kilek. Mathi and Tyar were farther along, then Sir Eciven and Zenia, leaving Florique and Alira farthest away – their task hardest.

Kilek found himself breathing hard.

The wings were now visible – long and clear like a dragonfly as they beat almost too fast to see but they still hummed. A row of jagged legs were curled up beneath it, the feet lined with talons. And now that the Cabeku had drawn close enough, Kilek understood Florique's fear of letting it near a city.

It had to be the height of a barn and half again as long.

"What by the Gods is it?" he breathed.

Orange eyes blazed down at them from a pointed face, purple ichor dripping from the jaws. It had slowed a little now, hovering above them and stirring dust, tail swaying as the segmented body quivered.

"Ready?" Florique shouted.

Zenia and Mathi cried out, their voices joined by Sir Eciven. Tyar had an arrow ready but Kilek fought to still his trembling limbs.

How could they face such a thing? No. He set his feet and his jaw.

This wasn't like with Nakir; he had his friends with him and he had to be strong for them. And just maybe he was lucky after all, and that would be enough.

Florique flung his arms up. Black, glowing chains shot forth to wrap the Cabeku around the mid-section. It struggled against him, wings blurring, but Alira added her own magic and together they seemed to be dragging it closer to the earth – yet she did not send chains into the sky herself, instead, she held one of Florique's hands, a glow meeting there as though she lent him strength.

The Cabeku continued to thrash in place.

"It's working!" Tyar cried.

The chains snapped.

Chapter 51.

Florique shouted but the shrill chattering that burst from the creature buried his warning. Before the black chains had even faded, the Cabeku shot down. Its hard body smashed into the earth with a thunderous crack.

Stone and dirt burst forth in all directions.

Kilek shielded his face with his arm. Dust and smaller pieces of stone pummelled him as more shouts rose from their circle. He ducked, struggling to see. The Cabeku beat its wings, clearing the dust.

Tyar and Mathi were rising from the earth, Zenia and Sir Eciven nearby.

The creature darted forward. Two legs lashed out, knocking Tyar to the dirt. Bones snapped and Kilek flinched.

But he was frozen to the spot, even as his mind screamed to act. Move, fool!

The Cabeku's tail flashed next. Sir Eciven deflected the barb with his blade but the point ran by him and pierced Zenia – striking her collarbone or throat.

"No!" Kilek cried out.

Mathi, snarling with rage, ducked under the Cabeku and thrust her sword up into its underbelly – the blade sunk but not deep; and the insect twitched, flinging her aside.

"Quickly," Paxoph shouted as he charged.

Kilek swayed, his body trembled, but his feet remained locked in place.

"Move," he ground out from between clenched teeth. Sweat formed upon his brow.

Fear turned him craven. All he could see was blood, Nakir's slicing blade, the talons of the Cabeku and its blindingly fast tail, the purple drool from its wet mouth. "Move," he spat at himself now, knuckles whitening around his blade.

His heart crashed against his ribcage but still he failed.

Florique spun into view, swinging his arms. As they whirled, white hot flames burst from his hands and splashed across the insect. It reared back and Florique kept up his attack, jaw clenched and eyes blazing. He drove it further from those who'd fallen, Alira using her light – this time it lanced forth to focus directly onto the Cabeku's head.

Sir Eciven had circled the creature and now he leapt up to swing his blade in a massive overhand blow.

It sheared a leg clean, purple spraying across the earth.

The Cabeku stumbled but its tail swung around.

The knight twisted but was too slow; the point dragged across his shoulder, tossing him to the ground. His greatsword clanged across the hard earth. Sir Eciven rose to one knee but he was already breathing hard, his face turning pale.

Yet even the warmth of the War Heart against Kilek's chest was not enough to start his feet moving.

He would die if he attacked – he knew that, Herisman amulet or no.

Paxoph knelt over Tyar and beyond them, Mathi held Zenia, her hair matted with blood. Were they even alive? Kilek flinched as his stomach lurched. And Sir Eciven? He was no longer moving either.

But the Cabeku seemed to shrink beneath Florique's onslaught.

Its eyes were closed and its head appeared blackened in glimpses between the lashings of flame but it had not fallen yet.

They needed him – whether it was luck or something else he'd been given, it mattered not – he had to use it, had to do something.

Go!

Kilek surged forward.

The blade felt light in his hand now; he had too much energy all of a sudden, he was so fast! Something, maybe adrenaline surged through him, overriding his fear at last, as his feet pounded across the earth.

He raised his sword as he neared the massive creature and leapt forth with a cry of frustrated anger.

The Cabeku's leg flashed out.

Kilek twisted – and it struck anyway. His sword shattered. Pain exploded as the strike sent him spinning through the air, crashing to the ground with a cry. He rolled, gasping for air and clutching his chest.

Had it been a glancing blow only? Or had the War Heart helped?

And still he could barely make his feet.

Through watering eyes he saw Alira dim her light,

bending to scoop a handful of dirt. She ran forward and cast it over the Cabeku. While the dirt still hung in above its body, she lifted her hands and swung them down with a scream.

The dirt streaked down like spears – impaling the insect in dozens of places.

It thrashed, twisting in pain as its legs twitched. But it slowed quickly, the wings too, shattered now, and then the enormous Cabeku grew still.

Florique let his fire fade.

The still-smoking head of the insect crackled in the morning light, acrid scent filling the clearing beside the road.

Alira exhaled, then fell to her knees, slumping to the ground.

"Kilek!"

It was Mathi, her dust and blood-covered face streaked with tears. She had carried Zenia over to Tyar, where Paxoph knelt, examining Tyar for wounds. Tyar did not seem to be bleeding but he was awfully still – and worse, his eyes fluttered uncontrollably. Mathi had her hands clamped over the princess's chest, where blood seeped through her fingers.

Kilek dragged himself closer, stumbling on his knees to Alira's side. Clenching his teeth at the pain, he rolled her onto her back... her eyes were closed but she was breathing. He turned. Florique knelt beside Sir Eciven, whose pallor had turned a pale blue, visible even from a fair distance.

"He is poisoned – I do not know how to counter it," Florique said, frustration clear in his voice.

"Zenia too!" Mathi called. "Her wound's deep, I don't think I can fully stop the bleeding either."

Kilek ground his teeth. What by the damnable gods were

they supposed to do now? He slammed a fist into the ground. Is this what Avendria had in mind? His friends dying before they were strong enough to protect the world?

Everything falling apart before he'd even grown strong enough to help?

Was she watching them even now, refusing to take part in events?

"And you," he muttered at himself. "You filthy coward."

Florique held his hands above Sir Eciven's face, a pink glow spreading like delicate petals falling. Yet the mage's expression was not one of confidence. Sweat dripped from his forehead too and dark rings had appeared beneath his eyes, as though he hadn't slept in a week and suddenly the exhaustion had caught up with him. And maybe that was true.

"What do we do?" Mathi demanded.

But Kilek had no answers.

Paxoph's voice rose above the panic, deep and rich. It turned even Florique's head, causing him to look up, the petals to fade. "Lady Avendria, please hear my prayer. If your plan is for us to carry out your wishes then I fear you have released us into the world too soon, as this day has shown." He lifted his voice further. "Have I failed you? Is that why I was powerless today? Because I believe you know my heart; I will do anything for my friends."

Kilek glanced away; he'd been so caught up in his own endless whining about not having any gift that he'd too easily forgotten Pax – his friend must have been fighting his own doubt and worry, and Kilek hadn't seen it at all.

Paxoph craned his neck as he shouted now, voice raw with desperation. "Please, show us your mercy – if we are truly who you believe us to be then let us fulfil the promise you saw in the temple; let this not be an end for your servants!"

A golden light welled where Pax held Tyar's head.

Kilek gasped.

The light came from Pax's hands; the golden glow was glittering, yet not bright – it was like his hands had turned gold themselves, and with the change came a faint chiming as if from sweet bells.

"Look!" Kilek said, pointing as he spoke.

Paxoph's eyes widened but his surprise was only momentary – he lowered Tyar's head to the ground softly, then moved around to lay his hands across their friend's chest and side, murmuring as he did. The golden glimmer spread into Tyar... and then his chest began to rise and fall, his eyelids calming to what appeared to be restful sleep.

Paxoph moved to kneel with Mathi then, smiling over at her. "Let me, by Her grace I will save the princess."

Mathi swallowed as she nodded, shifting only when Pax's own hands rested beside hers. Blood spilled but only a moment. Once again, he murmured as the golden light spread into Zenia, easing the blue pallor to her skin.

And when her breathing had also returned to normal Paxoph rose and strode to Sir Eciven, where he repeated the healing ritual, the gold of his touch restoring natural colour to the knight.

Kilek shuddered in a moment of relief... yet it was fleeting.

He turned to the sky, having no other direction to look.

"Why?" He spoke softly, not a question for his friends; Mathi was stroking Tyar's hair in any event, and Florique had moved to watch over Alira. No, it had been aimed at the Goddess... and maybe himself too. Kilek spun, wincing as he snatched up someone's sword. Why had he been so useless when it mattered most?

Tears blurred the edges of his vision. His whole body trembled. He ran at the Cabeku, blade lifted as he shouted again. "Why?"

He'd let everyone down.

Kilek screamed again, a wordless sound as he swung the weapon.

It bit deep into the insect's ruined face, sinking with a wet splattering sound. He swung again, harder. Another splatter. Another lance of pain from his rib. He didn't stop, hacking away as stinging ichor splashed across his face. The smell of char was stronger than the nauseating scents and his rage seemed hotter than the faint burn the ichor caused.

Someone called to him but he heard no words.

He roared as he destroyed the last of the head, raining blows until he struck the shell. Each stroke won a clang now and dimly, he knew he was dulling the edge of the sword but what did it matter? He threw his arms back behind his head and brought the weapon crashing down, time and time again, his voice rasping, rasping until something snapped and he stumbled back, chest heaving even as it burned, naught but a broken blade in hand.

Chapter 52.

The blessed shadows of night had fallen when he woke, blanket covering him and something soft beneath his head.

A dull pain returned to his ribs and with it, an avalanche of shame. He closed his eyes to the stars through the branches above, as if their light was revealing his failure anew. His useless limbs. Why couldn't he have trusted the Goddess before? Trusted his friends? Maybe it *had* been Luck that he'd been given, and maybe he'd been helping everyone all along? He scoffed.

Either way, he had been useless against the Cabeku.

And even though everyone had survived, that didn't excuse his cowardice. He'd let fear enslave him; hadn't fought hard enough. Kilek clenched his hands beneath the blanket.

That would change.

Now.

He turned to the faint sound of horses – a nearby picket-line. And there, Fleet would be waiting. Kilek pulled the blanket aside slowly, rising with a wince. Yet he was able to move at least. It seemed the War Heart had done its job.

"And now I will do mine," he whispered, swallowing back sudden tears.

It was the only thing he could do.

And then, when he returned to face everyone – it would be as someone worthy instead of a cowardly youth. They'd forgive him then. He'd go now, slip away before dawn and find Lady Wen's mansion. It couldn't be too far. Once there he'd find the Clarion Song. Because he *was* Lucky. *That* was his gift; he had a responsibility to use it.

To help everyone else as they'd helped him.

No other way to make up for his betrayal.

Kilek took the sword that lay beside him and threaded his way through the sleeping forms of his friends, placing each step carefully. Once, Florique snorted and turned, and Kilek froze, but the mage settled quickly.

He kept on, whispering soothingly to the horses as he approached.

Fleet swished her tail and he reached up to pat her neck. "Want to take a little trip, girl?"

He glanced back at the camp – no movement, only a faint glow from embers. He saddled Fleet then led her slowly from the trees. With every step he tensed, glancing to his friends but no-one stirred, and he soon found himself on the road heading east.

Once he'd put a little distance between himself and the camp, he swung into the saddle with a grunt and kicked Fleet into a trot. Her hooves echoed in a muted way between the thinning trees but hopefully it wouldn't be a problem.

The night was clear enough for a canter at best, and as much as he trusted the sure-footed Fleet, he would wait until he found more open road. By that time, if anyone noticed him gone, they'd not be able to catch up... assuming he could find Lady Wen's mansion. If nothing else, he could wake whoever owned the first home he came across and ask for directions. It wouldn't make him popular but being useful was more important.

He rode along the quiet highway but came across no homes beyond the fields and meadows, all dark and still. It seemed fewer people lived near the coast now... yet once, the old capital had made the area a place of plenty, awfully popular with Luargot's nobility wanting to escape the bustle of the former capital. The change in royal line shouldn't have been enough to turn the east into such a quiet place either, even after the port closed. Or was the tragedy upon the water all those years ago truly so horrifying as to make even regular people abandon the land?

He had no answers, but the road seemed level enough under the rising moon that he pushed Fleet into a canter. Yet he had not done so long before coming across light atop a hill – a mansion. It stood ringed by a small wood below, its many windows gleaming a faint yellow. The house was awake at least. Good. Someone would be able to help him.

Yet at the foot of the trail leading up the hill, a sign proclaimed the Wen Manor and he smiled. "So, my luck holds."

Here, he'd find the Clarion Song and redeem himself.

Kilek climbed the path through the hush of the trees then approached the house, dismounting before steps that led to wide double doors. Marbled arches lined the stair, and twin sculptures of harps waited before the entry. Kilek glanced around; above, the windows were empty now... no light, no sound, no movement from beyond them either.

Sought their beds of a sudden?

He tied Fleet to a post then started up the steps, the silence keeping his hand on his hilt. At the top, he reached out to use the iron knocker, shaped as a wren.

His knocking echoed across the pale grass.

Kilek waited but no sounds echoed from within the mansion. He knocked again – would the Master Bard be furious? He'd apologise and mention Dionarc as soon as possible. Hopefully that would work.

He glanced up at the building once more – cobwebs had formed beneath the eaves and around windows; not covering them, but enough to suggest no broom had touched them in some time. And still, not a single sound from within.

Kilek knocked harder this time and the door swung inward, revealing a large reception area with another stair, both lit by the moonlight falling through a wide skylight.

He frowned. No noblewoman would leave her home unlocked, surely?

"Lady Wen?"

His words echoed then seemed swallowed by corner shadows.

Kilek stepped inside. It was sparsely furnished, with a single painting of a young woman singing to a dove, and a stand where withered flowers had turned black upon their stems.

Open doors led to other rooms. There, plush red rugs stood empty; the chairs did not even bear creases or indents from use – and still, no sounds save for footsteps as Kilek searched, unease growing. Dionarc had spoken as though his master would be home... surely someone would have woken by now. Kilek called again, but his voice echoed in a flat tone like that of a tomb.

Was something wrong? There had been lights before.

Kilek drew his sword, the blade hissing from its sheath as he started up the stair. At the top, a balcony led to another door, this one standing ajar. He prodded it open with the tip of his blade, dust falling from the wood.

"What is happening here?" he whispered.

Another door stood ajar at the end of a corridor, moonlight visible beyond. Kilek strode forward with a growl, as if to banish his growing fear. He still had the War Heart, his sword, the Luck of a Goddess.

He could handle whatever he found.

He had to, had to make up for his failings with the Cabeku.

At the end of the passage he stood to take a breath, then pushed the door open. A circular room lined with shelves and instruments waited beyond. Dust motes floated on moonlight streaming in from another, bigger skylight. A small shadow passed overhead, fleeting. A bird?

Kilek's feet stirred more dust as he crossed the carpet to reach out and run a hand across a gleaming harp, the strings responding beautifully to his touch – and so did yet more dust. He moved to another instrument; it, too, seemed unused.

None of it made any sense.

Next, one of two small tables. Both their surfaces and that of several stools lay covered in books, parchment and scrolls – Dionarc clearly took after his teacher in that regard. Even the steps of a ladder which rested against the upper shelves bore a few tomes, and all dusty. A wealth of knowledge lay within, hundreds of books and scrolls, their spines speaking of half a dozen languages, it seemed.

He found no clues as to the cause of the seemingly abandoned house, just a dry inkpot and a half-finished song. The notes on the page were faded, though a date written in the corner suggested it was not so old at all.

But there was another mystery he could solve for the time being – the Clarion Song. He could find it himself, with or without Lady Wen. Then, all he had to do was ride back to the camp so everyone could return and discover the truth about the mansion.

Kilek approached the shelves where coloured lacquer divided its sections, though the moonlight leeched most of their hues. He squinted at the books. Some were in an unfamiliar script, others perhaps Minjao, but beside those rested books with Luargot words on each spine.

He ran a fingertip across the spines. Who was the writer he needed? Hadn't Dionarc mentioned Orille? Kilek kept searching, stretching or kneeling to check on the tomes until his fingers came to a halt. Two thin volumes bore the Bard's name – *Songs of Glory* and *Rituals*.

"Yes!"

Dionarc had mentioned *Songs of Glory*.

Kilek pulled the book free in a rush of excitement. Success at last! He now held the Song of Clarion, surely. It was simply waiting within the pages and all he had to do was open it up to be sure–

Someone was watching him.

Kilek lowered the book.

Nakir stood within the doorway, his sword drawn, gleaming beneath the skylight. "It is good to see you once more, Kilek."

A Note from Ashley

Hello! I hope you enjoyed *War Heart* and thanks for reading.

Kilek and co have more work to do – and you can pre-order the sequel to their first adventure, *Scales of Fire*, by visiting the link below:

https://books2read.com/u/3GEVOP

I'd also like to ask if you could help me out by leaving an honest review of *War Heart* at your place of purchase? Long or short, bad or good, it all helps!

You can also join my newsletter (https://ashleycapes.com/newsletter/), where you'll be the first to know when *Scales of Fire* is released. You'll also have first access to preview chapters and pre-release editions of the story, in addition to being automatically added into the draw for giveaways.

Acknowledgements

For Brooke, you really do make all difference, thank you!

I must once more thank both my families for years of unwavering support and especially my editor Amanda for always finding ways to make my stories better. Thanks also to Devin and Glenda too. I'm also in debt to Marcel Mosqi for the amazing cover art!

Ashley

If you're looking for more epic fantasy while you wait for *Scales of Fire*, you might like one of my other books: *Never: Prequel to The Amber Isle.*

Here's the blurb:

A nameless rogue. A priceless treasure map. An abundance of bad choices.

The rogue Never wants two things – his blood curse lifted and to know his true name. He's hunted down every relic and clue only to end up empty-handed. Until he hears of a treasure map to a sunken city full of potential answers.

Getting his hands on the map might prove to be Never's most dangerous heist yet. When the city is invaded in the middle of his caper, Never trades stealth for brute force to save the map before it burns along with the city.

But his violence has consequences. As he makes an enemy of the invading commander, can Never survive long enough to secure the map as well as his getaway, or will he go down in flames?

If you're looking for a different epic fantasy while you wait for *Scales of Fire*, you might enjoy yet another of my stories: *City of Masks*

Here's the blurb:

A bitter mercenary. A naïve mask-carver. A city in peril.

Sofia is a failure. The sentient magical mask with the power to compel, the Greatmask, refuses to choose her as its successor. Without it, the mask-carver will never succeed her father or have the power to protect her city. When palace conspiracies place a tyrant on the throne and lead to her father's disappearance, her only choice is to hide.

Notch wants revenge. After escaping imprisonment for a crime he didn't commit, the grizzled mercenary is more determined than ever to kill the king of Anaskar. It might have been impossible, until he stumbles across Sofia with her Greatmask and decides to protect her—his best shot at vengeance.

Taking Anaskar back from the tyrant is no simple task. With an uncooperative Greatmask and royal assassins hunting them down, staying alive is half the battle. Can they survive long enough to save their city, or will Sofia's shortcomings and Notch's need for retribution doom them all?

... yep, I've got even more epic fantasy that might interest you! This one is the Exiles Trilogy, and it starts with *A Drifting Sun*

Here's the blurb:

Mei has two sworn duties—protecting her village, and defending her brother.

When the village's prejudices drive her brother into exile, she chases after him. But with the hostile nation of Nasaru threatening the border, if she doesn't find him quickly, the telekinetic siblings risk being caught and executed.

Anyo is desperate to reclaim his honour. Only unearthing a lost, legendary blade will restore the Beggar Prince of Nasaru to his rightful place. So when he captures a young woman with useful powers, he agrees to spare her life in return for her servitude.

As Mei frantically searches for both the prince's sword and her brother, something ancient stalks her every step. A greater destiny awaits her—but only if she realizes it in time. For beneath the nation of Nasaru, a pitiless god is sowing the seeds of chaos, and if Mei can't find and unite those meant to defeat him, she'll reap the whirlwind.

Or maybe you'd like another YA fantasy? If so, *The Moss Dragon of Brittlekeep* follows a slightly younger heroine on a quest.

Here's the blurb:

Stay hidden. Stay alive. Stay free.

Penny has a power people would kill to possess. Fire magic forces her to hide in the shadows of the city of Brittlekeep, her only solace a mysterious talking locket that gives her hints about her lost family. She lives a lonely, cautious existence until her discovery of a dragon's tooth changes everything.

Brittlekeep's master is a dark mage willing to do anything to seize Penny's magic and her dragon's tooth. Fleeing the city is her only recourse. But outside the city walls, her safety is hardly guaranteed.

As tales of her fire magic continue to spread and her locket is stolen, Penny soon learns that it's not just dark mages who want to capture her. Desperate rebels are hunting her for her power. With danger closing in from all sides, can Penny outwit her pursuers and find her family, or is her freedom destined to go up in smoke?

www.ingramcontent.com/pod-product-compliance
Lightning Source LLC
Chambersburg PA
CBHW020548120726
47903CB00001B/175